SNOW
&
POISON

DISNEY DESCENDANTS SERIES

CHRONICLES OF NEVER AFTER SERIES

The Ring and the Crown
Something in Between
Someone to Love
29 Dates
Because I Was a Girl: True Stories for Girls of All Ages
(edited by Melissa de la Cruz)
Pride and Prejudice and Mistletoe
Jo & Laurie and *A Secret Princess*
(with Margaret Stohl)
Surviving High School
(with Lele Pons)

SNOW
&
POISON

MELISSA DE LA CRUZ

G. P. PUTNAM'S SONS

For Mike and Mattie always

G. P. Putnam's Sons
An imprint of Penguin Random House LLC, New York

First published in the United States of America by G. P. Putnam's Sons,
an imprint of Penguin Random House LLC, 2023

Copyright © 2023 by Melissa de la Cruz

G. P. Putnam's Sons is a registered trademark of Penguin Random House LLC.
The Penguin colophon is a registered trademark of Penguin Books Limited.

Visit us online at penguinrandomhouse.com.

Library of Congress Cataloging-in-Publication Data is available.

Manufactured in Canada

ISBN 9780593326688 (hardcover)
1 3 5 7 9 10 8 6 4 2

ISBN 9780593619780 (international edition)
1 3 5 7 9 10 8 6 4 2

FRI

Design by Marikka Tamura
Text set in Kis Classico

Love is poison. A sweet poison, yes, but it will kill you all the same.

—Cersei Lannister, *A Clash of Kings*, by George R. R. Martin

BAVARIA, 1621

CHAPTER ONE

THE DAY HAD FINALLY COME.

It was still very early when the sun crested over the Bavarian mountains, its light climbing up the walls of Duke Maximilian's palace to slip through its arched windows. But Sophie had been awake for hours. She'd spent most of the night staring into the dark velvet above her four-poster bed, and now she turned to watch the line of light that made its way past the thick tapestry curtains.

She jumped out of bed and threw the drapes open wide, squinting as the sunlight hit her pale skin. Lotte, Sophie's lady's maid, would be along in a little bit, but Sophie just couldn't wait any longer. She crossed the room to her dressing table and ran a hand through her thick, dark hair, studying her reflection in the wide gilded mirror. When she was younger, she had been nicknamed Snow White for her alabaster skin. At sixteen, people told Sophie that she was starting to look like her mother, the late Duchess Maria, who had been known throughout their land for her stunning beauty.

In the mirror's reflection, Sophie saw the raven-black hair, ivory complexion, sharp chin, and red lips that resembled her mother's features. But she was still just Sophie underneath. She hoped she would have even half her mother's elegance one day.

Duke Maximilian, Sophie's father, had veiled all the paintings of the duchess for a long time after her death. The portraits lined the halls of the palace in mournful black rectangles, darkening the mood of everyone who passed. Though Sophie had been nine years old when a fierce illness gripped Duchess Maria, the memories of the short life they'd spent together seemed to disappear more and more with each passing year. When the portraits were uncovered again, Sophie was struck by the image of her mother. It was like looking at a beautiful stranger.

Sophie looked away from the mirror and sighed. Today was meant to be a happy occasion, for that very evening Duke Maximilian would be wed, and the palace would have a duchess once more. But the memory of Sophie's mother seemed more present than ever. She reached for the carved box inlaid with mother-of-pearl, which remained always next to the mirror, and rummaged through its thin drawers until she found the necklace that had once belonged to her mother—a loop of thin filigreed silver inset with stones of opal. She clasped the jewelry around her neck, the cool metal on her skin bringing her a little comfort. The prospect of having a stepmother felt incredibly strange to Sophie, but she was happy for her father. And, in truth, a little relieved.

Her mother's death had made Duke Maximilian quiet and distant, causing him to withdraw from palace life and from Sophie, too. He'd spent many dark winter evenings alone in his quarters and sent himself on long trips to do business with other dignitaries. Years had gone on this way. For a long time, Sophie nearly felt orphaned in the big, silent palace, worried she was losing him. She wished he'd take her with him—Sophie would have loved to see where he went and to travel outside of Bavaria—but he said it was too dangerous.

So she spent her days inside, reading, studying with tutors, waiting and walking the long halls. She had little desire to do much else; though Sophie and her mother had often hiked into the mountains to enjoy the sun and the wind on their faces, Sophie found she didn't want to do that anymore. Not alone.

This pattern held father and daughter in its grip for many years too long. Yet on one of those long journeys, Duke Maximilian found comfort in someone new. While on a philanthropic trip to Khadjibey on the Black Sea, he and his advisers made a fateful stop in the principality of Moldavia, where they accepted the hospitality of a noble family—some of the only nobility the small state had. There in the dark, eastern fields, where anyone would have least expected it, he discovered the one person who seemed to wake him from his slumber. Her name was Lady Claudia. Though tonight was the wedding, Sophie hadn't met her yet. She had only heard the whispered rumors among the palace staff.

"I hear she's just a young thing—young enough to be Lady Sophie's sister!" the serving maid whispered to the valet at dinner earlier that week.

"They say her family is out of favor with the Kyiv nobility," the gardener murmured to the coachman the following day, unaware that Sophie was reading nearby. "And there's rumblings of war with the Ottomans in that part of the world. I certainly hope this isn't some kind of charity case—or worse—a spy."

Now the chamber door flew open behind Sophie, interrupting her thoughts, and Lotte burst into the gilded mirror's reflection.

"Are you ready to *debut*?" She squealed the question as she rushed to Sophie's side.

The mention of the second important event taking place today sent Sophie's stomach into knots. She'd been doing everything she could to avoid the subject. Even though it was a little early—her mother had debuted at seventeen, after all—Duke Maximilian had decided it was time for Sophie to be introduced to palace society. He feared she'd missed out on so much already, being holed away in his absence.

The arrival of Lady Claudia seemed to have turned his thoughts to romance in all areas of his life, and he had the unusual idea to conduct the debut and the wedding on the same night, in one operatic—and stressful—ceremony.

"What convenience," Duke Maximilian said, "with all the foreign dignitaries and guests gathered in one place already!" Her father looked at her keenly. "And we must think about your future as well."

"My future?" Sophie asked.

"You will have to marry, of course, and once you are introduced to society, we must make the proper arrangements. And you cannot marry just anyone," said the duke with a smile.

Marriage? Wasn't it just yesterday that she had put away her dolls? She rarely spoke to any boys—she had cousins all over the continent, but they hardly visited. There were few young men that she knew by acquaintance, though mostly she had spent years alone with only the servants for company. But she was the duke's daughter, a lady, and of course she would have to marry. This was expected of her, and in her dreams, she wished for the same happiness her parents had found—and perhaps her father had found once more.

"We shall find the best of suitors," her father assured her. "Someone who deserves you."

"Someone that I love?" she asked hopefully.

Her father's smile deepened. "One who adores you. It is my dearest wish to see to your happiness, my child."

"Thank you, Papa."

Still, the anticipation of so much change in one day was the reason she hadn't been able to sleep, and the reason her heart leapt into her throat at Lotte's declaration. Her future would begin tonight.

"Lotte," Sophie said sternly, rising and allowing the lady's maid to pull off her dressing gown and begin layering on the petticoats, "I'm trying not to think about it. And after all, this is Lady Claudia's special day."

She tugged at Duchess Maria's necklace again, straightening it between her collarbones. The stiff lace of her practice gown came up around her skin, feeling scratchy and tight as Lotte tightened the laces of her stays, made stiff with whalebone. It pulled in her waist and made her lungs feel shallow. Apart from her debut, Sophie was also trying very hard not to think about the fact that her mother wouldn't be there to see her.

Sophie's father; her governess, Frau Hilda; and her tutor, Monsieur Gustave, had been working to the bone, trying to prepare Sophie for her debut in the few short weeks since Duke Maximilian had made the plan. But despite arduous training and the many volumes she'd been tasked with reading, Sophie had little idea of what to expect. Her father and Monsieur Gustave were men, after all, and Frau Hilda had never herself debuted.

"Oh, you can't worry about that. It's going to be a dream, they will be banging down the castle door," Lotte said, pressing her foot on Sophie's back and yanking her laces. Sophie felt the breath push out of her and nearly doubled over. "You two get to share this. And Lady Claudia better not be envious of you if she's going to be a good fit in the palace."

Sophie winced. "We must make Lady Claudia feel at home. Papa seems happy, so I want her to be happy, too."

Lotte shrugged. "It's not easy being an outsider."

CHAPTER TWO

THE PALACE BUSTLED ALL DAY with final preparations for the wedding. Sophie tried to get a glimpse of Lady Claudia, but she'd arrived with all her maids and ladies-in-waiting that morning and was now hidden away in the north wing.

Sophie watched from her bedroom window as four whole carriages filed up to the palace doors. Sophie wondered what the lady was like. Would she be strict and regal? Would she keep close to her entourage or spend time with Sophie out in the gardens? Would they even have anything to talk about?

Sophie leaned on the window casement and sighed. She'd just have to wait to find out.

Instead of finding Lady Claudia, Sophie endured forty-five minutes of debut practice with Frau Hilda and Monsieur Gustave. In order to complete the ceremony, she would have to join her father—and by then, his new wife—on the ballroom stage and execute a low curtsy in front of the crowd. The slippery shoes she'd be wearing and the layers of heavy, billowing tulle only added to her nerves, not to mention the boning that almost prevented her from breathing entirely.

"Down once more. Lower. Now up—chin *down* as you rise!" Sophie's tutor barked. "No, don't look at us. You must keep your eyes demure! *Now* you lift your head. Smile! You're not smiling!"

"Monsieur Gustave," Sophie said. "I am going to break my ankle if I keep doing this."

"Would you rather break your ankle here, or in front of everyone? Again!"

When she finally escaped practice, Sophie was exhausted. In the rush of preparations and her own turbulent stomach, she realized she'd forgotten to eat.

Sophie slipped down a back stairwell and into one of the smaller pantries so she'd be out of the way of the anxious kitchen staff. Though Sophie theoretically had authority over them, the palace's chef—who answered only to "Chef"—was a tyrant who would not hesitate to call for Frau Hilda if Sophie was in the way.

Disappearing into the darkness, Sophie puffed out a breath of relief as she eased the larder door closed, alone at last with the cured meats and cheeses. Then she turned around and broke the silence with a scream. In the dim light, a face was staring back at Sophie.

"Who are you?!" a voice cried.

A tall young woman with a sharp face was standing at the back of the room, holding a block of cheese like a weapon. She looked like she was roughly ten years older than Sophie.

"I'm Sophie, I live here," Sophie said, her pulse returning to normal. She noted the servant's traveling cloak wrapped around the woman. "Can I help you with something? Are you looking for Chef?"

But instead of answering, the woman raised the hunk of cheese above her head, as if to throw it at Sophie, but she dropped it instead and ran for the door.

Sophie watched as the servant slipped away, finding it odd that she'd wrapped her traveling cloak around herself so tightly for such a warm day.

❦

It took two hours for Lotte and three other maids to get Sophie dressed for the ceremony. They scrubbed and scalded her thoroughly in the bath, then strapped and yanked and sewed her into a ball gown, ordered directly from Paris, with lengths of satin and embroidery. It had a blue bodice and sleeves that clung tight to Sophie's shoulders and opened, bell-like, edged with red lace at her forearms. The blue velvet paneling opened to a grand golden skirt, the fabric almost iridescent in its liquid smoothness. Sophie's maids pulled her hair tight around hot irons to curl and set it with a matching red band, then finished by batting her skin with all manner of powders and rouges. Sophie couldn't help coughing on Lotte, which made the girl buff even harder.

"Almost—there—" Lotte said through gritted teeth, attacking Sophie with the puff.

But Sophie was grateful for the distraction—the discomfort took her mind off the events that were to come. She reassured herself that most of the guests and dignitaries would be very old, already married, and with no more than a passing interest in her. Maybe the wedding would overshadow her debut entirely. She hoped so, at least.

In no time at all—far too soon—Frau Hilda came to fetch her. Arm in arm, walking carefully with all the weight and decoration piled atop Sophie, they made their way to the ballroom, which twinkled with hundreds of flickering candles.

Sophie found her seat in a balcony on the ballroom's second floor, where she would be partially out of the crowd's view for the

8

duration of the wedding ceremony. When the time was right, she would descend to the main floor and formally present herself to her father, Lady Claudia, and the full audience in attendance. As the guests began to fill the enormous room, each announced by the master of ceremonies, Sophie felt her heart climb out of her chest.

She watched them take their seats and marvel at the ballroom, which was adorned with garlands of red and white roses that cascaded down from the second floor and filled vases on either side of the room. Carved wooden statues of Duke Maximilian's and Lady Claudia's likenesses flanked the main stage, and a small orchestra struck up traditional hymns and folk songs.

Sophie wondered if things had been so grand for her own mother's wedding. She touched her mother's necklace and looked for her father but didn't see him anywhere in the sea of people.

All at once, the music of the orchestra died, and the lively crowd hushed. Duke Maximilian appeared at the head of the stage and looked expectantly to the end of the room, and everyone's eyes followed. Each guest hoped to catch a first glimpse of the bride.

Sophie stood as well, clutching the railing of the balcony and peering into the distance. She shook her head, reminding herself that this woman would not replace her mother.

The wide doors at the back of the ballroom opened once more and two figures stepped through. One was a tall, heavily veiled woman, dressed in a sea of pale lavender silk, who appeared to float as she clutched the arm of the other, a man—Lady Claudia's father.

The orchestra began an instrumental of "Die Vogelhochzeit," the sweet spring song about the blackbird who marries the thrush, and Lady Claudia and her father walked slowly down the aisle. Her father kissed the bride's hand gently and helped her climb the stairs.

From where she sat, Sophie could tell the duke was blushing. He looked younger and happier than he had in years, and as he reached with the utmost care for the hands of his new wife, Sophie felt a lump in her throat and swallowed hard.

Duke Maximilian brought Lady Claudia to stand in front of him and slowly lifted the opaque veil. Every duke, duchess, and lady in the room collectively held their breath.

Then the duke threw the veil back, revealing a young woman with light hair, sharp features, and radiant eyes. A ripple sounded through the crowd at the sight of her stunning beauty. Sophie gasped, but for a different reason—

It was the strange woman from the larder.

The one who'd almost chucked the cheese at Sophie's head.

Sophie felt a strange coil in her belly. This was her new step-mother? This was Lady Claudia? A woman who snuck into cupboards and threatened strangers?

Claudia smiled up at Duke Maximilian and took his hands in hers. The celebrant began the ceremony, and from her place in the balcony, Sophie could hear their voices as they spoke the vows.

"I promise to be loyal to you in good days and bad, in health and illness . . . ," Duke Maximilian said.

". . . to love and respect, until death separates us," Claudia finished quietly.

The audience watched in rapture, and Sophie noticed the comfort and ease in the faces of the couple.

Sophie felt, again, a tightening in her chest as her father and his new bride, now Duchess Claudia, embraced, the orchestra playing joyfully and the crowd unleashing applause and cheers.

Then a hand clamped on to Sophie's shoulder. Frau Hilda appeared at her side. "It's time!" she hissed.

Sophie's stomach twisted hard. It was her turn.

CHAPTER THREE

SOPHIE BARELY REGISTERED THE RUSH to the main floor of the ballroom as Frau Hilda pushed on the small of her back, and suddenly, she was out in front of the crowd. Hundreds of pairs of eyes were trained on her, the swell of people looking closer and much bigger than it had in the balcony. Sophie hadn't been in front of this many eyes since her mother's funeral.

She froze.

Her heart stopped. What was she supposed to do?

The orchestra began a light melody, an air on the "Bayernhymne," the Bavarian national anthem. Sophie touched her mother's necklace and looked to the stage. It came back to her—all she had to do was walk forward, climb the stairs, allow the master of ceremonies to introduce her, and execute the curtsy. It was simple.

Sophie took one wobbly step, then another. She lifted her chin as she had been taught, keeping her eyes demure. Somewhere beneath the music, she could hear murmurs of approval in the crowd.

"Ach du meine . . . just beautiful."

"The spitting image of Duchess Maria!"

Their words buoyed Sophie as if the sun was breaking through the clouds. Her confidence grew with every step.

Soon she was before the stage, and she looked up to face her father and Duchess Claudia for the first time. Duke Maximilian was positively beaming.

Duchess Claudia was flushed and looking a little unsteady on her feet. But she raised her eyebrows when she locked eyes with Sophie, evidently recognizing her from the larder as well. Sophie smiled, trying to communicate that there were no hard feelings about their earlier meeting. Claudia returned the expression with her own small twitch of the lips, pressing one hand to her neck and holding on to Maximilian with the other.

A servant at the stairs extended his hand to Sophie and helped her ascend gracefully. She reached her father and stepmother at last, feeling triumphant.

The music of the orchestra swelled; the guests beamed.

But then Lady Claudia's eyes fluttered closed and her head fell. She stumbled backward, sagging against Duke Maximilian's arm.

The crowd gasped as the duke caught Claudia before she fell, stabilizing her with a strong arm and pulling her back into a standing position.

Sophie was hardly able to process what was happening; the orchestra faltered and the music stopped. Claudia came to as Maximilian squeezed her arm, bending his head and speaking to her in a low voice. Her eyes darted, unfocused, and she shook her head as if trying to clear water from it. The master of ceremonies and another servant rushed forward as Maximilian led the duchess to one of the gilded chairs on the stage and helped her sit down. They whispered to each other for a moment, and Claudia nodded, her face bright red.

Then Maximilian smoothly turned to Sophie and bowed, extending his arm as an indication to proceed.

Sophie looked at him, then stiffly pivoted to face the ballroom, staring back at the silent, alarmed audience. Sophie felt sweat soak the back of her neck, suddenly understanding how Duchess Claudia must have felt.

The master of ceremonies broke in from Sophie's left. His loud, booming voice echoed through the huge room: "At the behest of His Right Honorable Duke Maximilian and his good Duchess Claudia, I present to you Lady Sophie of the Imperial Duchy of Bavaria!"

As he spoke the words, Sophie snapped back to life and placed one foot behind the other, sinking low into a curtsy almost by instinct and letting the mass of her ball gown pool around her. She held the pose as he called out each title, her leg shaking slightly beneath her dress, then rose slowly as he finished.

There was one more beat of silence—just a fraction as the audience recovered from their surprise—then the orchestra erupted into the national anthem, and the crowd broke into applause once more. Sophie bestowed upon them what she hoped was a gracious smile, turning and making another, smaller curtsy to her father and stepmother.

Duchess Claudia applauded politely from her chair, but her expression seemed as though it was carved from stone. Duke Maximilian clapped heartily and nodded, looking proudly at Sophie.

It was both all over and had only just begun.

❦

Sophie was so relieved to have both ceremonies finished with that she didn't care what happened the rest of the night. All the unfamiliarity of the new world in which she'd just been inducted could wait until tomorrow. Instead, she dodged greetings and well-wishers, trying to catch up with her father and Duchess Claudia making their way to the dining hall as the ballroom was prepared for the dance.

"My dear, congratulations," said someone who grabbed her arm, an elderly woman who dripped with so much lace and pearl that she rivaled Chef's layer cakes.

"Indeed," harrumphed a man bedecked with medallions and military garb. "It's about time your father returned to his own duchy and set his affairs straight. Not that you need worry about that, as I'm sure you'll keep him busy with your scores of suitors!"

"Thank you. I mean—I don't know," Sophie said, suddenly feeling very flustered. She'd never seen these people before—or at least, didn't recognize them—but they seemed to know everything about her and her father. The crowd pushed in closer, and Sophie realized how many eyes were still watching her, how they had not looked away though she had descended the stage. Sophie rubbed at her arms as the woman kept talking. Why couldn't her father and Duchess Claudia have waited for her?

"Dare I say, you certainly stood with more grace than *others* in this room tonight," the woman said.

"Caroline, watch your tongue! You must show some respect," the military man scolded.

"Well, isn't it what everyone thinks?" The woman's wrinkled face became scornful as she drew conspiratorially closer to Sophie, who tried to step back despite the crush of people moving through the hall. The woman kept talking. "Here we've been waiting for someone with the strength to support Duke Maximilian like your mother did. And what do we get? A fainter. Those poorer countries, they don't breed well—"

"Excuse me. I should congratulate my father," Sophie mumbled, ducking beneath the arm of another dignitary and slipping through the edge of the throng. Her urge to run outside for fresh air was overpowered only by her growling stomach.

By the time she reached the head of the main table, Sophie was so looking forward to the banquet that she didn't realize Duchess Claudia was gone. She leaned over to say something to her father, but at that moment everyone settled into their chairs at last and Duke Maximilian raised his glass for a toast.

"To new beginnings," he boomed. "And to Bavaria!"

"To Bavaria!" the guests cheered, and they dug into their first course.

Sophie took her time stirring the bowl of knödel soup before her, but still the chair next to Duke Maximilian remained empty. She leaned closer to her father. "Where is Duchess Claudia?"

He frowned. "She went to gather herself together. She's very embarrassed about losing her composure during your debut."

"I really didn't mind," Sophie said, remembering how distressed Claudia had seemed in the larder earlier. She tried to forget the unkind comment the old woman had made, about poorer countries and their weak-blooded women. "Is she feeling all right?"

"Oh yes," said Duke Maximilian. "She just needs a moment of rest. She'll be out before long."

Sophie scanned the room, grateful for the ebb and flow of conversation that came over the crowd as they enjoyed their food. From her vantage point, she was able to get a better look at all the guests. There were people from all different kingdoms and houses of nobility throughout Europe, from old French counts to Russian grand dukes.

Her eye paused at a table a little way from theirs, where a young man of about seventeen years of age was laughing with the other guests. The gold buttons on his dark scarlet dress coat flashed in the candlelight, and his smile was full and genuine, lighting up the entire room. He was handsome and confident, as if nothing or no one could faze him. His thick dark hair fell in a swoop over his forehead, and he often brushed it off his face in a way that Sophie found mesmerizing.

Reaching for her cup of honey mead, she found that she couldn't seem to look away from the boy. A drop of the drink sloshed onto her chin, and she swiped it away with her hand before anyone could see. "Papa," she said lightly. "Do you know everyone here?"

"Not everyone, to be honest," he said. "I would probably remember the names if you told me. But it's my obligation to invite members of the court. Even *I'm* not popular enough to have this many close friends," he said with a chuckle.

"I see," said Sophie. She looked around the room for someone to point out, still not quite sure why she was doing what she was doing. "Do you know that man over there?"

"Aha, a test? Well, let's see," Duke Maximilian said, squinting and putting down his fork. "Him? Yes, I believe that's the viscount of Rouen. He's a rather quiet man, but he can play a mean game of Trappola."

"And her?"

"The baroness of Sieradz. She's a skilled shot—we went hunting together once."

"And what about him?" Sophie said lightly, pointing out the handsome young man at the next table.

"Ah, that's Prince Philip, heir to the Spanish throne. Seems like a fine young man." Duke Maximilian picked up his fork again and speared a large piece of roasted potato.

"No interesting facts about the prince?" Sophie asked.

He raised his eyebrows at her, and Sophie had the urge to look away.

"Well, I don't know him quite so well. But his father . . . his father and I had words with each other once. For starters, the king of Spain is a terrible cheat at matzlfangen. It's my belief that any man who cheats at parlor games may cheat in other areas of his life as well, and King Ferdinand proved this tenfold."

"Oh. How?"

Maximilian shook his head and made a face. "It isn't pleasant, Sophie. Let's focus on the celebration, shall we?"

Sophie nodded, though she wanted to press further.

"Is there any particular reason you ask about the prince?" her father said, eyeing her. Sophie's neck felt very hot all of a sudden, and she tugged the sleeves of her dress farther up her forearms.

"Of course not."

As the two looked on, Prince Philip turned his head and glanced in their direction. Sophie immediately dropped her eyes to her plate, staring intently at her own roasted vegetables.

They were nearly through dessert when the noise of the room became quieter, more alert. Sophie looked up and, at last, found Duchess Claudia hesitating at the doorway. Duke Maximilian rose and led his new bride to the head of the main table without a word. When she reached her seat, Claudia gave a short nod to her audience and turned her attention to her food. Presently, everyone relaxed and continued with their meals, but plenty still cast quick looks in the direction of the head table.

Claudia peeked up from her plate and smiled sheepishly at Sophie. "Hello there," she said. "I'm sorry about earlier in the pantry; I was startled. I just needed something to eat very badly after that long carriage trip."

Sophie shrugged and returned the smile. "Don't worry about any of that. This has been a lovely evening, and I hope you're enjoying yourself."

Claudia nodded. "I am. And I'm grateful that I finally get to meet—"

At that moment, the voice of the master of ceremonies—now a bit hoarse—boomed through the hall once more. "Honored guests of Duke Maximilian and Duchess Claudia, at your leisure, you may return to the ballroom for this evening's entertainment!"

The volume of the room rose as the guests bustled out of their seats and chattered about the dance. Duke Maximilian extended his arm to Claudia, and Sophie moved around the table to walk with them. "You just can't manage to get any food around here, can you?" Sophie muttered to Claudia, who laughed softly. "We can talk again later," she said, taking her leave.

As she walked back into the ballroom, which had again been transformed to a wide-open space, Sophie felt a touch on her arm. She turned, a bolt of lightning running through her as she found Prince Philip at her side.

His expression was stern. "I saw you talking about me with your father."

"P-pardon?" Sophie stammered. The flush was back, creeping up her neck and making her layers of clothing seem like they would suffocate her.

"Discussing secrets? Wondering about the weaknesses in Spain's defenses?"

"No, no, of course we weren't—"

His austerity broke, and he laughed aloud. "I'm only joking! I apologize. But I really had you, didn't I?"

Sophie laughed with him. Her panic subsided, but the unsettling feeling in her stomach did not go away. She inwardly chided herself for the third helping of knödel she'd had, certain that it was the reason for the butterflies. "Yes, you did," she told him.

"I'm Philip, but I assume you already know that," he said.

"Sophie, my lord," she said, curtsying and remembering her manners.

"Lady Sophie," he said, and bowed. "A pleasure. I have to say, I was seated with the stuffiest people at dinner. And that includes my own courtier. I've been dying for a laugh all evening, and I'm afraid I picked you as my target. Do you mind terribly?"

Somehow, his friendliness put her more on edge. She wished they would open the ballroom windows, a need for fresh air overtaking her once more.

"You're ruthless." She shook her head. "But I suppose I should be happy to serve the prince of Spain in any way I can, if only to be the object of his entertainment."

"I'll make it up to you! Look around the room—what do you see?"

She saw couples in their fine regalia, sitting in the chairs that had been moved to either side of the ballroom, sipping from their cups of honey mead or twirling each other around in practice as the orchestra played a bar of music here and there, tuning their instruments. She saw her father and Lady Claudia, now Duchess Claudia, at the head of the room, deep in conversation as if nobody else were with them.

"A party?" Sophie ventured.

"Yes, but a party of old folks. Your new stepmother is probably the only one close to us in age."

It was true. Most were closer to Duke Maximilian's age; some were so wrinkly and bent that Sophie couldn't imagine them dancing at all. She had been introduced to society, and yet there were hardly any eligible bachelors in attendance. Except for one. Sophie looked back at Philip expectantly and was surprised to find he seemed nervous. A flush was coloring his own tanned skin.

"So, Lady Sophie," he said, "what do you say about doing us both a favor and dancing with me tonight?" He offered his elbow, lifting it toward her noncommittally.

Sophie grinned with pleasure. But he was probably just being polite. He was saving them both from the awkwardness of dance partners who could be their grandparents, as he had said. And she was the only girl close to his age.

"I would love to," she murmured.

"Good," he said, with a slight smile on his face.

A light musical sound echoed through the ballroom, but it didn't come from the orchestra. Sophie glanced over and saw Duchess Claudia with her head thrown back, laughing with Duke Maximilian.

The orchestra struck up its first song, a traditional folk dance to energize the guests. Then slowly, carefully, Philip put his hand on her waist and began moving the two of them, easing into the steps. Realizing they were one of the few couples on the dance floor, Sophie faltered and missed a step, nerves flooding back.

"Sorry," she whispered urgently as she stepped on his toes.

"You're doing just fine," he whispered back. "Also, please do me the honor of ignoring my father's courtier, who is our chaperone tonight. He really doesn't know how to enjoy himself." Philip jerked his head behind him and rolled his eyes.

Sophie looked over to find a man leaning against one of the marble pillars, arms crossed over his chest. He was staring directly at her with a frightening glare. When Sophie met his gaze, he moved his head slightly to one side, as if to shake it in warning. Sophie felt a coldness at the back of her neck, as though someone had trailed a drop of ice water there.

"What is he—" she began.

Then Philip spun her around and she caught the eyes of her own father. He watched her, beaming with approval, looking like his heart would burst. Duke Maximilian winked at Sophie and smiled proudly. Warmth replaced the feeling of ice.

Sophie smiled back and shook off her fears, pulling Philip closer to her and leaning into the dance as the tempo quickened. She looked directly at him.

"Your chaperone doesn't bother me," she said.

Philip looked back at her with amusement and matched her speed. They moved with each other, a little disjointed at first, then finding the rhythm of the music with their bodies so they didn't even have to think about what their feet were doing. They whirled and jumped, in tune with each other, spinning off into space but always connected at one hand, then coming back and colliding again and again.

Her cheeks flushed, and his smile grew broad. One song became another and another, until all blurred into a mess of chaos and joy.

CHAPTER FOUR

THE YOUNG COUPLE HELD THE floor even after many of the guests had paused to rest. The orchestra themselves looked a little tired by the time Sophie and Prince Philip slowed their dancing, still laughing and full of energy as they made their way off the floor. But after holding each other for so long, it was as if they didn't want to let go, their arms and hands still brushing into the other's as they walked away.

"Summers in Madrid are nothing compared with the heat in this ballroom," Philip said, laughing and wiping the sweat from his brow. A servant came by with cordials and spring wine on a tray, but Sophie shook her head at accepting one.

Sophie lightly took his hand, pretending not to notice when his fingers squeezed back. Her stomach pitched forward, and she looked away. "Let's go outside," she said.

Philip turned back to look at the courtiers, who were trying not to look as if they were watching them.

"What's wrong?" she asked.

He hesitated, then shook his head. "Nothing—lead us."

It was already late in the night, but the garden was lit with hundreds of lanterns hung from the trees and set on the walls. The fragrance of roses and pine drifted through the night air. Sophie and Philip made their way along the footpaths of mountain tassel flowers and moonwort, settling on a stone bench beneath a tall spruce. In the distance, faint lights dotted the mountain range and alpine valley, the moonlight reflected in the snow-capped peaks.

"Beautiful country," he said.

"Is it very different from Spain?" she asked.

Philip looked around and shrugged. "We are more southern, so the port cities are warm—almost desertlike. I suppose they are more sun-bleached. Not as green." He shivered a bit from the breeze and wrapped his arms around himself. "Is it always cold here?"

"Even in summer," Sophie replied. "Right now, the hills are covered with wildflowers, but soon all of that will be a blanket of snow."

Philip's eyes crinkled. "I'd like to see that."

"Maybe you should stay awhile," she said.

"Is that an invitation?"

"If it was, would you accept?" she teased.

"If I could, I would," he said, his voice low.

"Can't you do what you like?" she asked, her voice light. "Earlier—you seemed unsure about whether you could walk outside. Is your life so restricted?"

Philip sighed. "It is your debut, isn't it? And you know what it entails?"

Sophie laughed. "Oh yes. My father has made it quite clear I'm on the marriage market now."

Philip nodded.

"The old auction block. Sold off to the highest bidder," she said gaily.

"That's a rather mercantile way of looking at it," he said, his gaze piercing.

She shrugged. "I'm just being honest. You're lucky. You're a prince. An heir. You can marry anyone you choose."

"You'd think, wouldn't you?" He frowned, lacing his sturdy hands together. "But all marriages are political. My father and mother's was arranged. As was your parents', I am sure."

Sophie reflected on that. Her parents had been in love, but perhaps they had just been lucky. Sophie's maternal grandmother had been the empress of the Holy Roman Empire.

"And has your marriage been arranged as well?" she asked lightly.

She knew it was a mistake the moment the words left her mouth. Too playful, too direct. His face turned from interested to stony, and he glanced away from Sophie, shadows cutting across his cheekbones in the lantern light. Her heart faltered. He *was* spoken for. That was clear.

"We shall see" was all he said. His smile had lost its ease and was tight around the edges. Sophie didn't know what to say, so she said nothing.

Philip shook his head and shoved his hands in the pockets of his jacket. He stood, walking closer to the edge of the bluff and scuffing his dress shoes in the gravel. He faced her but kept his eyes down. "It's my fault—I'm worried I've given you the wrong impression."

"How is that?"

He ran a hand roughly through his thick, dark hair once more; Sophie's stomach flipped over on itself.

"I can't stay here. My father and I have spent the season visiting with family in our house across the valley, but I'm to leave tomorrow morning with him to travel to England." He cleared his throat. "His Majesty wishes for me to be very focused. 'Enfoque e intención ante todo,' he says. 'Focus and intent above all.'"

Philip rolled his eyes at the words. "I was only able to come tonight because I beat him at chess. I've been so very bored these past months by myself, you see." He smiled wryly. "Pity I didn't know you were over here, probably just as bored as me. But my father is already impatient with my delay."

"Oh," Sophie said, turning over his words. It didn't seem as bad as she'd feared, though England felt farther than one of the stars that hung above them. "How long will you be in England?"

"A while, I'm afraid." Philip's face fell. "My father wishes me to become well-acquainted with the king for matters of state. And then we'll go back to Spain."

"Ah—I understand." A sudden irritation at King Ferdinand kicked up inside Sophie, but she shook it from her head.

"I'm sorry," Philip said. "I don't know why I didn't mention it. I was just really enjoying myself, more than I have in a long time, and I began to forget everything else going on in my life. I hope we can still be friends."

"Please," Sophie said, standing. "There's no need for apologies. I wish you well in England."

She thought she saw a flicker of disappointment cross his face, though it was difficult to see in the low light. Sophie took a breath to say something, anything to change the subject and get them back to the casual friendliness they'd had before, but a sudden voice broke through the darkness.

"Your Highness!"

Both Philip and Sophie jumped, turning to find King Ferdinand's courtier emerging from the shadowy garden path. His eyes flashed even in the dim light and the expression on his face contrasted sharply with the lighthearted mood of the evening.

"Good evening," Sophie said, determined to remember her manners despite her disappointment with Philip and the way this man

25

unnerved her. "I am Lady Sophie, daughter of the duke. I trust that you're enjoying the party?"

"Sir Rodrigo." The courtier gave only his name and nodded at Sophie with suspicious eyes. Then he turned his attention to Philip. "My lord, we must go. We will only make it back to the household for a few hours of rest before setting out again in the morning."

"We do have rooms prepared for the guests," Sophie said. "It's already so late—my father wouldn't want anyone to have to go out into the night."

Sir Rodrigo shot a glance at Sophie so clearly meant to be in warning that she was tempted to take a step back. She did not.

"That is unnecessary. We will leave tonight," Rodrigo said.

"My good man, you're being quite impolite to our host," Philip said. His voice was suddenly as cold as the man before him. "Lady Sophie has offered us her hospitality, and I do not wish to refuse it. My father wouldn't be pleased to hear that you snubbed the duke of Bavaria and his daughter."

The courtier's eyes glinted like knives in the light. Then he lowered them as if in repentance. "Forgive me, Your Highness, but the carriage is already prepared and waiting. It is my sworn duty to your father to keep you safe and rested at home, not in a dark garden with the duke's daughter . . . unaccompanied."

Sophie did step back this time, as if his words had physical force. "You can't be insinuating—"

"Sophie, it's all right," Philip broke in. "I'll go. I know I must. Please forgive me."

The prince shoved his hands in the pockets of his jacket once more and looked quite defeated. Sir Rodrigo, on the other hand, raised his chin in satisfaction. Sophie sighed and smoothed her dress, composing herself.

"Yes. Well, it was lovely to meet you, Your Highness, and I wish

26

you safe travels. And you, Sir Rodrigo . . . as well," she said, looking with some difficulty at the courtier. An overwhelming feeling was fighting its way up her chest at the turn the night had taken, but she swallowed hard and ignored it.

Sir Rodrigo gave a sharp nod. "You will entertain many suitors now that you've debuted, Lady Sophie—perhaps a nice baron, or even an earl." His words were objectively encouraging, yet his tone was anything but. "I wish you success and bid you good night."

Philip frowned and Sophie flushed, hot with embarrassment.

Philip bowed briefly, his hand on his chest. He seemed to be feeling just as foolish as Sophie, his eyes darting around and failing to meet her gaze.

"Lady Sophie, it was a pleasure," he said again. "I'm sorry I have to go, I really am—"

Then he backed away from the stone bench and into the darkness, following Sir Rodrigo. Sophie was left alone in the night, silent save for the singing of the crickets.

CHAPTER FIVE

SOPHIE WOKE WITH A HEADACHE.

She'd hardly been able to sleep last night between the excitement of the party, her curiosity about Claudia, and, most of all, the thoughts of Prince Philip that raided her dreams. She'd been such a fool—too forward, too awkward, at a loss in the end. Sophie lay on her back and stared up at the velvet cover of her four-poster bed, replaying their conversation again and again, remembering the way he had looked at her when they had been dancing, as if she were the only girl in the room. The only girl for his heart.

Could one fall in love so quickly?

Surely it was nothing—just a dance at a ball, and as a prince, he probably attended so many. It was just another night for him.

But for her . . .

She had been cavalier about her debut, laughing about arranged marriages. But now, having met him, it hurt to know that there was someone out there who made her feel this way. Someone who could never be hers.

If only she could forget about him, but all she could think about was the way his hand felt in hers as they walked outside together.

Then there was the matter of Sir Rodrigo, the king's courtier. It stung to think of his sly words and the subtle jibe about being unaccompanied in the garden. Sophie had never been in trouble before—not once—and she found herself gripping the bedsheets in a fist at the thought that she might possibly be such a wanton girl, a girl with a reputation, someone who would ensnare a prince.

But none of it mattered now. Perhaps it was for the best that Philip had gone away for good; Sophie wasn't sure if she could face the embarrassment of seeing him again, anyway. There were more important things ahead: namely, the unclear, foreign landscape of palace life after her debut.

Lotte came in as Sophie was gathering her thoughts, carrying a tea tray with steaming Assam.

"Oh, bless you, Lotte," Sophie muttered. "This will help my head."

"How are you feeling, my lady?" Lotte said, using much too high-pitched of a voice for Sophie's current state. "You were just stunning! And I do believe I heard a rumor or two of you and a certain princeling who couldn't stop dancing together."

Sophie could feel her cheeks heating up and tried to frown, but she couldn't help giggling awkwardly. "Stop that. Prince Philip is long gone by now."

Lotte clucked her tongue. "You could always write letters."

"I don't think so. He was rather clear that we won't meet again."

"I don't know about that! I wouldn't be so sure he's gone for good. You should have seen the two of you, carrying on." Then the maid's eyes got wide. "I was sorry to hear about what happened, though. The way you were snubbed."

"You heard what Sir Rodrigo said?" Sophie asked, surprised. How many people had been lurking in the garden last night?

"Who's that?" Lotte wrinkled her nose. "No, I mean Duchess Claudia. She made such a scene just as you debuted."

"Claudia? Oh, come now, Lotte, she fainted." Sophie shook her head. "I'm sure her nerves only got the better of her. When I was up there myself, it was very unpleasant—bright and noisy, with everybody in the palace staring right at you."

Lotte knitted her brow as she herded Sophie over to the dressing table, then set to work brushing and plaiting her hair. "I wouldn't be so certain, my lady. She's made an odd impression on the staff so far."

"How is that?"

"Well." Lotte bit her lip as she concentrated. "She talked down to one of the other servants who was trying to assist her with her luggage—sort of pushed him a bit and picked it up herself. She's kept to her room as much as possible, using only her own staff who came with her. One of the kitchen maids tried to bring tea up to her as a gesture of goodwill but ended up getting a lecture about how poorly it was made."

"Hmm," Sophie said, thinking of how Duchess Claudia had almost thrown a hunk of cheese at her the first time they met. "Don't you suppose all of that could be to do with nerves, or moving to an entirely new country?"

"Perhaps." But Lotte didn't look convinced.

When she was dressed, Sophie hurried downstairs to the dining room for breakfast. On his days home, she and Duke Maximilian sometimes ate together before he went into his study to work. Sophie always tried to get up early enough to get a few extra moments with him before he disappeared once more.

But as Sophie entered the dining room, she saw servants clearing away one set of plates and goblets. She had missed him. And Claudia was likely still asleep.

Sophie sighed, taking a seat at the table anyway. She worked slowly through breakfast, nibbling small bites of toast and sipping a second and then third round of tea in the hopes that Duchess Claudia would come down. But an hour or so passed, and still the dining room remained empty, save for the servants who stood silently near the doorways.

Sophie tried looking for Claudia in the gardens instead. This was the part of the palace she enjoyed most, and as long as things were blooming, she spent time out here whenever she could. There was a constant and comforting hum of bees, crickets, and hundreds of other flittering bugs that made their home there, mingling with the splashing of the palace fountains. Sophie started back in the kitchen gardens, where fennel and basil and sage wafted fragrant in the air, and then through the rose garden filled with deep red and snowy-white blooms.

She settled at last on the stone bench where she and the prince had sat the night before, under the tall Norway spruce. Duke Maximilian's palace was built high up on the foothills of the Bavarian Alps, overlooking the duchy villages he governed and the mountain range beyond. The main road twisted and ran like a river from the palace and off into the distance, the same road that Philip had taken the night before. Sophie squinted, trying to see if she could see the family house he had mentioned way off the distance.

But it could have been anywhere above the villages, in the foothills, or nearer to the mountain range that stretched even farther into the horizon.

Sophie sighed, grinding her foot into the ground. She felt very silly for wasting so much time and thought on someone she barely knew, but he would not leave her mind. She sat with her chin in her hands, making up imaginary scenarios in which they might meet again.

She soon gave up. Every single one involved Sophie leaving the palace or traveling somewhere new, even to England in pursuit of him. And she knew her father would never allow that.

"Good morning," a voice said nearby.

Duchess Claudia emerged from the tangled vines by the path next to the bench. She had been so quiet—or perhaps, Sophie so distracted—that she had made no sound in her approach at all.

"Good morning," Sophie replied. "You startled me a little!"

"I apologize." Claudia frowned. "I seem to be having that effect on others lately. Do you mind if I join you?"

"Of course not." Sophie patted the bench next to her. They looked out onto the valley and rivers below as a blackbird sang above them. Sophie wasn't sure what to say, so she waited for Claudia to speak first.

After what seemed like a long moment, she did. "I'm sorry we haven't gotten a real chance to talk since our incident yesterday," Claudia said. "Did you enjoy yourself last night?"

In the alpine sun, Sophie was once again struck by Claudia's impossible beauty. Her skin was so dewy and her features so smooth and sharp that she looked as though a marble statue had come to life.

Sophie nodded. "I had a very nice time—almost too nice. Did you?"

"Your father is a wonderful person," Claudia said, returning Sophie's nod. "And I—I want you to know that I love him to bits." She cleared her throat before starting again, her face looking troubled. "I'm sorry I lost control of myself as you debuted last night. And about the larder as well. I really have been feeling so overwhelmed coming here. To be honest, I'm having trouble believing my luck. This place is so beautiful that I must be dreaming."

Sophie smiled. Lotte had to be wrong; this woman was no one to worry about.

"My father," Sophie said, "has seemed like a dead man since the day my mother died. You must be someone very special if you can bring him back to life as you do."

Claudia looked solemnly at Sophie for a long moment, then gave her the tiniest of smiles. "Thank you," she said.

Sophie nodded, then glanced back out at the valley.

"Are you all right?" Claudia asked.

"Oh," Sophie said. "Do you see that road, way off in the distance?" She pointed far down the valley. "Over that way is where Prince Philip was staying. I met him last night and—I was just a bit sad to see him go."

Claudia raised her eyebrows. "Do you think he'll come back to visit soon?"

"No," Sophie said, biting the inside of her cheek and trying not to let the disappointment show on her face.

"Ah," Claudia said. She let the syllable of understanding fall between them, losing itself in the whisper of the pine branches. They watched the valley for another long moment before she spoke again. "I see. I'm sorry to hear that. You both danced beautifully."

Sophie sighed.

"I wouldn't give up too much hope," Claudia said slowly. "Things work themselves out in mysterious ways, you know. And perhaps you shall meet someone else. Your father will make certain to introduce you to a great many suitors now that you have come out to society."

Sophie pulled a white rose petal from a nearby bloom and rolled it between her fingers, thinking that she did not want to meet a great many suitors at all. Just one. "Philip said marriages are arranged, but Papa said he would listen to me."

"He will, indeed," agreed Claudia. "Your father will not give you up so easily."

Sophie let the petal fall, avoiding Claudia's eyes. "But what if I don't like any of them?"

Claudia shrugged. "You will." She took great care smoothing the front of her dress, running her hand over the dark blue silk and watching the way it rippled in the sunlight.

Sophie wrinkled her nose. "How do you know?"

Her new stepmother hesitated before answering. "You must remember how fortunate you are. Your father holds significant authority, and the duchy is wealthy. If all goes well, you will have much greater say in who you marry. This isn't to say your father wasn't my choice," she said quickly. "I am very fortunate in that respect, too. But for a long time, it looked as though I would be lucky to marry at all. Few noblemen are interested in a woman from a failing household. It is said she will bring down their own fortune."

Sophie remembered the rumors she'd heard last night.

"Well, I don't think that," she said. "Do you miss your family and your home? Do you think we'll see them soon?"

Claudia's smile was confused and sad. "Oh—I do miss them, very much. I miss the smell of the barley in the fields, the frozen grass in November. White storks nesting in the spring. I'm sure I'll get some of that here, though not in the same way. But—I won't be seeing them again."

"What? Why not?"

"Sophie . . . I'm part of your father's household now. The maids and ladies-in-waiting I arrived with returned to my father's home; they had no place here. My family is too far for easy travel. My mother has passed away; my sister has been married off. My father is old. This is my new life now, you and your father. I have to make a new family."

There was some greater meaning behind these last few words, but Sophie was so preoccupied with the unpleasant feeling growing inside her that she didn't notice. Claudia now seemed the bearer of some very bad news indeed.

"Is that—is that what happens when you get married?" Sophie asked, her voice catching slightly. "You leave forever and don't come back?" Was that what her own mother had done, too?

"I don't want to upset you," Claudia said. "It may be different for you. You may end up somewhere very close by, or you may be able to travel more. You are Maximilian's only child—perhaps your father and I will be able to visit *you*."

"Or maybe I won't marry."

Claudia smiled at her, but the expression looked doubtful. "I know you are still young and don't understand. But a woman in our society without a husband is often dismissed, or worse, vulnerable."

Sophie looked at Claudia for a long moment, feeling challenged, but there was nothing defiant in the woman's eyes.

"We'll see," Sophie said with a heavy sigh that was as good an end to the uncomfortable conversation as any.

The sudden chill of mountain wind came through the trees and rustled the leaves of the rosebushes.

"Would you like a tour inside so we are more comfortable?" Sophie asked, eyeing Claudia.

Sophie led Duchess Claudia through the rooms of the palace, pointing out each one and explaining the difference between the libraries—the larger one was for law and record-keeping, the smaller for literature.

Sophie seemed to walk off her worries, which faded as Claudia's wonder grew. Sophie showed her young stepmother how to orient herself between the north wing and south wing and helped her climb to the highest tower to see the best view.

"This is incredible," Claudia gasped. "I have never before been up this high."

Claudia held on to the stone ledge of the tower with white knuckles, and Sophie grinned.

As they continued, Sophie found herself relaxing more and more. Claudia seemed eager to understand the palace and interested in what Sophie had to say.

"This is our biggest fireplace—you'll love it in the winter," she said, and, "Here's where we have our tea after dinner," the collective plural slipping naturally into her speech.

The palace itself seemed new as she saw it through Claudia's eyes, imagining the young woman in the places they would occupy together. Sophie and Claudia raced from one end of the dining hall to the other and slipped down corridors to hide from dour-faced servants, doubling over in stifled laughter with stitches in their sides.

The list of places to see having dwindled, Sophie hesitated before their last stop. But Claudia had confided to her in the garden, and the way she'd talked about her own family made Sophie feel it was important.

She cleared her throat, to sound a bit more formal, as they reached a corridor near the back half of the palace.

"What's down here?" Claudia asked.

"These are . . . the portraits of my mother," Sophie said.

The long hallway contained mismatched frames of all different sizes and gilding, pulled from all the other bedrooms, parlors, and halls in the palace to remain in this one place as a memorial to Duchess Maria. Sophie knew her father never came down here. But

Sophie looked straight back into her mother's flat, painted eyes with familiarity.

Claudia quieted, moving forward when Sophie gestured for her to come closer.

The young duchess gasped. "She looks so much like you."

Sophie looked into the painting at the smooth, pale skin; the dark, sharp eyes; the graceful neck and luminous black hair. Her mother looked so perfect in these renditions, almost formidable. Sophie certainly didn't feel like that.

"She's very beautiful," Claudia murmured.

"She was," Sophie said. She glanced at Claudia. "They called her 'the fairest in all the land.'"

"That is what they say about you, too, you know," said Claudia.

"Me?" squeaked Sophie.

"Oh yes," said Claudia, and they both fell silent. The light of the sun was growing shorter as it came through the arched windows, signaling the late hour of the morning. Sophie suddenly remembered Monsieur Gustave, who would be waiting several floors above.

"I have to go to my lessons now," Sophie said, breaking the moment. "But we'll talk some more this evening, yes?"

"Yes." Claudia smiled.

Sophie nodded at her, finding it strange to see this flesh-and-blood woman next to the two-dimensional versions of her mother she'd come to know. Suddenly uneasy at the sight, Sophie waved and left Claudia in the portrait hall alone.

Claudia kept staring at the portraits of Duchess Maria, lost in thought, as if attempting to memorize every feature of her predecessor.

CHAPTER SIX

SOPHIE WENT THROUGH HER STUDIES with Monsieur Gustave quickly, relieved to do something familiar and boring. There was too much change in the palace lately. Though Sophie didn't always enjoy the lessons, they at least gave her the chance to talk about different subjects and challenge her brain. It was more interesting, to say the least, than sitting quietly on her own as she often did when Maximilian was away.

She was, however, getting frustrated by today's lesson, which was yet another lecture on French verb conjugations. If she was to get involved in the palace's affairs at all, this wasn't the topic she needed today.

"Monsieur Gustave," she interrupted him, "I've actually had a question on my mind, lately, about the palace. And the history of Bavaria, as well."

Monsieur Gustave scowled. "En français, s'il vous plaît."

Sophie tried not to roll her eyes. "J'ai une question sur le palais et—et l'histoire de la Bavière."

"Pourquoi?"

"Parce-que je pense . . . because . . . Oh, listen, Monsieur, I just think I should be learning more about our current affairs, shouldn't I? Now that I've been introduced to society?"

"What difference could that make?"

Sophie drew back in her chair. "Well, I—I'm part of the court now. I should know what's going on. Am I misunderstanding?"

The tutor rolled his eyes. "Eh, d'accord . . . I suppose we could review the basics, if only so you'll have something to discuss in polite conversation. There are several volumes I've penned, in fact, on this very subject. I'll retrieve them from the library."

"I can do it myself," Sophie said. She couldn't risk Monsieur Gustave changing his mind and bringing back books about Rome or something else he considered more suitable. "I—uh—wish to see if there are any other volumes there that interest me."

"I suppose. I'll sketch together a brief lesson plan while you're gone."

Sophie escaped from the room. She walked slowly, in no rush to return to her tutor. Deciding to give herself a break, Sophie took a brief detour down to the kitchen, where she retrieved a spritzkuchen and a small cup of cocoa before meandering in the direction of the library.

Sophie was just thinking that she might see what Claudia was doing—perhaps she might have an interest in attending the lesson, being new to the palace herself—when a sharp crash and the sound of something shattering echoed out from the library door.

Sophie rushed into the room and stopped short at the scene. Frozen near the entrance were two maids, one clutching a duster. Their expressions stricken and terrified. In the middle of the room was Claudia, standing above a very old and ornate porcelain vase, now in a thousand pieces on the library floor. Its blue-and-white china pattern was unrecognizable.

"That was my mother's!" Sophie cried. A sharp ringing sounded in her ears.

Claudia stared wide-eyed, her face and throat bloodred. "I'm so sorry!"

"What have you done? That was my mother's vase!" Sophie heard her voice rise as if she wasn't in control of it. It had been Duchess Maria's, a thing of her own, one of the few possessions she'd brought to the palace long ago.

Claudia said nothing else but charged into the hallway, nearly colliding with Sophie on her way out, her face red and wet with tears. Sophie ignored her, kneeling to scrape together the broken shards. "What on earth happened?"

"We came in to dust and polish, Olga and me," Ada, one of the maids, said behind her. "Just as we always do this day of the week. We didn't realize anyone was in here."

"The duchess surprised us," Olga continued, wringing her hands. "She must have overheard us talking. We were just discussing the wedding party, that's all! But she got so angry, Lady Sophie, so angry. And she scared us—we backed away—and—we hit—we dropped the vase!"

The pieces were jagged and grainy in Sophie's hands; there were so many of them. "What did you say about her?" she asked.

"What did we . . . say?" Ada sounded uncertain.

"Yes. What did she overhear to make her angry?" Sophie said. "Tell me."

The two looked at each other, guilt written on their faces.

"We just—" the first started. "Well, you are so lovely, my lady. And you know how loyal the palace is to Duchess Maria's memory. All we did was to suggest that Duchess Claudia may be envious of your beauty. Anyone would be."

Annoyance bubbled alongside Sophie's anger. She'd rather everyone stopped talking about the way she looked and just left her alone, especially right now. It was embarrassing.

"Anything else?" Sophie asked.

Olga shrugged, rubbing her neck. "Just that . . . we hope she'll bear a child, soon. A boy." She cast her eyes down.

Sophie felt heat in her neck, her ears. She hadn't even thought about the possibility, but of course Claudia would be expected to bear a child, to produce the sign of a strong marriage. And if the child was a boy . . .

"Why a boy?" Sophie spoke very slowly in order to keep her voice even.

Olga looked back blankly. "Well, the duke—your father, he . . . he has no heir."

Of course. That was why her father had remarried. As of now— the title, the duchy, the fortune—it would all go to their closest male relative, some cousin across the country, if her father did not have a son. She knew this. She was the child of a duke; she knew the rules. How could she forget?

She was only a girl, cattle to be married off, like her mother, the daughter of an emperor, who found herself in this faraway place. Her mother had found love and happiness, but she was a rare case. Most royal and aristocratic marriages were made for political convenience. Not love.

Sophie felt the blood moving through her, as though the anger Claudia had left in her wake was infecting her, too. She expected the maids to apologize, to correct themselves, but their expressions were ones of pity instead. They said nothing.

"It's all right," Sophie said at last. "Clean up and fix it somehow."

The maids nodded quickly and hurried to work, keeping their heads down and backs turned to Sophie.

Stepping around their bent bodies, Sophie retrieved the books she'd come for and left the girls to their work.

CHAPTER SEVEN

As THE FIRST MONTH PASSED, a friction grew between Sophie and Claudia. Maybe it was the incident with the vase, or maybe it was Claudia's uncanny ability to find Sophie when she preferred to be alone. Though Sophie tried to find space to herself in the library or the gardens, she would hear footsteps and look up to find Claudia with the same infuriating, placid smile on her face.

Sophie had never been sought after this way, not even by the servants. Sometimes she would jump when Claudia called her name, its shape sounding odd and unfamiliar in someone else's mouth and with Claudia's slight Moldavian accent. When she could, she would invent some new task she needed to do or an errand she needed to run—alone—somewhere else in the castle. At times she felt guilty about this avoidance, but then she would catch sight of her mother's vase, which now stood safely in Sophie's room. The palace potter had done his best to restore it to something of its former self, but it would never look the same again. She and Claudia didn't speak of it.

Claudia's elegant movements were growing, to Sophie, stilted and unnatural. She began to dress in simpler, slimmer clothes and, somehow, looked more ethereal than on her wedding day. Though Sophie kept a sharp eye on the duchess's physique, nothing seemed to change. Sophie wasn't even entirely sure what she was looking for, but she figured she would sense something different if Claudia were to conceive a child.

At times, Claudia's smile seemed frozen on her face like a clay mask, especially when the servants gave her sideways looks in the hall or quickly broke off their whispering when the woman passed by. The rumors that began before Claudia's wedding to Duke Maximilian had only grown and sharpened as time went on. Even Lotte whispered that the duchess had taken to talking to herself in the mirror and was feared to be going a bit mad, and that she was often seen sneaking out of the palace and going off to the woods for some mysterious errand or another. The servants said she was consulting some kind of witch deep in the forest. Sophie knew it was wrong and unkind—even a form of treason—for the servants to speak this way about the duchess, but she didn't feel it was in her power to stop it. What was more, she couldn't help listening with uneasy fascination to the strange tales the palace spun about her stepmother.

"She sent her dinner back to the kitchens last night," Lotte said one morning as she set Sophie's hair. "Didn't even touch it."

Sophie winced as one of the hot irons came close to her ear. In the flurry of social invitations that had descended on the palace in the weeks following Sophie's debut, Duke Maximilian had finally found one close enough to the palace that he would allow her to attend. It was a ball at the nearby home of Baron and Baroness Ziegler, thrown to celebrate the end of summer and the beginning of the harvest season.

"Save the ones in Sweden and Italy for when you're a bit

older"—the duke had chuckled, though a slight look of panic reached his eyes—"there will be plenty of time for extended journeys in the future."

Now Lotte was inundated with hundreds of tasks to prepare Sophie for the ball, but she tackled them all with relish. "Sorry," she said, pulling the hot iron away to a safer distance before continuing her gossip about Claudia. "She turned her nose right up at the räucher-fisch. Chef has never been so insulted."

The two of them had an unspoken agreement that Lotte would relay what she heard to Sophie so they could both make sure the rumors weren't getting out of hand. But the zeal with which Lotte took to this role wasn't lost on Sophie, who did her best to ignore any feelings of similar glee.

"She did say something about seafood disagreeing with her stomach," Sophie said doubtfully. They'd all eaten separately yesterday, with Maximilian attending to some work in his study and Claudia, looking tired, taking her dinner in her own room. Sophie hoped this wasn't a sign of her father slipping back into his old habits. "Perhaps she just has a sensitive palate."

Lotte eyed her mistress in the old glass of Sophie's dressing mirror. "Lady Sophie, do you know what Duchess Claudia does when you're not around to accompany her? When you're in lessons or getting dressed?"

"I don't. What does she do?"

"Nothing." Lotte cast her eyes back down to the work she was doing on Sophie's hair. "She does nothing. She simply sits, bides her time in a room somewhere until you come out again. That huge, gilded mirror your father gave her for their wedding—like the one in front of us—they say she stares and stares into it and stays very still. She's frightened more than one servant who went in and made up the whole bed before realizing she was there."

Sophie had the feeling of a spider crossing the back of her neck. She twitched under Lotte's touch.

"And what of it?" she said, wishing she sounded less bothered.

"That's just the thing; no one knows quite what to make of it. But the opinion of the staff—if I may say, Lady Sophie—is that she's very vain. And it follows that she must be particularly envious of you. Her behavior at your debut proves it to be so, and now she watches you closely, follows you everywhere. I'm glad you're allowing me to be a lookout for you, because you never know what designs she may have on your well-being."

"That isn't quite what I asked you to do," Sophie muttered. "And I wish you'd stop bringing up the debut."

But Lotte was no longer listening, distracted by the valet who announced himself at Sophie's door.

"Your father would like to speak with you," he called.

When Sophie arrived at the duke's study, Claudia was already there, seated in a chair by the fireplace. She didn't look like she knew much more about why Maximilian had summoned them than Sophie did. But as he saw her, Sophie's father smiled.

"Ah, Sophielien. Thank you for coming—I can see I interrupted your preparations for this evening." He eyed the handful of hair across Sophie's shoulder that wasn't yet curled. "Please, have a seat."

Sophie smiled and nodded at Claudia as she came closer to the fire. Though her gesture was returned, she noticed the tightness in Claudia's face and felt a twinge of guilt. The rumors and gossip that went around the household couldn't be lost on her stepmother. Sophie realized she was probably doing a poor job of hiding her own doubts about Claudia.

"What an exciting night this will be for you!" Maximilian said, settling into his own seat. "Sophie, this is the first time you will truly participate in palace society as an eligible young woman. You know your responsibilities in this engagement: Behave well, be polite, and get to know as many guests as you're able, particularly the young men."

He winked at her, and Sophie laughed nervously. She was hoping to avoid the topic of marriage as long as possible, though it seemed to come up often these days.

"On that note," the duke continued, "it is important for you to bring a chaperone. You must not go anywhere unaccompanied, especially not with a young man. This is very important to your reputation."

"Yes, Papa, I understand," Sophie said. She remembered the scornful look of Sir Rodrigo in the garden, and she wished Maximilian hadn't brought it up. "Frau Hilda is accompanying me. I thought we'd already agreed."

"We had, yes." Maximilian folded his hands. "But in thinking it over the past few days, I believe it would be much better if Claudia were to go with you."

"What? Why?" Sophie said quickly. Next to Maximilian, Claudia raised her eyebrows; this was news to her, too.

Maximilian looked at Sophie in surprise, and she immediately regretted her tone.

"I thought that would be welcome news," Maximilian said. "All respect to Frau Hilda, but I do know how dry your governess can be."

"I'm sorry," Sophie said. "I didn't mean—I just don't want Claudia to feel burdened with having to be my nursemaid all night."

"I wouldn't feel burdened at all." Claudia shifted in her chair, looking uncertainly from Sophie to Maximilian. "But this is Sophie's first night out. She doesn't need me along."

"Nonsense," said Maximilian, now frowning at both of them. "It will be a good experience for the two of you. I didn't expect this to be a discussion."

Sophie wasn't sure what to say. As nervous as she was for the ball, she'd been looking forward to getting some space from Claudia.

"I—I don't know, Your Grace," Claudia said before Sophie could speak.

Maximilian sighed and ran a hand through his hair, just beginning to grow salt-and-pepper gray. "Now, I didn't want to have to be frank about this. But we've all been through a great deal of change in the past month or so, and I know not all of that has been easy."

He looked pointedly at Sophie as he said this, and she dropped her gaze to her lap.

"I thought it would be good for the two of you to spend some time together," he finished.

Sophie opened her mouth to say they had spent time together—far too much—and they could benefit from spending a great deal of time apart. But out of the corner of her eye, she caught the movement of Claudia twisting the end of her shawl round and round her fingers, staring at the embroidered rug on the floor of the study the same way Sophie had a moment before. Something in the thinness of her frame and the bend of her neck looked to Sophie incredibly pitiful.

"Claudia," Sophie said, fighting to keep a sigh from slipping out. "Of course you can come with me if you'd like. I'm—I'm sorry I didn't think of that myself, in fact."

Claudia's smile was nervous. "You're certain?"

Sophie bit the inside of her cheek. "Absolutely."

The duke clapped his hands. "It's settled! Off with you, then; you both have much preparing to do!"

CHAPTER EIGHT

As Maximilian's large oaken carriage bustled them down the hill, through the village, and toward the other side of the valley where the party was to be held, the early autumn chill made its way into the cab.

It had been years since Sophie had come down from the foothills and traveled through the village. She tried to think of the last time. It had been with her mother and father, going somewhere on business or to visit relatives, though the only relatives she knew were distant in both geography and demeanor.

She would have liked to sit quietly by herself, watching the quaint little town go by as it was bathed in dusky twilight, trying to remember the finer details of that long-ago memory and defining its shape. With Frau Hilda, this certainly would have been possible.

But not with Claudia. The duchess's nervous energy caused her to babble on, ignoring Sophie's short responses. Between Claudia's questions and the jostling of the carriage, Sophie began to develop a headache.

"I do hope I haven't overdressed," Claudia fretted. While Sophie wore a pale blue gown that cinched close at the waist and billowed around her legs, the sleeves similarly open and flowing at her forearms, Claudia was dressed in a simple frock, so dark green it was almost black, that showcased her slim figure. Her attempt to look less conspicuous had the opposite effect, rendering her more stunning, a natural, effortless beauty straight from Paris itself. The dark, tight fabric contrasted strikingly with her pale skin and gave her an angular look.

Sophie wondered if she would even be noticed next to Claudia. "You look fine, Your Grace." Sophie tugged down her own sleeves, which suddenly felt clownish.

"Please, call me Claudia," said the duchess. "We don't have to stand on ceremony in private. I thought I told you that already."

"Well, if I can say so, your attire is wonderful, Claudia," said Sophie.

"I'm sorry, I don't have much experience being matronly yet. I thought this would serve. I suppose I'll need to have more dresses made."

"You could have borrowed one of Frau Hilda's," Sophie said innocently.

"I hadn't thought of that. I'll consult with her next time," Claudia said with a raised eyebrow and a hint of a smile.

Sophie sighed and turned her attention to the window, trying to tell how much longer she had to endure this ride. Even Frau Hilda's scratchy wool garments would probably look like the opening of the spring season in Paris on Claudia's frame.

"Are you nervous?" Claudia broke in again. "It's all right if you are. I daresay I haven't felt quite this alive since the wedding. I do hope their orchestra is in tune. These nights are getting rather cold, and you know how bad that is for the instruments . . ."

By the time they reached the house of Baron and Baroness Ziegler, Sophie was ready to throw herself out of the cab. "We're here!" she cried and accepted the hand of the valet who appeared to help her out of the carriage.

An enormous Bavarian mansion stood there, with swirling Baroque columns before the door and dozens of high, beveled-glass windows, each of which glowed and sparkled with the party lights inside. It was all Sophie could do not to leave Claudia behind as they ascended the stairs and entered through the grand doors.

They were announced with great fanfare, all eyes suddenly turning at the names of Duchess Claudia and Lady Sophie. It was clear that Claudia's arrival and wedding ceremony had made news in Bavarian high society. Sophie felt Claudia clutch her arm; to steady herself or to use Sophie as a shield, she couldn't tell.

Within the great hall where the foyer opened up were hundreds of people, many of them as young as Sophie. It was not so large as the palace ballroom, but still the scene was ablaze with glittering chandeliers and the bright music of the orchestra that reverberated against polished marble. Servants ducked through the crowd bearing shining silver trays of appetizers and pastries. There was an energy in the air, something thrumming and taut, that hadn't been present at Claudia's wedding and Sophie's debut. At the loud thrill of the youthful nobility around them and the sight of the couples whirling on the dance floor, Sophie suddenly felt cement lock her feet to the marble tiles beneath her shoes.

She didn't know anybody here. Not a soul.

Someone nudged her elbow. "Go on," Claudia said gently in Sophie's ear. "It looks like fun. I'll be right over here." She jerked her head toward a group of older noblewomen near the window, flanked by a governess or two. They eyed Claudia with raised eyebrows and curtsied slowly to the duchess.

Sophie felt Claudia leave her side, but still she could not move. As the orchestra neared the end of their song, she became more and more aware of the need to step forward, to blend in with the crowd and act normal. But she'd never done that before, not with so many people her own age. Sophie tugged at the hem of one of her sleeves and then the other, sweat pricking at her neck and under her arms in the stuffy, crowded hall. Why did this have to be so hard?

The song finished, the room erupted into applause, and Sophie took a step. In the lull before the next dance, she took another.

Suddenly a young man with sandy-brown hair was at her arm. He said something, but Sophie couldn't hear over the noise.

"I'm sorry?" She leaned closer, hit with the scent of sweat and the powder that must have been in his hair.

"I said—*may I have this dance?*"

"Oh. You may. You can have—yes." She felt so silly.

The boy grinned, his smile a bit lopsided and too wide for his face. Then with a yank of her arm, they were out on the dance floor. The song had a fast tempo that Sophie found difficult to follow, and she had to concentrate hard to avoid being stepped on or smashing her own feet into his. At one point she tried to find Claudia at the side of the room, but they were moving so dizzily that Sophie lost her bearings on which end of the hall was which.

"May I have your name?" she shouted.

He shouted back, something that sounded like *Lord Maximilian.*

"Did you say 'Lord Maximilian'?" She hoped not.

"No, Lord Manfred! My father is the baron!"

"Ah. It's nice to meet—"

But at that moment Manfred flung her off into space and let go of her hand. Sophie cried in surprise, but quickly realized that everyone was doing the same thing—they were switching partners. She was now with a stocky boy, shorter than her, who squeezed her hands hard.

The orchestra repeated their phrase and he too spun her off to be caught by a tall blond boy with a smirk. As he put his hand around Sophie's waist and swung her in a circle, she felt her shoulder hit against another couple in the dense crowd.

"Oh! I'm so sorry," she said pointlessly, her words drowning in the music. She glanced over her shoulder to see whom she'd bumped, and her heart stopped cold.

The shock of dark hair over the forehead, the wide shoulders. The boy looked just like Philip.

But her dance partner caught her attention.

"Not the best on your feet, are you?" sneered the blond boy. "You're that new girl from those godforsaken mountains, aren't you?" he said, dismissing all of Bavaria as a backwater nation.

Remembering her manners, she tried not to flinch. "Lady Sophie, my lord, and you are?"

"Lord Dietrich. My father is the archduke," he sniffed, holding his nose high. Archdukes outranked her father's title, and he knew it.

"A pleasure," she told him even though he was holding her too tightly and too closely for her comfort. There was something cruel in his eyes that she did not much like and almost feared.

He snorted, "Of course," as if every noblewoman in the surrounding areas would swoon to dance with him.

She was saved by Manfred, who was back again, pushing her arm out at length and galloping her across the ballroom, followed by the rest of the pairs. He turned her around once more in a circle, easing up with the slowing of the music. Sophie took the opportunity to look for the boy she'd glimpsed for a moment.

Oh! There he was—mere feet away—and he was looking back at her. His eyes glittering in the candlelight.

It *was* Philip, his hand around the waist of his partner, a rather gorgeous young lady.

A moment of shock passed, and Sophie came to her senses, just in time to see that Manfred was bowing to her. The song was over. Quickly, she dropped into a curtsy and ducked her head.

"Thank you," she said. "It was a pleasure."

"The pleasure was mine!" said Manfred. "Would you like—"

"I would!" she said, not knowing what he was about to ask but wanting to get away from Dietrich, who was leering in her direction.

Manfred looked positively thrilled and led her toward the tables where lemonade and wine were being poured for guests. Sophie looked over her shoulder to see if Philip noticed where she'd gone. If he had, she couldn't tell, as his face was turned to his partner's.

Philip had stayed, and he hadn't told her. He was in this very room, dancing with another girl. Sophie didn't even know what to say; she wanted to talk to him herself. But the noise rose and fell, and another song started; the crowd swallowed him up. And then another terrible thought occurred to Sophie: What if he'd never planned to go to England at all? What if he'd only said that to let her down gently?

Sophie turned to search once more and found Philip staring right at her. She felt a thrill, and a naughty desire to punish him.

She faced Manfred again and laughed gaily at something he said, which caused him to turn an even deeper shade of red and fumble with his cup, when she felt a tap on her shoulder.

"Lady Sophie?"

A hand on her arm and he was there, real, slightly different from the picture she'd built up of him in her head over the past month. Sophie took a step back, hit with a wall of nerves and emotion as he looked earnestly into her face.

"Your Highness," she said breathlessly.

CHAPTER NINE

"FANCY MEETING YOU HERE!" SOPHIE continued, her voice a bit overbright. "A long way from England, aren't you? Lord Manfred, will you excuse me?"

"Oh, uh, yes, of course," said Manfred, who bowed and took his leave.

She turned her attention back to Philip. "So, England?"

He smiled sheepishly. "Uh . . . I think we took a wrong turn somewhere," he said lightly.

Sophie cleared her throat, wishing one of the servants would come by with food or drinks so she had somewhere to put her hands. It was awful seeing him again—awful and wonderful.

Philip looked to his shoes and then back up. "I decided not to join my father on his business. It was a last-minute decision."

"Oh. I see. But why?"

He shrugged. "A whim, I suppose."

Sophie frowned at the response. "Do these whims hit you often? That seems like a rather large one."

He laughed aloud and shook his head at the floor. "Well, no. I—"
He looked around the room, sucking his teeth. "Would you mind
going somewhere a bit quieter? I can't hear a thing in here."

"I believe my dance card is full," she said, wanting to punish him
just a little more.

"Oh," he said, looking crestfallen.

"I'm kidding," she said. "I don't know where my dance card is."

He grinned. "Good."

She couldn't help it. She smiled back.

He held out his arm, and she took it.

Sophie scanned the room as they headed into the next, Claudia
still nowhere to be seen. But, after all, she had said this was Sophie's
night, and surely one couldn't really be "unaccompanied" in a manor
house brimming with guests. So Sophie would do as she pleased.

There were other groups in the halls and corridors, taking a break
from the dance and resting in the cooler air from the windows that
had been thrown wide. Philip picked up two goblets of wine from
a passing servant and, mercifully, handed one to Sophie. She held
the stem with both hands and sipped, the bittersweet liquid burning
warmth into her throat. They walked very slowly, aimlessly, over the
lush carpet that ran through the halls.

"It's a fine night," Philip said, looking over the hallway's por-
traiture and away from Sophie. "It seems like the weather is really
starting to take a turn, though."

"I suppose," Sophie murmured. "I imagine the weather in
England is doing the same."

He leaned against an open doorway, a threshold that seemed to
lead into a large, darker library whose bookshelves reached high to
the ceiling. They could not go in that dark room together, not unsupervised, but they could hover at its edge.

"I imagine it is." Philip took a long sip of his wine.

"Did you beat your father at chess again?" Sophie said. Her tone was teasing, but she realized she didn't mind if he heard the slant of accusation. He had some explaining to do.

He grinned once more, shaking his head and swirling his drink in his glass. He took a deep breath. "Sophie, I'm sorry I didn't tell you I stayed. If you want the truth, I was embarrassed."

She looked at him incredulously, wrapping an arm around herself and tipping her wine back and forth. "*You?* Embarrassed? Whatever for?"

"Sir Rodrigo was quite unkind to you, but even so, he was right: I put you in an uncomfortable situation. I wasn't sure you'd like to see me again."

"You shouldn't worry about that. It was *I* who was embarrassed, leading you out in the garden like that. I should have known better than to kidnap a crown prince."

He laughed, shaking his head. "That's a crime, actually."

"Isn't your father cross that you didn't join him?"

"He's not pleased, to be sure." Philip pressed his lips in a hard line. "But it's a decision he's going to have to live with."

"You've heard from him, then?" Sophie watched him carefully, eyes wide. She couldn't imagine disobeying her own father, much less the formidable man she imagined King Ferdinand to be. And Philip was practicing *continued* disobedience; every minute he was not in England was an act of defiance against his father.

"Oh, I've heard from him," he muttered. "I told my staff to just throw the letters away, with how many we've been getting."

"I see. Philip, have you done anything like this before?"

He shook his head, in sharp movements, and threw back the rest of his wine. Sophie waited for him to speak again, but he stayed quiet, seemingly distracted by the muffled playing of the orchestra down the hall.

"He sounds like a strict man," Sophie said quietly. "But I'm certain that he cares for you."

"So you've heard the rumors?" Philip smiled but his eyes were cold. "He's earned himself a bit of a reputation . . ."

Alarmed by the change in his face, she worried she'd crossed a line. "No, he just seems—my father didn't say anything specifically, he only mentioned the king was—" What could she say? Surely not "a cheat," though those had been Maximilian's words.

"A liar? A tyrant?" Philip said, finishing the sentence for her.

"No, not exactly—I mean no disrespect to your father."

"Of course not." He looked into his cup as though he wished it were still full. "But I assume you have heard of his capture of the duchy of Milan, many years ago."

Sophie shook her head. "Not very much, actually." She had heard about the wars that had been fought within the continent but knew little of the specifics. The pained expression on his face told her the details were anything but honorable.

"He sent his men into Milan, letting them do as much damage as they could. You should know we have a great number of soldiers— more than most kingdoms," Philip pressed on. "The first troop became fatigued and was replaced with fresh fighters, then the next and the next, and the same happened with Italy—as their soldiers tired, their general called them back and sent out new men. The battle was evenly matched, and then it looked as though we were losing. As though we had run out of troops ready for combat."

His fingers closed tighter around his goblet. "Our soldiers stayed on the fields, fighting until they were completely exhausted. I was young, only six or seven—I was back in the general's tent with my father—but I am told our men were lying down and dying right there in the fields from fatigue alone. They believed they were Spain's last hope. Seeing our weakness, Italy rushed forward, ready to finish us off."

He sighed now, and his anger was gone, replaced by a tiredness that told Sophie he knew this story too well. "It was all a trap. My father never *technically* surrendered, and that is why he manages to maintain respect. But the moment Italy crossed onto our turf, my father sent in fresh, well-rested Spanish troops to attack from all angles. It was a bloodbath."

Sophie felt the blood pulsing hard in her neck. "But the Spanish soldiers who fell, the exhausted ones—"

"Sacrificed," Philip said flatly. "Even they did not know what was coming. So you can see—my father's practices are controversial. He has been determined to bring Spain back to prominence, especially after the defeat of his father's armada at the hands of the English. Since its loss, he has been bent on getting us back to where we were."

"I see," Sophie said at last.

"He is prideful, my father, and very intelligent, but I'm not sure that I wish to be like him." His voice was soft.

"I don't see how you could be, Philip," Sophie said.

They stood together, leaning against the doors of the library and watching the guests go past.

"So, why are you still here? I didn't think I would ever see you again," Sophie said, taking another sip from her goblet. The wine was making her bold.

"Why do you think I'm still here?" he asked.

"Hmm." She shrugged. "I haven't the faintest idea."

He looked at her for a long moment, the silence of the library growing louder and the raucous music of the party seeming very far away.

"Can you not hazard a guess?" he asked, taking one careful step into the room and setting his goblet on the arm of a nearby chair. Sophie followed.

They were standing so close together. When had that happened? She was so close to him she could see her reflection in his eyes.

His lashes were so dark, and his hair, always falling forward—she felt an intense need to push it out of his eyes herself. To feel how silky it was under her fingers.

"Not one guess?" he whispered.

She leaned ever closer.

As did he.

He was staring at her lips. She could feel the intensity of his gaze, the heat from his body and from hers. It was as if he were a magnet, and she was drawn to him. She could not help but close her eyes and—

"Sophie!" A voice echoed in the room.

Philip jumped back.

Sophie whipped her head to the source of the sound, her heart sinking as her stepmother appeared at the doorway, backlit by the hallway lamps. She had the urge to jump back across the threshold and pretend she'd never stepped inside the library unsupervised.

"Sophie, can I speak to you, please?" There was something urgent in Claudia's voice.

"I—I was just saying hello to Philip," Sophie said, strained, as she introduced them to each other. Claudia and Philip exchanged pleasantries, but Claudia soon shook her head, pressing her hand to her stomach.

"I'm sorry," Claudia said with a tight expression on her face. "But, Sophie, we need to go. Now."

Sophie turned in confusion. "Oh—we do?"

"Of course, Duchess Claudia," said Philip, bowing. "May I be of service?"

"Is everything all right?" Sophie drew closer to the hallway, and it was then that she saw Claudia's neck and chest were covered in bright red welts. As the duchess hunched over, leaning hard on the doorjamb, a sheen of sweat glistened on her forehead.

"Oh my goodness! What on earth happened to you?" Sophie cried. "Help—we need help!"

CHAPTER TEN

"SHH, PLEASE. IT'S ALL RIGHT. I must have eaten something bad," Claudia hissed, gesturing for Sophie to keep her voice down. "I'm sorry. Can we just go?"

"If the food has gone bad, the kitchen staff should know," Sophie said forcefully.

"Sophie, please don't make a scene. Let's just go home, please." Claudia's eyes were pained as she tried to stand straight.

"Lady Sophie, let's get her outside," said Philip, appearing at Sophie's side. "Come, Your Grace. Do you need my arm?"

They limped along, Sophie and Philip flanking Claudia at each elbow, moving through the back halls so as not to draw attention. They retrieved their shawls from the servants, and Claudia quickly concealed her neck.

Outside the grand house, the fresh, cold air seemed to revive Claudia a bit as their driver brought the horses around.

"Here we are," Philip said at last, helping Claudia climb through the carriage door.

"I'm sorry about this," Sophie said before she followed. It was unbearable to leave him, embarrassed and flustered by the circumstances yet again. "Write me?"

Philip frowned, shaking his head. "Don't be sorry, I only hope she's all right. Have a safe ride back." With that, he shut the door and waved as they pulled away.

But he had not said he would write.

Was he about to kiss her?

Would they have kissed if Claudia hadn't interrupted them?

Sophie watched him until he was just a figure in the darkness against the bright light of the house, then turned to Claudia. "What did you eat? How did this happen?"

"I don't know," Claudia groaned, slumping against the wall of the cab. "This is how I get when I eat seafood. But I was being careful! There were some chocolate pastries, a meat pie, a tart with—with hare, or they may have said krabben, I think—"

"Krabben? Claudia, that's shrimp."

"Oh, is it? Oh dear, yes, I can't—"

"So why did you eat it?" Sophie cried.

"Because I *thought* they said rabbit!" Claudia said, suddenly yelling. "I don't know, I couldn't hear anything in there! Apparently, I can't do anything right. I lost sight of you. You weren't supposed to leave me; I was supposed to be your chaperone! And I find you alone with the prince! And all those women wouldn't talk to me. I heard them say I was trying to draw attention to myself, the way I was dressed. I heard them laugh about how I'd fainted at my wedding. I—I—" And all at once she was crying, face in her hands, bent forward on her seat.

"Oh, Claudia," Sophie said, wincing. "Please don't cry, don't—"

The duchess broke off suddenly, her hand clamped over her mouth and eyes wide. With a fist, she pounded on the window behind her.

"Can we stop the carriage?" Claudia choked. Unheard, she pounded harder. "Stop the carriage, please!"

At last, the driver took the order and brought the cab to a jerky halt on the side of the dark, windblown road. Before Sophie could ask what was wrong, Claudia clambered out the door and retched into the fields. Sophie sat quietly and waited for her to finish, guilt stinging her every pore as she suddenly realized how very sick Claudia was.

After a few minutes, Claudia climbed, shamefaced, back into the carriage and wiped her mouth with her sleeve. She slammed the door and sat down across from Sophie, not looking at her. The rash on Claudia's neck had disappeared into a ghostly pale glow.

"Think I should be all right now," Claudia whispered as they started moving once more.

Sophie watched her a long moment. She looked so much like a child, sitting there staring at her feet, that Sophie remembered how young she truly was. "You really did send that dish back for a reason. That dinner a few weeks ago. You can't have fish."

Claudia nodded silently. "I can't."

"I'm sorry I got upset," Sophie murmured, her cheeks still stinging red.

"And I'm sorry about your mother's vase," she said.

"It wasn't your fault."

"I startled them while they were cleaning it."

"It's all right, Claudia." Sophie was surprised to find that she meant it. She moved across the floor of the cab to sit next to her step-mother, moving closer as the duchess shied away.

"You don't want to sit next to sick old me," Claudia said roughly.

"I do. I promise. None of us have been kind enough to you, have we?"

Claudia shrugged her thin shoulders. "I know it's been hard. I—I feel as though I'm doing everything wrong."

"You're doing fine, Claudia," Sophie said, taking her hand. "You're doing just fine."

They rode in silence the rest of the way home. Sophie listened to the beating of the horses' hooves and the rhythm of Claudia's breathing as she fell in and out of fitful sleep.

The next afternoon, Sophie sat at a desk in the library, fretting about what had happened between her and the prince. Was she mad to think he had been about to kiss her? What if it was all in her head? When she'd asked him to write her, he hadn't responded. Perhaps she was just imagining that he felt the same as she did. He was a prince after all; there were probably dozens of hopeful ladies throwing themselves at him. She cringed to think that she had joined their ranks.

She was lost in thought, doodling Philip's name over and over with a quill, when the door opened.

"There is a visitor here to see you, Lady Sophie," a servant called.

Sophie jerked her head from the table. "Who is it?"

"Prince Philip of Spain, my lady."

"Oh. Oh!" It was as though her thoughts had magically summoned him somehow. Sophie quickly flipped her paper over as though the prince would descend upon her that very moment. "I'll be right with—just let me, um—where is he?"

"He awaits you in the parlor," the servant said, eyeing her confusion.

"Yes. Good. One moment."

Sophie pushed all the paper to one side, rolling it to conceal her doodles. She smoothed her hair and dress, then looked at her ink-stained hands in horror. Sophie ran to the library door and yanked on the servant's cord, ringing for Lotte. The maid appeared in moments, all aflutter.

"I heard, I heard!" she squealed. "The prince!"

"Lotte, my hands!" Sophie hissed, holding them up in all their wretchedness. "Help me—could you make a run for my gloves? Please?"

"I'll meet you on the stairs."

In less than ten minutes, Sophie was tugging on the kid gloves and approaching the ornate front parlor where the family took guests, heart crashing in her chest.

You just saw him last night, you goose, she chastised herself. *He's only a boy.*

But seeing him there in her parlor, worriedly tapping his foot against the woven carpet, brought the events of the previous evening that had felt like a strange dream into a beautiful, concrete reality.

"Your Highness!" Sophie said, breathless, dropping into a curtsy. When she rose, she cleared her throat and set her chin. "Good afternoon. This is a nice surprise."

He jumped to stand, bowed low, and sat again as they both settled into their chairs. "Yes, well—hello. I'm sorry to intrude. Duchess Claudia just seemed in such a poor state last night that I couldn't stop worrying. I had nightmares, I confess, of you two not making it, that she may pass out on the road and leave you both without help." He shook his head. "I should have accompanied you, or insisted you stay with the Zieglers, or even given you my own carriage, which is faster. I don't know what I was thinking."

"Well, I'm sure you can see we made it back just fine." Sophie smiled at the thought of Philip having any sort of dream about her, nightmare or otherwise. "You worry too much. Your kindness was more than enough last night, and I'm certain Claudia preferred to be alone with her illness, anyway."

"Good! Fine, fine," Philip said, smiling. Silence fell between them as he eyed the servant who stood near the door like a statue, eyes cast down yet frustratingly watchful.

"You know, I'm not quite used to all this chaperoning," the prince said in a low voice. "I don't suppose you want my pity, but you have it. Makes a man feel he can't talk freely when there's others around all the time."

"You mean you haven't entertained many young women?" Sophie asked with sly surprise. "That's the only time when *you* would encounter a chaperone, I think."

He frowned, shifting in his seat and clearing his throat. "A— a few, once or twice, I suppose. Haven't had much time for courtship with all the work my father has me do. And the meetings with him—those are secret! No one but the most trusted advisers around, not even servants. I'm just used to a little more privacy, that's all."

Sophie sighed. "The lack of privacy is rather new to me, too. Almost makes me wish I hadn't debuted and just stayed a child in the eyes of society forever. But really, you're the one to blame—they let me alone when there aren't crown princes running around the place."

"As if we'd do something nefarious," Philip said, rolling his eyes. "Insulting, really. Where's the trust? Treating us like suspects . . ."

She laughed, though the topic hit a little close to home. They fell gradually to silence again. Then Philip stood, wiping his palms on his trousers and looking around the room. "Well—"

"You can't be leaving, can you?" Sophie said, alarmed.

"I've dropped in on you unexpectedly, and I don't want to take up the rest of your day—"

"Don't be silly! You didn't come all the way over here just to speak with me for five minutes, did you? Please stay for dinner."

From the crimson flush that creeped into his cheeks, it seemed perhaps he *had* found five minutes of conversation worth the long journey.

"Of course not. Inquiring after Duchess Claudia, you know—saying hello to you, and I thought I might have a stroll by the—in the—oh, dash it," Philip said, pushing his hair back from his face. "I guess I'd better stop talking and accept the invitation, hadn't I?"

Sophie laughed.

CHAPTER ELEVEN

Duke Maximilian eyed their visitor with great interest at the dinner table, and Claudia fell over herself with thanks for the night before. "You were a true gentleman, Your Highness," she said, raising her glass to him. "I felt well taken care of as you rushed me out of there with tact."

"My gratitude goes out to you," Maximilian agreed. "I heard of the evening's mishap and was about to send a note of my thanks. I'm glad I'm able to say it in person instead."

"It was my honor," said Philip.

The prince was a charming presence at the dinner table. He soon regaled the family with tales of his adventures in Spain.

"And King Ferdinand is well?" the duke inquired.

"As well as he can be," replied Philip, uncharacteristically brusque.

Duke Maximilian grunted and continued to saw on his steak.

"Have you seen much of our province during your stay?" asked Claudia politely, to change the subject.

Philip nodded. "A little. I walked around the villages a bit."

"Oh!" said Sophie. "I have not been outside the palace grounds in so long. Were you able to visit the bakeshops? They have the most wonderful treats."

He shook his head. "We did not stay long." He looked a bit uncomfortable.

"Did . . . you not enjoy your visit there?" asked Sophie innocently.

"Oh, no—I mean, they are very nice," he said.

"Come now, you may speak freely at our table," said the duke.

"Well, there's just something about them. Do *you* know what I mean?" He directed the question at Claudia, who looked as if she shared in his discomfort.

"I can't guess your meaning exactly," the duchess said, unfolding and refolding her napkin in her hands. "But I do remember how I felt as I rode here for the first time. I was . . . surprised by the size and grandness of the palace after passing through the villages."

It seemed to Sophie that they had some sort of shared understanding that she was not privy to, and that frustrated her. "Please. What is it you're trying to say?" Sophie asked.

Philip looked at her, sympathetic. "Well . . . would you say that they're thriving?"

"The villages are fine." Sophie frowned, trying to recall their image from the night before. Passing the twilit houses and shops in the carriage, everything had looked as picturesque and normal as she'd expected it to. "Aren't they, Papa?"

Maximilian nodded. "They do the best they can with what they have, and we help them out when they need it. It's been a slow year for farming and mining. My work takes me away from home often, but I trust that I leave things well enough in my absence. And though the villages may seem meager in comparison to the palace, it's really a matter of perspective."

With that, he shrugged and turned back to his meal. It was the same reassurance that Sophie had heard him give in the past, but for the first time, it rang a little hollower in her ears.

"Perspective—you may be exactly right." Philip smiled as though he sensed he'd treaded on delicate territory. "Anyway, this knödel is boiled to perfection," he said with a laugh.

But the dough felt lumpy and hard to swallow in Sophie's throat.

As the evening came to a close, Philip bid thanks and good night to Maximilian and Claudia and stood awkwardly with Sophie at the door. They lingered, both reluctant to part ways once again.

"Lady Sophie," he said. "The evening is so pleasant. Shall we stroll around the gardens?"

"Without a chaperone?" Sophie teased, then looked more carefully behind him. "Your courtier isn't with you, is he?"

"I've dismissed him. He returned to England when I was supposed to."

Sophie narrowed her eyes at this. It didn't seem like King Ferdinand was one to let his only son stay in another country without a guardian, and she began to wonder if Philip was giving the full story.

"You've been on your own all this time?" she said slowly.

"Of course not. I've got my servants and staff. Shall we?"

Did she need a chaperone in her own house? Sophie did not think so. It was late, and the brisk night air sent breezes rippling through the gardens. The light of the full moon cast a silvery sheen over the paths. Though they stayed in view of the palace and its guards, Sophie had a feeling—similar to the night before—that everything was tinted with some sort of magic when they were together.

"May I show you my favorite spot before you go?" Sophie asked, forcing the question out before she changed her mind. It would involve going off unsupervised, but Maximilian and Claudia were already up in their chambers, and Sir Rodrigo was, mercifully, far from here. They could sneak around the servants. Worried she may never get the chance again, Sophie felt she couldn't pass it up.

Philip glanced back at the palace, where the guards seemed disinterested in their movements. "You're sure?"

Sophie nodded. "We'll be quick."

She grabbed hold of his hand, pulling him through the autumn flowers toward the west side of the palace, where tall hedges formed a miniature maze. They slipped through the leafy corridors, Sophie leading by heart, until they reached a little pool of fish and a bubbling fountain that sparkled in the light of the moon. No sound reached them except for the movement of the water.

"This is lovely," Philip said, hushed. "I can tell why it's your favorite."

"My mother came here often to think and read. I like to save it for special occasions."

"Is this a special occasion?"

Sophie hitched as she became distinctly aware of the privacy afforded by the hedges, of how closely the two of them were standing together, of the way her heart rate galloped at the question.

"It's just a nice night," she whispered.

Philip looked at her for what seemed like months, years, studying her face and meeting her eyes so boldly that it was hard to return the gaze. Then he looked away, concentrating hard on the fish in the fountain.

"What I'd started telling you last night," he said. "Before Claudia fell ill. I wanted to tell you that *you* are the reason I did not go to England." Philip let out a long breath. "There—I said it."

Sophie could barely speak. "I was?"

He met her eyes at last, and it was as if a spark was lit between them. Sophie felt his gaze flooding her like warmth.

"Yes," he whispered. "Are you glad I am still here?"

"Yes," she breathed.

Philip exhaled. It seemed like he wanted to say something more, but instead he bit his lip and turned away.

"Is something wrong?" she asked, concerned.

He looked back at her and shook his head with a smile.

Time moved very slowly as Sophie watched him, framed by the hedges. They both looked up at the moon and the stars, sitting together quietly. She didn't know what to say but also felt that she needn't say anything at all.

"Your hair is so dark," he said, almost as if he were talking to himself, but he was staring at her with an awed look in his eye. "It makes your skin look . . ."

"Snow-white?" she asked, teasing. "It's what they used to call me as a child."

"Snow White," he murmured reverently. Then he shook his head. "I must go," he said, breaking whatever spell had kept them bound together in the center of the maze. "I musn't keep you."

"Of course. Nor I, you," Sophie said, louder than she'd meant to.

"My coachman has probably fallen asleep by now." He was grinning.

She grinned back, feeling out of breath and reckless. "I'll race you to the front."

Before he could respond, she was already off, tearing through the twisting and turning hedges and laughing as his footsteps sounded loud behind her. He caught her just at the entrance of the maze, lunging out to grab her arm and sweeping her around with his momentum. They stumbled, both laughing as they nearly collided with one of the old gardeners making a night inspection.

"Oops—excuse us!" Philip cried.

"Pardon me, my lady," the gardener said gruffly to Sophie. His eyes were wide and disapproving, but Sophie didn't care.

They ran to the palace drive, out of breath. Philip doubled over, clutching his middle and laughing. When he glanced up at her, she laughed. "I beat you."

"Did you now," he growled, and pulled her away from the front entrance so the two of them were hidden in the darkness. He had his arms around her, and she felt his chest, solid and strong—she barely reached his chin.

He leaned down, and without thinking, she reached around and pulled him even closer. They stood in each other's arms, even closer than they had been the other night at the party.

"Sophie," he said huskily, and his hand cupped her cheek. It was the first time he'd called her by her first name without her title.

"Philip," she whispered, doing the same. She closed her eyes and stood on tiptoe.

He bent closer, and she felt his lips brush the top of hers, but at the last moment, he pushed her away, breathing heavily. "I will not compromise you," he said, his voice strangled.

She held her breath. If only he would. "Oh!" She tottered on her heels, feeling his sudden absence from her body too keenly.

Instead, he took her hand and gently kissed it. Then he looked her square in the face, his eyes flashing in the darkness with an intensity that made her breathless. "We shall do this properly. I will return and ask your father for your hand in marriage."

"Oh! Philip!"

"If I have his blessing, I hope I can count on yours as well?" he murmured.

Sophie could only nod, filled with so much joy and excitement it was hard to contain.

Philip bowed once more with a boyish smile on his face. "Good night, my lady. Till we meet again."

"Good night, my lord," she said, her heart thumping in her chest. "I shall be waiting."

CHAPTER TWELVE

THERE WAS NO SIGN OF Philip the next day, nor the next. No letters either. But Sophie did not worry. She told herself he must be busy arranging everything—writing to his father, letting the court of Spain know of his plans. He was going to ask her father for her hand in marriage! It was too delightful and too wondrous a prospect. She had dreaded her debut, had worried about finding a suitor who would be kind. She had not even dreamed she would find someone to love—and to think she and Philip had found each other so easily! It was a dream.

In the meantime, the conversation at dinner about the state of the villages in the duchy weighed heavily on her mind. That morning, she found Claudia in the garden and thought her stepmother could help her with a new idea of hers.

"Good morning. What's that look for?" Claudia said when Sophie sat down and peered at her with narrowed eyes.

"Claudia . . . are the villages in disarray?"

The duchess set aside the book she was reading and cleared her throat. "I think it may be difficult for you to know what's happening when you're all the way up here. I know you haven't spent very much time outside the palace."

Sophie looked back at the towering palace, with its walls and turrets that had both protected and sheltered her through her youth and when Maximilian was far away. Maybe it had done too good of a job.

"Like I said, I haven't been down there—*really* there—in several years," Sophie said. "In fact, passing through the villages in the carriage before the Zieglers' party was the closest I've been in a long time."

Claudia looked thoughtful. "Then let's go."

Sophie's stomach pitched. "Really? When?"

Claudia stood and began walking back to the palace. "Right now."

Sophie followed the duchess, wondering if there was any way she could stop this trajectory. "We'll need an escort. Papa wouldn't want us to go by ourselves; it's not safe—"

"To be truthful, Sophie, I think you'll get a better picture of the state of things if we aren't there on an official visit."

"Without the guards? And how do you expect us to manage that?"

Claudia smiled. "We shall go in disguise."

Sophie laughed in shock. Claudia was nothing if not unorthodox. "You sure do like your disguises," Sophie muttered, thinking of their first meeting in the larder, when she had mistaken Claudia for a servant.

Then like a flash in the back of her mind, Sophie remembered something she hadn't thought about in a very long time. "If we are going alone, we must bring extra protection."

"And what might that be?"

Sophie led Claudia up to her chambers and closed the doors, then disappeared for a moment beneath the bed. When she emerged, she held a slim black-velvet box. She remembered the seriousness with which Duchess Maria had presented it to her, pressing the thin object into Sophie's hands as they sat near the window in the duchess's quarters.

You must keep this very safe for me, Sophielien, Sophie's mother had said. *There may come a time someday when you need it.*

Now she allowed Claudia to open the latch. Inside was a small silver dagger with a mother-of-pearl hilt, shining bright and sharp. Claudia took it out, marveling at its lightness. Sophie had kept it hidden ever since her mother's death, only taking it out on occasion, holding the handle up to the window and watching it catch the light. When she was little, she dreamed of training with it when she grew up, using it to fight enemies in the forest and protect the palace from harm. But in the wake of her mother's death and her father's absence, she'd all but forgotten it was there.

"It's beautiful," Claudia said. "Do you know how to use this?"

"I've never had to," Sophie said, dodging the question. It wasn't as though anyone had trained her in combat, and she'd hardly lifted more than a butter knife in her lifetime. "But I think I'll feel better about going alone if we take this with us."

Even though the maid's uniform was just another set of clothes, Sophie was surprised at how different she felt in the disguise. In the dull blue cotton dress, faded white apron, and cap, Sophie looked like any one of the hundreds of servants who freely moved in and out of the palace. Even better, it was much more comfortable than her regular clothes and miles away from the whaleboned stays and layers of heavy silks she wore for special occasions. Sophie took a few deep breaths, enjoying the way her rib cage could expand and her arms move without restraint.

And there were pockets, more than one, where Sophie could put her hands, or even a spritzkuchen if she really wanted to abandon any sense of propriety. She found an inner pouch close to her hip where she could hide the dagger away but still get at it easily. Sophie left a note for Lotte explaining that she would be studying with Duchess Claudia today, instead of attending what was left of her formal lessons.

Then, finally, Sophie and Claudia left through the servants' entrance and hiked under the bright blue sky.

There was a path winding through the forest that paralleled the main road and led to the villages. At first, Sophie jumped at every cracking twig and the rustling of the wind through the branches. But as the distance between themselves and the palace grew, a strange thing happened—she began to feel lighter, giddy. It was as though a heavy, invisible tether had snapped. The feeling grew as they made their way down the foothills, through sun-dappled forests and sparkling creeks. Birds followed them from tree to tree, and squirrels chirred in the canopy.

"Can I ask you something?" Claudia said as they walked. She'd seemed more comfortable around Sophie since the incident at the party, and Sophie noticed that her young stepmother was becoming equally relaxed as they put distance between themselves and the palace. "I'm not saying it isn't a beautiful gift—it is. But why did your mother give you that dagger? Especially at the young age you were?"

Sophie bit her lip as the memory came to mind. "She said it was for my protection. She told me she didn't want to frighten me, but that Papa underestimated the threat of danger to us—to any noblewomen, really," Sophie said. "Though I don't suppose she thought I'd be traveling outside the palace alone!" She laughed.

"I hope I'm not putting us in any of that danger," Claudia said, suddenly doubtful. "Perhaps we should turn back."

"We'll be fine," Sophie assured her. "Besides, it's too late now."

❧

At first, the villages looked normal as Sophie and Claudia emerged from the edge of the forest. There were clusters of wooden houses and buildings, pens of animals, some shops to serve the townsfolk, and an open town square. The homes were decorated with carved wood in the traditional folk style and held window boxes filled with cheerful edelweiss and hepatica.

But as Sophie looked more closely, her heart began to sink. She could see the weariness that filled the atmosphere; some of the buildings sagged and were in need of repair. A few men sat idle in the stoops and doorways, whittling at blocks of wood or simply staring. Their clothes were threadbare, and some even went without shoes. Seeing the town from the carriage had blurred these details; now, standing here in person, the feeling of hopelessness was palpable.

Sophie had spent her childhood imagining that the edge of the foothills held cheerful towns, as happy and colorful as she'd heard of in any bedtime story. Her father had led her to believe this. But Duke Maximilian's words from the night before rang empty, and Sophie could only guess at the reason behind his reluctance: shame? How could he have let their people down like this?

Sophie had always been proud of her father. Now something within her wavered. "What has happened here?" she whispered.

"Let's walk around," Claudia said.

They passed several shops, most of which were either closed or empty altogether. At the edge of the square, they found the village bakery. The two women forayed into the shop, whose floorboards creaked and groaned as Sophie and Claudia crossed the threshold. Despite its large windows, the room felt dim and damp, with more bare shelves than baked goods lining its walls. A burly woman leaned on the counter, eyeing the two women with indifference.

"Are there any tarts today?" Sophie asked politely.

"Tarts?" scoffed the woman, who did not return Sophie's smile. "No tarts. Only bauernbrot."

"Oh," Sophie said, unused to such a gruff tone. "We'll take some of that, then."

The woman said nothing, merely turning from the counter and thrusting a bread knife into the bauernbrot loaf.

"Tarts must go quickly, I suppose," Sophie said to Claudia, trying to fill the odd silence. "It's blackberry season, after all."

The baker looked back and narrowed her eyes. "*You* may have blackberries up on the mountain—the holy mountain—I see your palace uniforms, yes," she grumbled. "But you'll find none of that down here."

"I'm sorry—the 'holy mountain'?" Sophie repeated. "I don't understand. There are fields and berries down here too, aren't there? The palace gets its food from the valley. At least in part."

Sophie glanced at Claudia, feeling the stability she'd known most her life become more and more unbalanced with every word. But Claudia only watched the baker.

The woman snorted. "Hasn't been that way in years. You're a youngster, so you must not know. The palace used to work with us, provide us protection and resources while we provided them with food, crops, and labor for the copper mines. Then Duchess Maria died, and the palace stopped holding up its end of the bargain— moved all agricultural focus to its own grounds, shut itself off from us. They keep the little girl locked up in the tower. The new duchess is a witch, they say, and the duke doesn't care about us anymore. Goes off trotting around the globe. You should know this, working there."

Sophie felt like she was being hit in the chest repeatedly with every word the woman said. She hoped Claudia wouldn't feel too badly about being called a witch.

Sophie bit her tongue as Claudia took the pieces of bread for the two of them and paid with a few coins. They sat on the edge of the dry, crumbling fountain in the town square and tore into it with their fingers.

"I'm sorry about what that woman said," Sophie told her stepmother.

"Oh, it's all right. I'm used to it. Rumors, gossip, it's just part of court life and it trickles out to the villages." Claudia shrugged.

"It's so quiet," Sophie observed. She looked again at an old man passing and a woman, slightly older than Claudia, struggling to push an empty cart with a broken wheel. In her memories from when she was younger, there had been people in the fields—children bringing food and water to their parents as they worked.

At that thought, some small key unlocked a thought inside her head. "Claudia," Sophie said, very slowly, "where are all the children?"

Claudia's face was filled with foreboding as she swallowed a lump of her bread. "I don't know."

Sophie stood and ran back to the bakery, a sense of dread filling her throat. "Excuse m-me," she stammered to the woman at the counter. "Where are the children? Why don't I see any in the square?"

The woman's face narrowed into a hard glare. "Where do you think? They're in the mines."

"The *mines*? The copper mines? But—they're just children." Sophie shook her head. "How can they be down there?"

"We're out of resources. Out of gunpowder to open up larger tunnels. They're the only ones who can fit into the smaller spaces with their picks to get at what's left of it." Her face was blank. "There may be more deposits deeper down, but the duke and his men don't think it's enough to be worth it. Their interests are turning elsewhere, forgetting us once again."

Almost more disturbing than the news itself was the way the woman spoke. Her voice was devoid of emotion, matter of fact, as if

Duke Maximilian had already moved on. Claustrophobic in the small shop, Sophie backed out the door. Claudia was close behind her.

"Does your father know about the children?" Claudia asked, her own voice quiet and small.

"He couldn't. He couldn't know, or he would fix it," Sophie said.

For some reason she was breathing very hard, as though she'd just run a long way. Seeing the villages brought one fact into sharp focus: This was the absence of responsibility. This was what happened when leadership failed—and her father never failed. This must just be a fluke, and once she told him, he would fix everything.

"But he *should* know," she continued.

Sophie stared at the barren town square, seeing the village as if for the first time.

CHAPTER THIRTEEN

THE NEXT MORNING IT WAS Sophie and Claudia, not Duke Maximilian, who commandeered the palace's library, spreading themselves out across the wide tables and leather chairs. She had found her father on their return from the villages, going immediately to his study before she lost faith in him. Sophie wasn't going to waste this opportunity, not after her talk with the duke yesterday afternoon.

"Papa," she'd said, ignoring his warm greeting and going straight to his desk. "Do you realize that the villagers' children are working in the mines?"

The disquiet that flittered across his face was not lost on Sophie, and her heart began to sink. He was upset, not surprised.

"Where on earth did you hear that?" he said.

"I was—I mean, one of the servants mentioned—" Then she shook her head. "It doesn't matter where I heard it! Is it true?"

"Sophie, the servants can't hope to understand how complex these matters are."

"So, it *is* true?"

Though she wanted to look away, Sophie held his intense gaze, gripping the back of a carved wooden chair for support. For a moment it seemed he would chastise her, but then Maximilian dropped his head and sighed. "I had heard tell of it. But I'd hoped it hadn't truly come to that."

The blood kicked up to a boil in Sophie's veins. Suspecting the problem was just as bad as knowing about it, and in both cases, he had willfully looked the other way. Her father suddenly seemed weak and tired, sitting at the other end of the wide desk that separated them.

"What? Why on earth wouldn't you investigate if you'd heard of it?" Sophie said.

"I apologize, Sophielien. My mind has been on other important affairs."

"What could possibly be more important than this?"

"I know. I agree with you." He pressed the tips of his fingers together as he said it. Looking at him, Sophie wasn't sure what to believe. She'd always grown up thinking of her father as such a wise man, respected in his decisions and always sure of what to do. Their relationship had become complicated when he began spending time away, but Sophie had always trusted him unequivocally.

"Something must be done," she said through her teeth. "We can't stand for this."

Maximilian looked at his daughter for a long time, quiet as though he was trying to make a decision.

"I can tell that this matters to you," he said at last. "And I know you've been expressing an interest in palace affairs. If you look through the budgets and find resources we can use to help the villages, I will present that to my ministers. They are reasonable men, though they're very careful with how we allocate our funds. But I will talk to them."

"Me? Figure out the budget?" she asked.

The duke looked amused. "You could ask your new stepmother. She has a head for figures and may be able to help you."

Having gotten an early start this morning, riffling through Maximilian's study and examining the shelves of the libraries, she and Claudia found several rolls of paper and enormous leather-bound ledgers that contained the palace's financial state of affairs.

With Claudia's assistance, Sophie planned to study all these materials until she found the funds with which to assist the villages. In her mind, it had been as simple as tracing her finger down a page and locating an empty spot. But now she stared unfocused at the reams of notes, written in tiny, cramped scrawl. Additions and supplemental materials had been written in the margins, sometimes contradicting or dismissing the original numbers. And even though Sophie performed well at her mathematics lessons, it did not take long for a headache to kick in.

At length, she glanced up at Claudia, whose eyes were equally glazed over as she stared into the books.

"It's just awful, isn't it?" Sophie said. "But there has to be *something* here."

⚜

With Claudia's help, Sophie put together an analysis of the documents to present to her father. After much grueling work, they had deduced how the duchy's money was spent. To their surprise, much of the wealth left the country toward international causes like the Huntsmen's Club of Northern Italy, Stallion Breeders and Racing in Estonia, and the British Coterie of Ale Brewers. She presented the information to her father, who promised to bring it up at the next meeting with the council of ministers.

Four days later, Sophie waited with bated breath and followed her father out of his receiving room after his councilors had left.

"Did they agree?" she asked, suddenly nervous.

The duke shook his head. "Sophielein, I don't wish to upset you, but the ministers did not agree to allocate more funds toward the villages. They said we cannot afford it."

Sophie scowled. "But Claudia and I found mountains of extra money in that budget—*mountains*. It would cost them so little to bring the villages back on their feet. They would be heroes."

The duke grimaced, gently placing his hand on her arm. "It isn't just about the money—though that is an enormous part of it. They feel that their authority is being threatened, along with their lifestyle."

"But, Papa, you must," Sophie hissed. "You are the duke; these are your people!"

"As the duke, I must keep my council in order," he said gravely. "A leader is nothing without the trust of his advisers." Duke Maximilian sighed. "But you have given me much to think about, and I won't forget it."

"Thank you, Papa," said Sophie.

"At least it has brought you and Claudia together," he said. "All she does is berate me about the villages' cause as well."

"Does she?"

"Oh, much more than you," he assured her. "I cannot get her to stop badgering me about it!" He chuckled. "I am glad to see you are now good friends."

Sophie was disappointed to hear she had not done enough to bring change to the lives of the townspeople, but she was mollified by her father's observation. Claudia had been an enormous help in gathering the right information to present to the ministers.

Her father was right; they had become good friends.

But there were other things on her mind. Sophie realized with a start that she hadn't heard from Philip yet. It had been weeks now since he had visited, and there was nary a letter or message about his forthcoming proposal.

For the first time, she began to worry.

CHAPTER FOURTEEN

AS THE DAYS AND WEEKS flew by, Sophie tried not think of Prince Philip, trusting him to do what he had promised. There was the matter of his father, of course, but surely the king of Spain would want his only son and heir to be happy. Sophie knew she was being naïve, but she clung to the hope that Philip would appear soon, or at least send word. She wished she could confide in her stepmother, but Sophie was still a little shy around Claudia, even as they had grown closer by working together. This was not to mention that Claudia had taken to keeping to her room for the past several weeks now, and Sophie could not help but feel somewhat abandoned.

That afternoon, she stood outside of Claudia's door, listening for a sign of life inside. She'd sent a servant for Claudia nearly an hour ago, but neither of them had appeared at her chambers. Sophie was starting to worry that something was truly wrong with her stepmother, and with the duke away for business once more, it was left to Sophie to check for herself that all was well. No one had cared to look after Claudia, so Sophie had taken matters into her own hands.

Possibly Claudia was sleeping and hadn't heard her knock. She tried again, but there was still no answer. Sophie knew her stepmother must be inside; she hadn't been in the gardens, the library, or the dining room. Sophie had even checked the tower, but the high turret was empty, and clouds in the distance signaled a coming storm.

Sophie pressed her ear to the wood, but all was silent. She rapped her knuckles once more, a little louder, then eased the door open very slowly, finding it unlocked. She would peek in on Claudia, see that she was safe, and leave her be.

The chambers were dim, their heavy drapes pulled against the setting sun. Sophie squinted into the darkness, trying to make out the shapes of the bed and furniture.

"Claudia?" she murmured. "Are you in here?"

When there was no answer, Sophie moved all the way into the room and leaned over the bed. It was neat and made. But the room had a strange smell to it; the thick air was humid and earthy.

Sophie caught an odd shape out of the corner of her eye; she turned and inhaled sharply. Claudia was there, standing stock-still at her dressing table with her back to Sophie. Before her was the large, gilded mirror that Maximilian had given his wife for their wedding.

Claudia was looking at herself in the reflection, her face strange and distorted in the dim light. Sophie fought the urge to bolt from the room immediately.

"Claudia?" she said once more, her voice quieter and wavering.

But Claudia didn't answer. She clutched an object tight in her fist, staring straight ahead and murmuring very quietly so that Sophie couldn't hear what she was saying. Next to her on the floor was a dark, tangled mass.

"What—what are you doing? Claudia, what is that?"

Sophie rushed forward, grabbed her stepmother's arm, and shook her out of her trance. Surprised, Claudia seemed to see Sophie and squeezed her eyes open and shut a few times. "Oh—Sophie. I'm sorry." She shook her head and sank onto a nearby bench, avoiding Sophie's gaze.

"Are you all right? What are you doing?" Sophie asked.

"I'm just brooding. I'm sorry, this must look very strange."

Still unnerved, Sophie crossed the room to the window and pushed open the drapes, blinking in the sudden light. The strange mass on the floor was nothing but a small sheaf of old barley, limp and dull.

"Why is there barley on your floor?" Sophie asked.

Claudia smiled wanly. "It's a fertility test. I'm meant to—well—relieve myself on it, and if I'm with child, it will sprout. I've been doing it every single day."

"Oh." Sophie wrinkled her nose, disgusted and fascinated at the same time. She hoped she wouldn't have to do anything like that someday. She wondered if her mother had been subjected to it, too. Sitting next to her, she asked, "And . . . are you?"

Claudia shook her head. "I don't think so. It smells rotten, doesn't it?"

"Well, it's still early, isn't it?" Sophie said, ignoring the question and drawing closer to Claudia. "You've only been here a few months."

"They like to have these things done quickly, to—to make sure the duke hasn't, um, made a mistake."

Sophie frowned, feeling a sharp anger at the very idea. "That's ridiculous. My father married you because he loves you, whether you give him a baby or not."

"I hope so." Claudia laughed quietly, pressing her knuckles to her stomach.

Sophie nodded at the small object in her fist. "What's that?"

"Oh, nothing, really. It's just something my childhood nurse gave me back in Moldavia, telling me it would help with fertility. I don't really think it's working."

She passed it to Sophie. It was a smooth stone carving of a figure, a woman with a spiral in the middle of her belly. Sophie remembered the rumors from the servants about Claudia talking to the mirror and sinking into madness.

"I pray that it will send me a child," whispered Claudia. "It's become a bit of a ritual, trying with the barley, holding the talisman, and repeating what she told me to say—*May my body be open to new life*, or variations of that. I always feel foolish afterward."

"I don't think you should worry. There's no reason you shouldn't be able to conceive, is there? Not that it matters," Sophie said quickly.

"I don't know." Claudia ran her fingertips across her hairline. "I'm starting to wonder. I survived a very difficult illness when I was younger, diphtheria or something else. They couldn't say for sure. It left me weak, and I still feel vulnerable sometimes. One of these days a bite of fish is going to finish me off entirely." She chuckled darkly. "But I'm beginning to worry that my illness changed that part of my body too, somehow, the part that could hold a child."

"I'm sorry, Claudia, I didn't know," Sophie said softly. "Diphtheria was what my mother had, they say."

"Indeed, Sophie. I'm also very sorry."

"Thank you," Sophie said earnestly.

Claudia took the little stone figure back and tucked it away somewhere in her dress. She looked down, picking at one of her fingernails. "I'm sorry your work could not convince your father's councilors to change their minds."

"I won't stop trying," Sophie promised.

"I'm glad," said Claudia, smoothing out the lap of her dress. "You are a brave girl, Sophie. Unlike me."

"I hope you'll stop worrying about that," she said quietly, watching Claudia fret over the fabric of her gown. "That doesn't matter, not at all. Papa and I would never think less of you if it doesn't happen."

"Your father is kind, but his advisers will not be," said Claudia. "A barren duchess is cause for annulment."

"It will not come to that," Sophie said grimly. She glanced at the pile of barley on the floor again. It was still hard to ascertain exactly what she was seeing. Sophie stood and opened the rest of the curtains, letting more light into the room. "There, that's better," she said as Claudia shielded her eyes from the sun.

"Are you sure you are feeling well?" Sophie asked.

"To be honest, I have been quite ill," said Claudia. "Even though I haven't had any seafood."

"Perhaps a fresh bunch of barley will work better?" Sophie moved to clean up the stinky mess on the floor when she noticed something. Was there— Was she seeing— She looked up excitedly. "Claudia! There's something! Look!"

"Are you sure?" Claudia gasped. She leaned over and rested a hand on Sophie's shoulder to steady herself.

"Yes! There!" Sophie pointed, and sure enough, in the deepest part of the pile, they could see several small green flowering spikes.

"They're blooming!" crowed Sophie.

"Oh my goodness!" cried Claudia, throwing her hands on her face.

"You're pregnant!" Sophie declared.

Claudia glanced down at the barley. There was no mistaking it had sprouted.

"I remember my nurse telling me my mother was so ill when she was carrying me. Perhaps that is the reason you have felt unwell," said Sophie.

Her stepmother almost collapsed on the bed from the emotion. "I am with child." Her eyes shone with happiness.

"It will be a boy," Sophie declared. "I am sure of it." She didn't know how she knew, but she felt it so strongly that it must be true.

Sophie would have a brother.

If only Philip would arrive for his long-awaited proposal. Then the family would be complete.

CHAPTER FIFTEEN

NEWS OF THE DUCHESS'S CONDITION spread quickly, and it was as if the household was suddenly bathed in sunshine. The duke's own physician examined the duchess and pronounced her definitively with child. The servants whispered that the duchess must be carrying a son from the way her belly was shaped. All in all, everyone in the palace was overjoyed with the news of the new ducal baby.

The duke was said to be hurrying home as soon as he heard the news, but he would not be along for a while, as it took a long time to get to Bavaria from Paris, where he had paid a visit to Louis XIII of France. Claudia was still pale and unsteady, but there was a lightness to her, and her face glowed with happiness more often than not. A few weeks after the discovery, she was able to join Sophie at the breakfast, luncheon, and supper tables once more.

"Is something the matter, my dear?" Claudia asked when she noticed Sophie looking out the window more than once during their morning meal. "Are you expecting someone? You keep looking at the mountain path."

"No, no," Sophie replied. "It's nothing."

"Strange that Prince Philip hasn't paid us a visit since the lovely dinner," said Claudia. "Did he join his father in England?"

Sophie shrugged. "I don't know."

"I am certain he will call again," said Claudia. "He seemed quite besotted with you."

Sophie's cheeks flushed. "I thought so too—"

"But?"

"But he hasn't come back!" cried Sophie.

"We must be patient—you and I both," Claudia said, smiling shyly and placing a hand on her belly.

"I hate it," said Sophie, wringing her napkin. "I wish I could be out there—doing things—"

"Instead you are stuck here with me," said Claudia. "I do sympathize. But perhaps you can find something to occupy your time."

Perhaps her stepmother was right. Sophie had to find something to keep herself busy while she waited for Philip, or life would become unbearable. In her room after breakfast, she held up her mother's dagger to the light of her bedroom window. Sophie turned the weapon over and sucked in her breath as the blade brushed across her ring finger. She dropped the dagger. A razor-thin red line appeared on her skin, with blood beading at one end. Sophie brought her hand to her mouth, thinking. Perhaps she could learn how to use it properly. If only she could find someone who could teach her. But any man of her father's would scoff at such a suggestion; women were meant for needlepoint and ballroom dancing, not for throwing and using a knife.

There was a little leather sheath also folded in the dagger's box, and Sophie used it to cover the blade. She tucked it away in a pocket—having asked Lotte to sew some into her petticoats, after realizing their usefulness in her maid's disguise—and resolved to find a better place for it. She would keep the dagger with her whenever she could.

Sophie wandered around the empty palace slowly, aimlessly, her thoughts once again turning to Philip. Where was he? Had he changed his mind? Why did he not return to the palace or send a letter? Perhaps his father had forbidden the marriage. From what she could gather, King Ferdinand was decidedly not a romantic.

She found herself near the pantries where she had first met Claudia, some impulse having guided her there. The palace kitchens were interconnected rooms that held enormous ovens and long tables for different purposes, depending on what was to be prepared. Being midmorning, it was quiet, with just a few cooks in the back putting together small plates for lunch. The largest room stood empty before Sophie, its wide butcher-block table clean and bare. Running along the wall opposite were knives of every kind hanging from leather-strapped handles, everything from the widest meat cleaver to the smallest paring knife.

Sophie walked along, watching the glint of their sharpened blades in the dusty light. Coming to the end of the collection, she carefully lifted one closest in shape and size to her dagger—a fish-boning knife—and examined its silver shine.

"You'll draw blood with that," a voice said behind her, startling Sophie. The knife clattered to the floor, narrowly missing her foot.

Sophie turned to find Chef, a woman known only by her title, leaning against the kitchen table and surveying her with a suspicious eye. The chief of all kitchen-related duties and staff, Chef was a hard-faced, burly-armed woman who ruled with an iron fist. Legend was, she had worked as a scullery maid at a famous culinary school in Paris that did not enroll women, picking up the craft in secret. She shocked the headmaster by presenting him with a flawless coq au vin out of the blue. Then she quit.

Sophie might have been nobility, but here, she was on Chef's turf.

"I—I'm sorry. I was just curious." Sophie quickly retrieved the knife, setting it on the table before she could fumble again.

"Curious about what?" Chef asked.

Sophie could only shrug. She didn't know where to start with knives, much less daggers, which were two very different things. Chef eyed her for a tense moment, then slowly turned and sauntered out of the room. Sophie sighed, flicking the handle of the fish-boning tool to make it spin in a circle on the wood.

Then Chef returned, slapping a large, cold speckled cod down on the tabletop. Sophie flinched once more.

"You'll learn," Chef said. "That Frenchman Gustave might be able to teach you lots of things upstairs, but he can't teach you how to bone a cod. Put this on." She tossed her a large white apron.

Sophie hesitated, eyeing the cold fish.

Chef beckoned impatiently. "Come on, come on. Don't be squeamish."

She slipped the apron over her head and tied it in the back.

With a knife of her own, Chef traced the slippery, scaly gills. "First thing we do, we cut off the head. But you don't want to lose the extra meat beneath. We'll call it the cheek of the fish." She ran the knife tip in a crescent shape from the gill.

"Oh dear," Sophie said. "I actually have something to—"

"Go on, get a good grip." Chef ignored her. "Handle against the palm, finger on top of the blade, just like that. Gives you good control over your cut."

Sophie did as the woman said. She *could* tell the difference when she moved her fingers, feeling the leverage it gave her. Grimacing, she pressed the sharp tip into the fish's skin and cut. The curved angle was difficult; the head sloughed away awkward and ragged.

"Don't saw, this isn't a steak." Chef frowned. "Don't be afraid of it—*you* have control. You have the power. Cut smooth."

"I don't know why it's so hard," Sophie said, suddenly much more frustrated with cod than she ever thought possible.

"You don't trust yourself. You don't think you know what you're doing." Chef gripped Sophie's hand in her own, skin callused and rough from years of hard work, scratching Sophie's knuckles. Chef dragged their hands together, scraping the knife over an empty space in the table over and over until Sophie got the cadence. "Which means you're not stupid, not arrogant; you *don't* know what you're doing," Chef continued. "But you will."

She shoved the rest of the cod back in front of Sophie. "Now. One cut, straight down the middle, head to tail. Cut that fish in half. Give us a nice smooth line."

Sophie shifted from one foot to another. She peered at the shimmering scales, gauging the middle and lining up the tip of the blade. It hovered, barely piercing the flesh, at one end.

Chef nodded. "Go."

And Sophie cut, in one fluid motion, slicing through the fish's soft body like butter until she reached the tough matter of the tail.

"Oh!" she said, impressed with herself. "That wasn't so hard, actually."

Chef nodded, pulling the halved pieces apart with her hands. "No. It wasn't." She placed one in front of Sophie. "Now it gets trickier. You want the blade at an angle, horizontal, cutting off that meat like the layer of a cake."

Sophie worked the knife, a little clumsy at first, but finding the leverage. As she went slowly, Chef peeled back the skin of the fish, revealing the ridges of bones beneath.

"You see the bend in the blade?" Chef asked, pointing to its flexibility. "That's what you want in a good boning knife. Other knives, you should know, they won't have that. The ones for cutting through hard vegetables, flesh—they'll have a stronger blade. You'll want to practice with those, too."

"'Flesh'?" Sophie asked, somewhat startled by the word choice. She looked up at Chef, but the woman kept her eyes on the table.

"Meat, of course." She looked amused as she picked up the other half of the fish, slicing through it with alarming skill. "But yes, these sorts of skills come in handy for all sorts of situations."

Sophie looked around, making sure they were still alone in the kitchen. "Chef . . . what do you mean, exactly?"

But she already knew the answer. It thrummed through the air like a cello string.

Chef shrugged. "No one sees us palace staff down here, and no one cares what we do as long as our jobs get done. It has its drawbacks, but I like it that way. You, my lady"—she slit the flesh from the bones: a perfect fillet—"you must take care. There are those who do not love your family as we do."

Sophie's skin went cold. She gripped the handle of the boning knife harder. "You mean my father's enemies?"

Chef nodded. "And others. Those of noble blood are often targets."

Sophie digested this information with a frown. "Then I must make certain I am not an easy one."

For the next few days, Sophie snuck back into the kitchens to learn more knife skills. One day, Sophie had finally worked up the courage to show Chef the dagger she owned. "So you ended up with this, did you? Good," Chef said. "I trained your mother with this. You must also learn how to throw it." And so, this morning, Sophie quietly had Lotte set up some wooden targets in the trees behind the palace for practice. She stood in a small clearing on the side of the hill, her home looming high behind her.

Working with the weapon felt incredibly good—with each toss, Sophie's breathing was a little calmer. But the actual practice wasn't going well. She had missed with every throw. Sophie found the dagger's shining hilt beneath the dark leaves and brought it to the small clearing before the targets. She couldn't keep going back and forth like this. Could she really have such bad aim?

She gathered a handful of stones and lobbed them at the targets one by one until she could hit the middle with fair accuracy. There. She could aim. Then she examined the way she was throwing the dagger. She figured it had to do several full turns in order to stick in the wood—many of her tries had seen it bounce off at the hilt. She flipped it straight up in the air once, stepping back, to see how many times it rotated. Then she tried again.

Sophie took a deep breath, wound up, and threw.

The dagger flew once more. It hit the wood with a *thwang*, point in, sticking several inches away from the center.

Sophie yelped in disbelief. A new feeling surged through her body, something powerful and unfamiliar. She removed the knife from the target and tried over and over again, using the rest of the afternoon to run back and forth, practicing her throw.

She slipped up to the palace kitchens and borrowed a handful of paring knives, launching them one by one from the same spot until she had a rhythm down. As Sophie worked, a thought occurred to her. Hitting the targets and seeing herself tangibly improve made her feel like she could do anything. Knowing she could protect herself made the ministers, the villages, the forest, and unknown dangers less frightening. Sometimes, when she felt mischievous, she imagined the targets were Philip's face.

The practice put Sophie into a sort of trance as she turned the idea over and over and continued her training. She kept at it every day until the dagger was part of her arm. One afternoon, Chef came out to watch and cheered every hit.

Sophie and Chef were so engrossed in the practice that neither of them noticed a servant walking up to them. "Ah, Lady Sophie. There you are."

"Yes?" Sophie asked, slipping her dagger back into her skirt.

"My lady, the duke has returned and wishes to see you in his study."

"Papa—he's home!" Sophie cried, and on an impulse, hugged Chef. "Thank you for your help."

Chef was taken aback but patted her shoulder lightly. "You take care now, my lady."

CHAPTER SIXTEEN

"PAPA!" SOPHIE CRIED, THROWING HERSELF at the beloved duke. "You're back! Have you heard the news? Of course you have! Isn't it wonderful?"

But Duke Maximilian looked far from happy. He removed Sophie's arms from his person and sighed. "Sophielein, yes, I am happy Claudia is expecting."

"So, what? Is something wrong? Why are you looking at me like that?"

"Where have you been?" her father asked, frowning at the state of her dress. "Why are you so dirty?"

"Oh! I was with Chef," she told him.

His mouth pressed in a hard line, and his eyes flashed with an emotion she'd never seen before—at least not directed at her, not until now. He sat at his desk, his back to the sun. "What were you doing?"

Sophie shook her head, casting about for an answer that wouldn't sound as bizarre as the truth. "Just—just talking. About tonight's supper."

"I see." He rubbed his hands over his face and frowned hard. "I'm going to cut directly to it, and I want you to be honest with me. A few months back, at the Zieglers' ball and when the Spanish prince was over for dinner, did . . . did something happen between the two of you? Has he taken liberties with you?"

"What on earth?!"

"Answer the question, Sophie!" the duke roared. "Has he?"

Sophie shook her head. "No—never! He has been a perfect gentleman!"

Maximilian sighed in relief. "Are you certain?"

"Papa! Of course I am!"

The duke still looked troubled. "Alas, the news around the continent is very different."

"Wh-what are they saying?" she whispered. "They were talking about me? And the prince?"

Maximilian folded his hands and looked at her from beneath his brows. "You were seen coming out of a secluded part of the garden with Philip on the night of your debut, at the Zieglers' ball, and the evening he was here for dinner. Servants have witnessed you display affection with each other. More than that, you've been caught"—he wrinkled his nose as he said it, like it was distasteful to imagine—"kissing at our entryway."

"That isn't true!" Sophie cried. But she remembered Philip pulling her into the shadows after leaving the maze. Her every movement had been watched, judged. Humiliation washed through Sophie; she remembered the gardener's shocked gaze. Who else had seen them? The guests at the ball—so many must have seen them slip out that evening.

"Did you or did you not go into the garden unaccompanied?" Maximilian demanded, voice and temper rising. "And were you together in the palace out of view of household staff?"

"Well, if they saw us, then obviously we weren't out of view! And we weren't *doing* anything!" Sophie's face and throat could not possibly grow hotter; she was on fire inside and out. "We were just *talking*. That is a normal thing for two people to do, may I remind you, and not suspicious at all."

"Sophie," he said, his voice in a tremor as if he was trying hard to control it. "I thought you understood the importance of chaperones. I know you're still very young, and it's easy to get carried away with your infatuations. I blame myself for neglecting you, for failing to teach you better, but you must realize that young noble ladies do not—"

"But why? Why?" Sophie's voice grew more incredulous with every word. "Does our own staff not know who I am? Do you? How could those who practically *raised* me think so ill—"

"Try to understand!" Maximilian said through gritted teeth, slamming his fist upon the desk and making Sophie jump. "That is not the issue at hand. You know how this works as well as I do. You are a young, unmarried woman whose prospects depend solely on reputation. This could ruin you. It might already have."

"But I have done nothing wrong, Father," she insisted. "Nothing! And the prince was a true gentleman."

Maximilian raised an eyebrow.

"He didn't—he wouldn't—he said he would return to ask you for my hand in marriage. He promised." There. She said it. She had been keeping the information for herself, not wanting to share it until Philip arrived, glorious and heroic like a knight out of a storybook.

This time, the duke's face turned ashen. "He told you this?"

She nodded, tears forming in her eyes. "I was waiting..."

Maximilian held his head in his hands. "Sophie, I have something else to tell you. When I was at court in Paris, there was an announcement."

"Yes?"

"There was a letter from the king of Spain, inviting the king of France to the upcoming nuptials of his son and heir."

Sophie held her breath.

"Prince Philip of Spain is betrothed to marry Elizabeth, princess of England."

And though Sophie was still physically in her chair, she was sent reeling, flung far out into space. "But isn't she so much older than him?"

Maximilian let out a long, hard breath that buzzed through his lips, then slumped back against his own seat. "Eight years his senior. But it does not matter. He is betrothed. He is not here, he will not be coming to visit you, he has been packed off to England immediately."

So that's why there had been no visit or letter.

Philip was getting married.

But not to her.

To someone else.

It hurt. It hurt so much. He had not even thought to write her, to tell her the truth. He had just disappeared, like a ghost in the night.

"I was able to tamp down the whispers, and hopefully I have salvaged your reputation. Now there is only one way to ensure your future," the duke said, his brows knitted and angry.

Sophie braced herself for the worst.

"You must marry immediately. Before word of your clandestine affair with Prince Philip is more widely known. Because the prince was involved in these rumors and yet will marry someone else, it will look as though he's rejected you—or worse, that he used you and cast you aside. You will be married in a fortnight. I have invited several suitors to the palace. You will choose one."

"No!" cried Sophie. "I cannot marry someone I do not love! I know Philip; he will come back for me!"

"I will brook no argument on this," Maximilian said, his face hard.

"No! Father, if you do this, I will never speak to you again."

"That's fine with me, as I have nothing more to say on the matter."

CHAPTER SEVENTEEN

SINCE DUKE MAXIMILIAN'S DECREE, LOTTE roused Sophie from bed early each morning, and each morning Sophie wished she could burrow six feet under the ground. She sat before her dressing table mirror, barely noticing her reflection as Lotte brushed and powdered and yanked her into her best finery. Then the maid practically pushed Sophie down the stairs and into the front parlor, where her suitor awaited.

First was Lord Peter of the Slovene Lands, a painfully thin young man with a shock of red curly hair and equally red pimples all across his face and neck. He stared openly at Sophie while she curtsied, then took her for a hunting outing up the mountain. They rode horses along the Pöllat Gorge and carried bows and arrows, aiming idly at different targets. Sophie wasn't sure she could actually shoot an animal, but it felt good to be outside and to practice her aim.

"So, Lord Peter," she said grudgingly. Sophie had considered staying silent and cold through these outings, but it wasn't Peter's fault he had to be here. The way it was, she was sure his parents had planned his life just as Duke Maximilian had for her and King

Ferdinand had for Philip. "What do you like to do with your time?"

"This." He looked at her and absentmindedly stuck his finger up his nose.

"Ah," she said, trying not to grimace. "You mean—you're an avid hunter?"

"Mm-hmm." He took aim and shot into a tree; a squirrel dropped from underneath the branches. "Oho!" cried Peter, dismounting his horse. He ran over and picked up the dead squirrel. "Right in his ribs! Those are very tiny, you know. A very small target."

He smirked at her. Sophie cleared her throat.

Then, to her horror, he brought it over to her. "My lady," he said shyly. "Would you like to keep it?"

"*Keep* it? Why, no—I—why would I keep it?"

"Just as a small memento of our time together." He shrugged. "Not only am I an adept hunter, but I've learned how to mount and preserve my trophies. I enjoy creating tableaux of historical scenes using small animals. It's simple, really; one must only prepare a salt bath and create a small hole to drain the fluids from—"

"That's very kind of you," Sophie said, urging her horse to back away. "I'll just—cherish the memory. How about that?"

"Just like every other woman on this godforsaken continent," Peter muttered to himself, tossing the squirrel into the river.

❧

The next day, there was Count Gunter von Zürich, a large man with a sweaty brow who was significantly closer to Duke Maximilian's age than Sophie's. When they met in the parlor, he kissed Sophie on both cheeks and squeezed her hand so hard it felt like it was being crushed.

"My dear," he said. "Do you have a music room?"

"Yes, we do," said Sophie through her teeth, rubbing her hand. "We have a harp as well as a harpsichord."

He winked. "How about some harpsichord music?"

"That sounds very nice."

Sophie led the way through the palace, thinking that at least it might be relaxing to sit and listen to some music for an hour or so. It had been a long time since she'd had someone play for her; not since her mother had died, in fact.

"Here we are," Sophie said, leading him to the harpsichord made with warm wood and inlaid with mother-of-pearl.

"How beautiful!" the count said, beaming at her.

"Yes, my mother had it specially made. It's quite old, but it's tuned regularly and sounds lovely." Sophie waited for him to take a seat at the bench, but he simply stood near the keyboard. An awkward silence fell between them.

"Do you play often?" she asked.

His eyebrows shot up and he laughed. "Oh—my dear, I do not play. It's much too delicate and feminine an instrument for me. My bride, however, must be able to entertain me."

Sophie groaned inwardly.

"Ah," she said. "Well, it's been several years since I've practiced, but let me see what I remember."

He winked, and Sophie's smile froze into what must have been a very strange-looking grimace. "Do you know 'To Thee and to the Maid'?"

"Um. Let me see." Sophie started slowly, plunking out the melody.

"Did your mother teach you?"

"What's that?" It was very difficult to concentrate on playing while he was asking her questions.

"Your *mother*? Did she teach you?"

"Oh—yes. She did."

He nodded as Sophie continued to work at the song. Then he started humming—then singing, in a loud, off-key baritone.

"*To thee and to a maid*—no, that's not correct—mmm ... da-da-da ... *to thee and to THE maid* ... Oops, I do believe I just heard a wrong note, Lady Sophie! Tsk-tsk."

Sophie huffed. She wished she could throw the harpsichord at him.

❦

A few days later, there was Lord Dietrich of Austria, the same arrogant boy who had danced with her at the Zieglers' ball. He was as disaffected as ever, crossing his arms and regarding her with that smirk of his.

"Lord Dietrich," she said, curtsying.

He nodded.

"How would you like to spend our visit?" she asked, trying and failing to force a smile.

"I can think of a few ways to spend the time," he said, raising his eyebrows at the open door.

"Oh, uh ..." Sophie blushed furiously. The door was open because she had no chaperone in the room, but there was something about Dietrich's manner that was so inappropriate it bordered on terrifying. She did not want to be alone with this man.

Dietrich studied his fingernails. "If I'm to propose marriage, don't you think I should be allowed to—hmm, how shall I put it—inspect the goods?" At her shocked face, he sighed.

"Excuse me?" she said.

He rolled his eyes. "My father, fool that he is, considers this duchy to be relevant to our interests. Let me be clear, when we are married, you will be my wife, but I will do as I please. And I will have what I want, marriage vows or not."

Sophie felt her blood grow cold in her veins. Gently bred ladies of the nobility were like lambs to the slaughter when it came to matters

111

of the flesh. Her mother had died too early to give her much advice concerning the wedding night. But she thought about the dagger she owned. If he made any untoward moves toward her, would she be brave enough to use it? She hoped so.

"After all," he carried on, "you must marry someone to save your reputation, don't you? You've been soiled. I hope he hasn't used you up so well."

"My lord! I have never!"

"Just as I thought." He sneered. "Well, we shall soon see about that. You won't be a backwater virgin for long."

This time, Sophie was stunned speechless.

"You shall come visit me in a week's time," he said, a threat more than an invitation. "And we shall see then if you are worth all this trouble."

To her great relief, Lotte entered the room and informed Lord Dietrich his time was up, as a new lord had come to call.

The next suitor was none other than Manfred, the clumsy but sweet boy from the dance as well. His father was Baron Ziegler, lower in rank but well respected. He smiled broadly at Sophie. "My lady," he said. "It is good to see you again."

"Lord Manfred, hello." She greeted him, relieved that the awful Dietrich was finally out of her company. "Shall we go sit in the garden?"

"Anything you want."

She led him to a sunny bench near their pool of golden trout. He contemplated the fish deeply, staring into the rippling water, so at least watching them was better than nothing.

"I wrote you a poem, you know," Manfred said at last.

"Oh," said Sophie, genuinely surprised. "That's very kind of you.

Would . . . you like to read it for me, or would you rather I save it for later?"

"I'll read it." He pulled a beautiful piece of fine vellum from his pocket and unfolded it to reveal several handwritten verses in sonnet form. He cleared his throat quite loudly.

"So fair thy beauty like the dawn of day / My mistress's voice rings an angel song / And thus, run I to greet her, come what may / And meet her there on sunny, dew-dropped lawn . . ."

Sophie couldn't help but to be impressed. No one had written a poem for her before, and it seemed passable enough.

He cleared his throat and continued. "But fairer still the sweet embrace of death / I long for Her more than my earthly love / And eagerly await my final breath—"

"Oh!" Sophie said. "Uh, that took a turn. Rather dark, isn't it?"

Manfred looked a bit hurt. "I'm following a long tradition of Stoic poetic expression. You may not understand." He sighed. "And please don't interrupt me while I'm reading my poetry."

Sophie stared at him. "I . . . apologize."

"And eagerly await my final breath / My dying heart, a-beating like the dove . . ."

Sophie glanced over at the page. The stanzas continued down the front of the vellum and onto its back as well. She wished she was one of the trout.

At dinner that evening, Sophie told her father and Claudia that none of the suitors were acceptable. Lord Peter was dull, Count Gunter von Zürich too old, Lord Dietrich—the less she thought about him the better—and Manfred would torture her with his abominable poetry for the rest of her life.

"I shall not marry any of them, Father," she said.

Duke Maximilian said nothing, though Claudia looked at him as she dipped a spoon in her oxtail soup. "I'm very sorry, Sophie," she said. "I know it's a difficult situation to be in."

"I shall not have you spoken of as no better than a wench," Maximilian said at last. "You are my daughter and a lady of Bavaria. You will not bring shame to our name. It is your duty to have a respectable marriage. A successful alliance with another great house will do much for our country."

"I think I have a greater duty to the people of Bavaria than to any preconceived notions of romance," Sophie retorted.

"It isn't about romance—it's about saving your hide," the duke muttered.

"Maximilian," Claudia said, low and reproachful.

"It is the truth!" the duke roared so loudly that the soup tureen wobbled. "You were seen unchaperoned with the prince of Spain on more than two occasions. You are lucky there are those who still do not believe the rumors about the end of your chastity."

Sophie gulped.

"You are lucky to have any suitors at all," the duke growled. "You will marry, Sophielein." It was the first time he did not call her by that name in an affectionate tone of voice. "You must, or you bring disgrace to yourself and to all of your family and country."

Sophie looked down at her untouched plate, her stomach sinking lower than the floor underneath. "Yes, Father," she whispered. She would marry. She had no choice.

CHAPTER EIGHTEEN

THE NEXT MORNING BROUGHT NO new suitors and instead a letter from the Archduke of Austria. Duke Maximilian called Sophie into his study once more. Her father was clearly in good spirits, smiling at her when she entered.

"Sit, sit—I have news!" he crowed.

"Yes, Father?" she asked, hoping it wasn't the news she feared.

"The archduke writes that his son is enamored of you and has asked for your hand in marriage. You are to visit them in Vienna at the end of the week, and so you must leave tomorrow to be able to arrive in time."

It was exactly as she'd feared.

"Lord Dietrich?" she whispered. "He wants to marry me?"

"Indeed!" said her father. "You shall be a princess of Austria! Your mother would be so proud if she were here today."

"But, Father—"

"I won't hear any objection! This is better than I'd hoped. Austria! We will be aligned with one of the richest kingdoms in the region!"

"But, Father—"

The duke wasn't listening. He was still reading the letter. "Hmm, they would like you to travel on your own, they will provide you with a lady's maid when you get there, and all will be taken care of. Neither myself nor Claudia has been invited to accompany you. Oh, it must be so you and Dietrich can get to know each other better."

I should be allowed to inspect the goods.

You won't be a backwater virgin for long.

"Father! No! I will not! Never!" she cried. With that, she ran from the room without looking back.

But the adrenaline that allowed her to speak so boldly against the engagement didn't last long. By the time Sophie got back to her room, she was a wreck, tears streaming down her face. She crawled into bed, still fully clothed, and pulled the quilts all the way up to her chin. She sobbed for a while, muffled by the blankets and wrapped in as tight of a cocoon as she could manage.

Later in the evening—Sophie couldn't say when—someone sat on her bed and pressed a handkerchief into her hand. A gentle pressure came onto her back, moving up and down in slow circles.

"Shh," came Claudia's voice from somewhere above her. "You'll be all right. You'll be all right."

Sophie pulled the covers away from her head and wiped her eyes with the handkerchief.

"Thank you," she said hoarsely.

"I am sorry," said Claudia. "But your father is only doing this to protect you."

"Is it so terrible not to marry?" asked Sophie.

"A woman in our society without a husband . . . you would not be protected. You would be too vulnerable. Or worse, discarded."

"I have already been discarded." She had not let herself think of Philip, but his memory was there still. How could he have abandoned and disgraced her?

"Surely, Lord Dietrich is not so terrible. He is very handsome, is he not?"

He was as handsome as a lion about to eat an antelope. Sophie thought about it. Could she possibly grow to love him? He was not Philip, but was there a way she could? Then she remembered his lecherous smile and the way he leered at her. The way he'd joked about conquests and the threats he had made to her person. He had ordered her to his palace like a serving girl and made certain that there would be no one to protect her when she arrived. She would be alone in a strange palace, with no maid, no father, and no stepmother.

"He is awful." She drew in a breath between sobs. "He is . . . he is . . . he said he would . . ." And she told Claudia what conspired between them.

Her stepmother was not shocked, but she was distressed. "There are stories about men like this, but I never thought one would be so bold as he."

"He thinks he owns me because I am ruined, that I have no choice but to accept him," Sophie said.

Claudia sat up straight. "I shall talk to your father."

"He won't change his mind."

"But he will not give you to a monster!"

"Claudia, why must I marry? Why can't I just stay here, with you and Papa and the baby?"

Her stepmother's shoulders slumped. "Because if you do not marry now, the rumors will only grow in viciousness. And soon you will have no prospects at all."

"I can't marry Lord Dietrich. I won't."

Claudia studied the brocade on her sleeve and did not meet

Sophie's eyes. "Then choose someone else. Perhaps if encouraged, one of the other suitors will offer for your hand."

Sophie thought about Manfred. She could marry him. He would be kind and dull and recite atrocious poetry and step on her feet every time they danced. She could marry him, and her life would be peaceful, at least. He would not hurt her like Dietrich clearly meant to. But she would be consigning herself to a life without love, without passion. Without Philip.

"I can't. I don't want to marry anyone. I'll run away if I have to!" Sophie cried.

Claudia paled at Sophie's words. "Do not say such things! You will feel better tomorrow. The shock will wear off. Would you like some tea?"

Sophie sighed. "I suppose. I can call Lotte . . ."

"There's no need," Claudia murmured. "I'll get it myself."

She returned a few minutes later with a steaming tea tray that she set next to Sophie's bed. Claudia helped her stepdaughter up to a sitting position and handed her a cup of amber-colored liquid. It smelled unusual, like raspberries and cinnamon, and shimmered slightly in the waning light of Sophie's bedroom.

"What kind is it?" Sophie sniffed. "Lotte usually brings me chamomile. I like the smell of this, though."

Claudia shrugged, tracing the embroidery on Sophie's blankets with her finger. "It's made from the bark of the balsam trees outside."

"Is it safe to drink?"

"Perfectly."

Sophie lifted the cup. The moment the tea passed her lips, she felt immediately comforted and very drowsy.

"That's nice," she murmured.

"I thought you'd enjoy it." Claudia helped her settle back into the pillows. Sophie took one more drink of the tea before Claudia took it back from her, catching it from spilling.

The room swam and Sophie closed her eyes.

"Just get some rest," Claudia said, her voice echoing into darkness.

When Sophie woke in the morning, her body felt unusually rested and her mind surprisingly clear. The events of the previous day felt far away, muted by the long night of sleep she'd had. As Sophie stretched in bed, she saw Lotte setting out a tray for breakfast next to the window.

"Ah, good, you're up, my lady."

"Good morning, Lotte." She frowned. "What time is it?"

"Nearly eleven, ma'am."

"What?" Sophie rarely slept past nine. She flung the covers back and swung her feet over the bed, trying to get her bearings.

"What—what do I have today?" she said, fearing that Lotte would tell her that she was already late for the days-long trip to Vienna.

"It's all right, Lady Sophie," Lotte said, smiling. "You're not going to Vienna after all."

"I'm not?"

Lotte shrugged. "Apparently the duke sent a letter to the archduke this morning and everything's off. But there is something exciting!"

"What?"

"Baron Ziegler is on his way! With the young Lord Manfred!" she said. "Oh, I wasn't supposed to tell you that—I think it's meant to be a surprise!"

While Sophie had been sleeping, the duke and the duchess had plotted her future. She would not be forced to marry Dietrich, but she would have to settle for a life with Manfred.

Out of the frying pan and into the fire.

She should have run away last night. She had meant to, truly, except the tea that Claudia had given her to drink had made her so sleepy, almost as if it were enchanted.

Sophie chewed her lower lip, thinking as she looked out her bedroom window. It was a nice view, though she rarely stopped to appreciate it. The casements in her room were wide and reached nearly up to the ceiling, overlooking the forested foothills and into the valley. She couldn't see as well as she could in the tower, of course, but she caught glimpses through the branches of the trees. Through the forest was freedom.

"They will be here soon!" said Lotte.

By the time Sophie finished her breakfast, she knew what she was going to do.

Manfred proposed, just as Sophie had known he would. He did it with great ceremony, reciting a sonnet as he bent on one knee, seeming more pleased with himself than enamored with her. Sophie bore it as best she could, accepting his offer in front of her father, her stepmother, and Baron Ziegler, trying to look enthusiastic so as not to hurt Manfred's feelings.

But Lotte had a hard time helping Sophie out of her clothes that night—Sophie's limbs were quite weak. The lady's maid was overcome by the engagement and couldn't stop talking about it. A light rain pattered against the window, punctuating her words.

"Lady Sophie!" she squealed. "You just can't *imagine* how excited I am! Oh, we'll have so much to do—the hair, the makeup, the gown. I've been having Chef send out for fashion advice from her friends back in Paris. She hates it, you know, but I've been getting what's left of those berries far up on the mountain, this late in the season—Chef really will do anything for a basket of hand-picked whortleberries. All the better for us. And I believe I know just the gown you'll want to wear . . ."

But Lotte's babbling faded to background noise as Sophie plotted her escape. Manfred was kind enough, sure, but there had to be more to life than being married off to the least offensive lord in the land. There had to be *more*.

Claudia stopped by the room to see how Sophie was feeling, offering her another cup of tea, but Sophie demurred. She suspected her stepmother knew her too well and had put something in the tea to keep Sophie in bed. She wanted to be alert.

Sophie had to go tonight, because tomorrow the word of her engagement would be all over the duchy, and then the continent, and there would be no turning back. She had her mother's necklace, some jewelry, a purse of gold coins. Her mother's dagger was her only protection. Perhaps she could make her way to England—*what a thought*—and surprise Philip there. No, she would have to live among the people of Bavaria, free, but common. She would do it. She would make her own way.

She left through the stables, where she found a small lantern and headed out into the darkness. She slipped past the night watch, jogging opposite the way the guards were walking around the palace's perimeter. The rain had picked up and now came down in sheets, pressing the weight of her cloak on top of Sophie and making it difficult to see. She slipped down the path, now a small landslide of mud, holding on to trunks of trees and low branches to keep her balance. A crack of lightning came, briefly illuminating her way with purple light.

She looked back at the palace looming above the grove in dark silhouette, light from the tower windows shining faintly. She would never see her home again. But she knew that soon it would not belong to her either. She would be a married woman, and she would have to live with her husband. There was nothing here for her anymore. She gulped and moved forward.

In between the rush of wind and loud hammering of rain, there came a sound from the trees behind her—something like a branch snapping in two.

Sophie froze.

It could be something harmless. An animal making its way through the forest. The wind causing storm damage. But a rivulet of icy fear traveled down her spine all the same. She was exposed by the noise of her poor footing on the side of the hill and by her bobbing lantern, easily spotted in the storm. In the darkness beyond her circle of lamplight, a whole army could have her surrounded and she would never know. She kept moving.

The storm howled even louder but she kept to the path, now working against the flood of water coming down the trail. Sophie dug her shoe horizontally into the mud, trying to create small notches that she could use to push off with her legs. She grabbed trunks and branches for balance, fighting gravity and her sodden skirts at the same time.

Sophie was three-fourths of the way down the path when she heard it again: the same snap as before. A quick *one-two*. It sounded much closer now and had the volume of something broken by a person or a large animal. Her heart threw itself against her rib cage. Already out of breath from trying not to be swept away by the mudslide, she paused to check her way. Raising the lantern as high as she dared, Sophie peered out into the stark contrast of trees and murky shadows.

"Hello?" she called. "Who's there? Show yourself!"

She heard nothing but the hard rainfall.

Then there was a rustling somewhere to her left. Sophie fumbled with her skirts, checking for the hilt of the dagger. She knew she'd gotten much better at throwing in the past few weeks, but could she fend off an attacker now? Even worse, engage in hand-to-hand combat?

Just then, a flash of lightning brightened the forest to reveal a dark figure frighteningly close to Sophie.

She reeled, nearly losing her balance. She grabbed at a nearby branch, dropping the lantern, which quickly snuffed out in the wet. Plunged into darkness with the stranger, Sophie's adrenaline soared. *Turn back now,* her intuition told her. *Run.* She began to scramble up the hill, hand over fist, using the lights of the palace towers to guide her.

The noises continued behind her, footsteps scuttling around in the darkness and struggling against the same mudslide to catch up with her. These sounds beneath the whistling wind forced Sophie on faster.

Muscles aching, lungs on fire, Sophie knew she could only run so far. As the approach of her pursuer drew closer, she reached into the pouch at her hip and felt the hilt of her mother's dagger there.

The footsteps behind her sped up, crashing through the brush. Sophie steeled herself against the trunk of a birch and gripped her weapon, prepared as well as she could be for whatever she was about to face.

All at once, a figure burst through the branches. Sophie raised her dagger, screamed, and lunged.

CHAPTER NINETEEN

"PHILIP?!" SHE SCREAMED WHEN THE clouds parted and the moonlight revealed his face.

"Sophie! Snow White!" It was him, for real, in the flesh. It was him, crashing into her in all his bewilderment and outsized joy and handsome grin.

"How did you— What are you—" Sophie gaped, immediately lowering her knife, as he embraced her and swung her around, unsteady on the side of the hill and flinging mud left and right.

"I'm here!" he said. "I'm here! I made it! I'm back!"

"But—but how?"

"I told you I would come back for you, didn't I?"

Sophie paused to take him in. He had never looked more beautiful than he did now. She felt that it would take a great deal of time to regain her breath once more.

"You were about to kill me," Philip said with a laugh, seeing the dagger she held in her hand.

"I'm—I'm so sorry," Sophie said. She fumbled to put it back in its pouch, still dazed. "You frightened me . . ."

She pulled her hair back from her face with a flush, knowing it must look wild from the rain. Philip's own cheeks must have grown red, and he appeared to temporarily lose focus.

"I'm sorry, I didn't mean to— I meant to arrive earlier, but then it was too late. I thought I would try and see you tonight, anyway. Throw pebbles at your window, you know," he said, looking abashed. "I couldn't wait to tell you I had returned."

"I—I've been waiting for you," she stammered.

He pulled her into his arms. "I wanted to come sooner, but I was delayed. Please forgive me."

"Forgive you?" she asked. When he held her, she could feel his heart thumping in his chest. He was all nerves and jittery like a horse.

"Yes." Philip cleared his throat, steadying himself. "I should have written, but I wanted to tell you in person."

"Tell me what?" Sophie watched as he shifted from one foot to another, face streaked with rain. "Hold on, should we go somewhere more comfortable?" she said.

"Please, let's."

After its downpour, the rain was beginning to lighten. Philip and Sophie trudged back up the hill, toward the palace Sophie had been so ready to abandon just minutes ago. Unable and unwilling to go in, given their current state, the two continued into the gardens. Philip held her hand tightly as if he would never let go. Sophie kept catching glimpses of him grinning at her; he would look away, and then she would do the same thing.

A voice in Sophie's head told her she should not dare to hope so much—Princess Elizabeth could be waiting for them nearby. He could have come all this way to tell her to her face that he couldn't ask for her hand in marriage.

They went to the old stone bench under the Norway spruce, the bench that Sophie, sheepishly, thought of as theirs.

"I assume you've heard about my engagement," he said.

"Yes," she said levelly.

"It was the reason I was supposed to go to England months ago. The marriage had been arranged for quite some time," he confessed.

"I see."

"The thing is—I wasn't supposed to meet you. You weren't part of my father's plan."

She nodded. The rain had stopped, and it was easier to see each other's faces.

"When I left you that night I came to dinner, I meant to write to my father and tell him I would never marry Elizabeth. But instead, I read a letter from him saying he had announced my engagement to the whole world. I wanted to come to you, but I needed to talk to him first. And I couldn't face your father without clearing everything up. So I had to go home to Spain."

"And?"

"I told my father I would not marry Elizabeth."

"What did he do?" Sophie asked, hardly able to speak.

"He ranted and raved and had a tantrum."

Sophie clutched his arm. "Oh no."

"But I am my own man. I had never disobeyed my father, not once, until I met you. And I would defy him again, I would defy it all, if it meant that I could be with you," Philip said, his voice gaining intensity. "He said it was too late—the announcement was out—we would be insulting England, and war would be on the horizon."

She shook her head. She could not be the cause of so much war, of so much suffering. "We cannot risk that, Philip. It's not worth it."

Philip shook his head. "There have been rumblings of war from England for years—they still have not come to terms with Spain about the new trade routes. They are just looking for an excuse for battle.

This marriage was supposed to bring the two countries together, but I have heard Elizabeth wanted this marriage as little as I did. Her heart is elsewhere."

"And your heart?" she whispered.

"Is right here," he said, gripping her hands even more tightly.

Sophie felt her heart leap in her throat. "So then what happened? How are you here?"

"At last, my father came to his senses."

"He let you off the engagement?"

"Well, not quite." Philip had enough sense to look abashed.

"Not quite?"

"There was a situation in Milan. He had to leave to attend to it. I am to join him shortly. But first, I wanted to come here. To see you." He drew a long breath. "We don't have time. We must be married before I go. I can arrange for a special dispensation from the Church. We can have a priest here as soon as possible."

Sophie found she couldn't speak, so she simply pulled him forward and wrapped her arms around his shoulders. He embraced her right back, burying his hands into her long hair.

"I'm so sorry, Sophie, I should have written. You must have thought me the worst kind of rogue."

She shook her head. "I always knew you would come back for me."

A shadow crossed Philip's face, but then vanished with a smile. "I am sorry for making you wait."

"You came just in time."

He ran his thumb along her cheekbone affectionately and gave a quiet laugh. "Oh?" Then he stopped, as he realized where they were. Out in the gardens, at night, in the pouring rain, alone. "What were you doing out here?"

"Running away."

Philip's eyes widened. "But why—"

She hung her head. "My father said I had to marry someone—someone who wasn't you. I didn't want to, so . . ."

In answer, he brought her hands to his heart. Sophie breathed in the smell of the pines and the wet earth, the warmth of the late-summer breeze, the flowers that surrounded them. She wanted to preserve this moment as long as she could. Philip was back. She would not have to run away or marry Dietrich or Manfred.

"I suppose you should talk to my father now," she said, removing her hands from his chest. "Although it is late."

But Philip stayed seated, looking once more very flustered and pale; the last few raindrops clung to his lashes like tears. At last he spoke. "Lady Sophie, it doesn't matter what your father says. Because the only one who matters is you. I will have to ask him because that is what we do in society, but I believe you should have a choice in your future."

He knelt on the ground before Sophie and again took her hand. Sophie's heart stopped.

"My dear Lady Sophie," he said, looking her straight in the eyes and offering a gold ring that glinted even in the wan light of the moon. "Would you do me the honor of becoming my queen?"

Sophie clapped a hand over her mouth. It was more than she dreamed. A lifetime of love and happiness and passion. She knew that she could not—would not—lose him again.

"Yes," she choked. "Yes, a thousand times over."

"My darling," he said, putting the ring on her finger as the whole sky lit up with a meteor shower. "You have made me the happiest man in the world."

Sophie looked up at a falling star and thanked the heavens, for her heart's desire had come true.

CHAPTER TWENTY

PRINCE PHILIP RETURNED IN THE morning and formally asked for Sophie's hand in marriage. If Duke Maximilian was shocked by this sudden turn of events, he did not show it. Mostly, the duke looked relieved.

"I've had my differences with your father, Philip, I'll admit," Maximilian said, clearing his throat. "But I must say, I find you quite a respectable young man. If your father is content with your decision, I believe this union will be beneficial for us all," the duke continued, offering Philip a cigar.

"He has no choice," Philip said tightly, shaking his head at the cigar.

"Ah," said the duke, looking troubled. "I wish no war with Spain over this. Your father would have my head if I went behind his back."

"There is nothing to fear from Spain," Philip assured him.

Maximilian stared hard at the boy across the table. "There cannot be."

"I guarantee it," said Philip. "It's my honor to be able to speak with you and to consider Sophie part of my future."

"Good," said the duke, taking a puff and filling the room with smoke. He leaned forward. "She was waiting for you, you know."

Philip nodded. "My deepest apologies for the delay in my arrival."

Maximilian meditated on the situation. Baron Ziegler's pride would have to be placated with a great many gifts from the duchy—the best ham from the cellar and cases of wine from the current harvest. It had taken more to assuage the archduke of Austria the day before, and Maximilian grumbled that at the rate they were accepting proposals and breaking them, Sophie would have no dowry.

"She does not need one," said Philip, his eyes flashing. "She shall be the queen of Spain."

"Right," said Maximilian. "Well, shall we tell the ladies all is set?"

When the men returned from the duke's study with smiling faces, Sophie and Claudia felt so much relief they almost fell backward. Claudia was especially overwhelmed when she heard the good news and clasped both hands over her throat. "Sophie! Prince Philip!" she shrieked. "Oh, I'm so happy for you. If you could have seen us the last few weeks, you would know how much we've missed you. How we've *all* missed you. Oh, I didn't dare to hope—"

Philip smiled, happy and flustered as Claudia fawned over the two of them, while Sophie looked a tad embarrassed.

"Suffice it to say, we would be so glad to have you in the family," Claudia finished.

"Certainly," Duke Maximilian said, though his tone didn't quite match the graciousness of his words. Sophie watched him closely as he led them to the parlor, wondering how the conversation had gone.

There was tea, celebratory wine, and a silver platter of intricate springerle cookies on the table before the fire. The duke, the duchess, and the two newly betrothed settled down in the warm chairs next to the hearth. Philip took her hand in his—a display of affection, right in front of Maximilian and Claudia, to Sophie's surprise. And yet it was all right, now that they were engaged. The gesture promptly made Sophie forgive and, momentarily, forget the agony of the last several months.

"I must say, not only did Lady Sophie enchant me, but so too has Bavaria," Philip continued. "It's a beautiful place, and I've gotten to see myself that its people are steadfast. Though Sophie and I will be in Spain for much of the year, we will be happy to assist in any way with the concerns here."

Despite the reminder that she would have to leave Bavaria, Sophie smiled to herself. With Philip at her side, perhaps she would finally be able to bring the councilors to heel and help the villagers.

Maximilian paused as he poured more wine, then spoke casually. "Yes, well. That is very kind of you."

"I know allocating funds to the common cause may not be the most popular plan among the nobility. But I think there should be no argument. A country, no matter how large or small, should ensure that its own citizens are cared for," said Philip.

Sophie could see her father's face beginning to sour.

"Another cookie?" Claudia gracefully changed the subject, offering the plate around.

While Maximilian and Claudia busied themselves with the refreshments, Sophie squeezed Philip's hand, feeling as though she were in a dream. She had spent so many years by herself, missing her father, her mother, and her childhood. Now here she was, sitting before the fire with her loved ones, feeling as though she'd been reunited with a family she'd never met before. She touched her mother's necklace, unsure whether she deserved this much contentment.

As they sipped their wine, the palace steward came into the room and went to Duke Maximilian's side. "I apologize for the interruption, my lord," he said in a low voice. "But there's a small security matter I wish to bring to your attention."

"Go ahead, Hans," Maximilian said. "It's all right to speak in front of our guest."

Hans looked uncomfortable as he cleared his throat, but he continued. "One of the cooks saw an unknown man near the kitchens. We don't believe he's one of our staff, and the cook wasn't able to speak with him before he disappeared into the woods."

"Hmm," Maximilian said, his face yet unreadable. "Could he have been a lost traveler? Perhaps he was hoping to get something to eat. Did he take anything?"

Hans shook his head. "Not that we know of. And he wasn't dressed like a traveler, my lord. He seemed to wear the clothes of one who would work for a house of nobility, but it wasn't a uniform that any of our own staff recognized."

The duke frowned, deep in thought. "Perhaps an employee of one of the suitors sent for Sophie?"

At the word *suitors*, Philip breathed in sharply but played it off as a cough. She felt her cheeks grow warm.

"Describe his clothes, please," Maximilian finished.

Hans rubbed his jaw. "They said he was dressed in something very dark, perhaps scarlet, with gold trim." He nodded down at his own uniform, white and blue, as was the standard throughout the duchy.

At the response, Maximilian turned slowly to Philip. Sophie's heart sank to see suspicion clouding in his eyes. "Scarlet? Could that be one of . . . ?" the duke asked.

"There's a chance it's one of my father's men," Philip said, his tone optimistic, though not as bright as before. He withdrew his hand from Sophie's and clasped both tightly together, elbows resting on his knees. "The king, gentleman though he is, has learned not to be overly trusting as a leader—even in the matters that involve his own son. I wouldn't be terribly surprised if he sent someone to check in on me; he likes to have eyes on a situation from afar."

Sophie felt a prick of doubt in her chest. Nothing she had heard of King Ferdinand made him seem like a kind or reasonable man. And as the night went on, she was getting the keen sense that Philip hadn't been completely truthful about his father's reaction to their plans. Philip had never mentioned that Ferdinand consented to the match after all, only that he would have no choice but to accept it. Kings did not like to hear that they had no say in such matters.

"I see," Maximilian said, the lightheartedness now fully gone from his voice. "Thank you for the information, Philip. Hans, let's set a watch out tonight, just in case."

Hans nodded and left the room.

"I'm certain you wouldn't have misrepresented your father's feelings to me, Philip," Maximilian said, though his face looked as though he was not certain at all.

"It's just my father's way," Philip answered, peering into his wine.

They all sat quiet for a moment, thinking. Then Claudia broke in with another question—"Now, what kind of cake would you like for your wedding?"—and lifted the mood of the room once more.

∿

Work and lessons were canceled for the rest of the day so the family and staff could celebrate and begin the wedding preparations. Lotte was extremely giggly upon being introduced to the handsome prince and would not stop blushing when she saw Sophie and Philip together. The excitement could be felt everywhere in the palace, as the young couple's love had brought happiness to all. There would first be an engagement banquet in two weeks to announce Sophie and Philip's plans to the nobility and the duchy of Bavaria at large. The wedding would take place only a week later, followed by an exciting ball similar to the wedding feast for Maximilian and Claudia but smaller in size due to the time constraint. The four spoke late into the evening, consulting with the head butler and head housekeeper on the work that would need to be done. There was the matter of urgency and time, but also the matter of propriety and tradition. Both had to be served.

Eventually, Maximilian stretched his arms and stood. "Sophielein," he said, "would you mind if I stole your beloved away for a brandy in the study? It's traditional to plan a hunting party for the men, and I'd like to spend some time with my son-in-law-to-be."

Sophie nodded, hoping the matter of King Ferdinand wouldn't come up again. "Of course, Papa. Don't be too difficult on him."

Maximilian winked, and Philip lightly squeezed her shoulder on his way out. Once they were gone, Claudia melted in her chair, beaming like an excited child. "Oh, Sophie, he is lovely. Are you happy, my dear?"

Sophie pulled at the sleeves of her dress. "I feel like none of this is real"—she smiled and shook her head—"yet here we are. I can't believe how quickly things have changed."

Claudia nodded. "It can happen like that. It's a strange and wonderful thing." She absentmindedly patted her stomach, which she tended to do more often now.

Sophie was quiet for a moment, rolling the edge of the paper on which they'd been drawing up wedding plans between her fingers. The only noise in the room was the crackling of the fireplace and a light drizzle starting outside the windows.

"I don't want to think of bad things," she said. "But I am a little worried about King Ferdinand. I fear he's less pleased than Philip is letting on. I don't want his disapproval to cause problems."

Claudia sighed. "Families can be very complicated, and the fact that the king is a powerful man doesn't help matters. It sounds like Philip and his father disagree on some things, but none of that is a reflection on you. If you trust Philip, and he can trust you, the bond between you is what matters most."

Sophie picked at her fingernail. "I know it was very hard for you, wasn't it—to move somewhere brand-new and try to fit in?" she said. "I don't know how to do . . . any of this."

The duchess glanced at the floor and shook her head. "It isn't easy. But Bavaria and Spain would benefit from an allegiance—the king will see that if he hasn't already. It wasn't the same in my homeland. With two rich nations, it is fitting that you'll protect the interests of both of your homes."

"I suppose so. I just can't shake the feeling that something bad is going to happen."

Claudia joined her stepdaughter on the sofa and put her arm around her. "You and I are fortunate to be marrying men we love; many don't have even that luxury. But I believe Philip is a good match for you. And"—she cleared her throat, dropping her eyes to her hands—"and I'm sure it must be difficult to do this without your mother. She would have the best advice for you. But I'm always here."

Sophie leaned her head against Claudia's shoulder. "Thank you," she murmured.

"Also," Claudia said, patting her belly again, "if you have any questions about the wedding night—"

Sophie's cheeks turned the deepest crimson. "Uhhh . . ."

"I can certainly talk through any questions on *that* subject as well."

There was a pause. Then Sophie snorted and Claudia threw her head back, laughing. They dissolved into giggles together until their stomachs hurt.

CHAPTER TWENTY-ONE

WHEN MAXIMILIAN AND PHILIP RETURNED from the study, Claudia bid them all good night and Maximilian soon followed. The servants bustled in and out of the room, clearing away plates and setting everything aright for the morning.

"What a day we've had, Lady Sophie," Philip said, aglow in the light of the fire.

"Indeed." She smiled, leaning back in her chair.

"I don't wish to end it early, but you look as though you're about to fall asleep this very moment."

"Nonsense."

"Now, my lady," he murmured, rising and taking her hands. "If I am to take care of you, I must ensure you get your rest."

"I believe we're meant to take care of each *other*, Prince Philip."

"Well said."

They walked the halls together. Sophie had the strange sense of being older, different; her status as an engaged woman was bringing her to another plane that was even more foreign than the one she'd entered when she debuted. Soon, the thought of chaperones and ill reputes and horrid suitors would be a thing of the past—or so she hoped.

"Philip," she said quietly, not wanting to break the comfortable silence between them. "What will it be like in Spain?"

He smiled so warmly that she blushed. "It will be beautiful. I can't wait to show you the mountains of my own homeland, the Cordillera Cantábrica, the beech forests. You can try mojama and fideuà; we can go to the ocean. I'll take you everywhere."

"That sounds wonderful." Hearing the anticipation in his voice, she suddenly wanted to do all of those things as much as he did, to go right now. But she laughed nervously. "And your people—what will they think of me?"

Philip looked at her solemnly. "They will fall in love with you as I have. You won't be some ornament on my arm, but someone who listens to Spain's needs and cares fiercely for them—and for Bavaria's, too. That's the kind of princess they want." He smiled wryly at her. "And eventually . . . queen."

Sophie took a deep breath, nodding and telling herself to believe his words. But something nagged at her, still. "What did my father discuss with you in the study?"

"Just the hunting party." He smiled. "And a few other things about being a man, doing nothing to hurt you, ever, lest I answer to him—the usual spiel. Why do you ask?"

She stopped, tugging where their hands were still attached. "How does your father *truly* feel about the marriage? You must be honest with me."

Philip's smile faded. "Oh. Let's not talk about him tonight. Please?"

He looked so sincere, so pained about the subject, that all Sophie could do was drop it. "All right. I can't say no to that face," she said, grinning ruefully. "Promise we will, though? Sometime soon?"

"Promise."

He led her upstairs and paused in the hall before her quarters. Sophie suddenly felt wide awake as they stood in the dim light, close and alone.

"This is where I leave you," he said quietly.

"I hope you sleep well," she whispered.

Then he lifted her hand to his face and very, very gently pressed his lips against her skin. At his touch, Sophie felt electricity coursing through her to match the autumn thunder rumbling outside.

He broke away, grinning, and pressed his hand to her shoulder.

"Good night, my lady."

✦

When Sophie woke up on the morning of the engagement banquet two weeks later, she spent a few moments in fear, wondering if everything had been a dream. This surely could not be happening, after so many weeks of disaster.

But no; there on the chair by the window was the dress that Lotte had laid out for the banquet, its dark-red silk chosen for the colors of the Spanish royal family's coat of arms. Burnished layers of scarlet draped around the waist and at the shoulders to reveal another layer of fabric beneath, gold and delicately embroidered. The bodice would cinch tight above the full skirts, and the sleeves would billow around cuffs of lace at the wrist. It had been made very quickly. "Costly but worth it," Lotte had said. They owed gratitude to the palace tailor and her team of seamstresses and lacemakers who had worked themselves to the bone day and night.

Sophie wrapped her arms around herself and shivered, partly from excitement, but mostly from nerves. They'd been so busy with preparations since the proposal, and Sophie still hadn't had a chance to speak with Philip about his father. And the relationship between Philip and Duke Maximilian was cordial but had cooled; Sophie got the sense, from snippets picked up from the servants and observing her father, that the duke had sent a few messages to establish a conversation with King Ferdinand. But as of yet, there seemed to be no reply.

Philip assured them his father would come around. The king was busy with the duchy of Milan and had little time to spend on the matter of his son's marriage. He didn't seem too worried. But Sophie wasn't convinced. If one of King Ferdinand's men was already here, skulking around in the forest somewhere, what did it mean? Would the king spirit his son away? The thought made her stomach lurch.

Lotte's knock at the door forced Sophie out of her spiraling worries.

The maid set out the breakfast tray, but Sophie was too nervous to eat any of it. Everything had happened so fast her head was still spinning from it. Only a short time ago, she was to leave for Vienna to marry a man who did not love her, then she was to marry a lord who would bore her to death. But now she was engaged to the right one, the only one. Except his father was a powerful king who was known to be something of a tyrant bent on conquering as many kingdoms as he could.

Lotte glared at Sophie as she hustled to her dressing table. "You've got to put something in your stomach, or you'll faint away just like the duchess!"

"I'm sorry, I'm sorry!" Sophie picked up another roll and tried to eat as Lotte set to work on her hair, but the bread was cold and sticky in her mouth. She swallowed what she could, too agitated to finish.

It would be a strange feeling, standing in relative triumph before the nobility that had mocked her and scorned her as little as a few days ago. She found it hard to believe that they would truly congratulate her and applaud, but that was the way high society worked, she supposed. Perhaps she would even feel vindicated.

The day was a blur of preparations, with a whole team of maids descending upon Sophie to make her presentable. They gathered all her hair into one braid that thickened as they teased and powdered it, then wound it as a heavy crown around the top of her head. Behind it, they placed a stiff headpiece that haloed the braid, red velvet to match the scarlet dress, embroidered with gold thread, and set with pearls. A veil of translucent fabric came down from the headpiece and fell past Sophie's back. The maids oiled and curled any flyaway hairs into ringlets that framed Sophie's face.

Sophie was deafened by her maids' constant chatter, more to each other than to her, and wished she could be anywhere else in the palace. And Sophie knew Claudia hardly had it any better, as she was in charge of the major preparations and would spend the better part of the day wrangling the staff, who were colder to her than they'd ever been to Sophie.

Sophie knew it would be beautiful. She could tell Claudia had been working very hard on the planning and hoped she wasn't over-extending herself, especially with her condition.

Through the flurry of servants, a footman entered the room with a small crystal glass on a silver tray.

"What's this?" Sophie asked as he set the tray on the dressing table next to her.

"A blackberry cordial for my lady, sent by Prince Philip," he said.

"Oh! Thank you."

She eyed the dark red drink as the maids continued to work.

"Would you like to pause and have your cordial, my lady?" Lotte asked. Sophie could tell she spoke through gritted teeth; with the evening fast approaching, the women had no desire to stall their progress.

"No, no," Sophie said lightly. "Please continue."

She reached for the glass and swirled it around in her hand as they began to set the finishing powder. It was a bit strange. She thought Philip knew she didn't care for cordial, which was too syrupy for her liking. But knowing he must have forgotten, surely nervous about the day's events, it was a sweet gesture all the same.

Sophie brought the glass to her nose, the heavy blackberry fragrant in the air. Beneath the smell were notes of the sugary, medicinal liqueur that made her already unsettled stomach flip-flop. She quickly set the glass down before she gagged. The maids had finished her hair and makeup, so it was time to step into her gown anyway.

She would drink the cordial later.

CHAPTER TWENTY-TWO

AS THE WOMEN PULLED THE silk bodice tight around Sophie's chest, Claudia swept into the room. She wore a dress similar to Sophie's in a shade of blue so pale it was almost white, looking pearlescent against her fair skin. Its bodice was let out slightly, just barely disguising that the duchess was with child. The dress's outer skirt was the same shade of blue with a white silk underskirt beneath. The sleeves opened into wide, draping fabric, and she wore a headpiece like Sophie's for the occasion.

Her stepmother was truly glowing and now looked positively giddy, whirling in front of the mirror and bending down to plant a kiss on Sophie's cheek. "Oh, you are going to be too lovely," she said, clasping her hands. "What a perfect day this is. One to be remembered, for certain!"

A few of the maids glanced up at these declarations, and even Sophie felt they seemed a little grandiose. But she laughed with her stepmother. "You'd think *you* were the one getting engaged again, instead of me," she said.

"Is this the cordial from Philip?" Claudia picked up the crystal glass from the dressing table and swirled the dark liquid.

"Oh yes, I think he sent it. Did he say something to you?"

"No, no, I saw a servant carrying it up earlier. He was a bit gruff to me, but then, who isn't?" She laughed a strange, high-pitched giggle, a little wild in the eyes. Claudia raised the glass to her nose, sniffed deeply, and nodded.

"Blackberry is my favorite," she said, giving the glass back to Sophie. "He's very sweet to you."

Sophie smiled and nodded, but returned the cordial to the table as the maids completed their finishing touches.

"Shall we?" Claudia asked, hooking her arm around Sophie's.

Sophie eyed her stepmother as they descended the stairs, seeing the wide smile on her face, the high color in her cheeks, her suddenly ramrod-straight posture. A forgotten thread tugged somewhere at the back of Sophie's brain.

"Are you all right?" she murmured into Claudia's ear. "Is something going on with you?"

Claudia turned, grinning conspiratorially. Her eyes were sharp and bright, reminding Sophie of the cold elegance that struck her, back when she and Claudia were strangers. The woman whose beauty had threatened the nobility and incited its envy on her wedding day was still there, perfect and hard as carved stone.

"The baby is kicking," Claudia whispered.

"Oh," Sophie said. "How wonderful! Babies kick?"

"We can talk more later," Claudia said, squeezing Sophie's hand and passing her on to Philip.

And then suddenly the world was coming back into sharp focus—she and Philip reentered the dining hall together to orchestral fanfare. Maximilian and Claudia followed closely behind.

There was too much to look at, so much noise and color. The room was filled with guests once more, already seated and warmed with honey mead and lively with conversation. Claudia had done a beautiful job—flowers and autumn wreaths adorned every inch of the hall and lanterns from the garden had been brought inside, mimicking the part of the palace that Philip and Sophie loved best. Claudia had even provided her own silver goblets for the banquet, ones that she had carried from home and saved for special occasions.

Everything was perfect. Claudia was pregnant with the duke's heir and Sophie was to marry a prince—not just a prince, but the boy she loved—and one day soon, as Philip had said, she would be a queen.

The two couples took seats at the head table, with Sophie and Philip flanking Duke Maximilian. "You sit here," said Claudia, meaning to let Sophie sit at the head of the table next to her father. "So you can be close to Philip."

"Oh," said Sophie, agreeing to the change.

Claudia settled in next to Sophie and looked down the room at other nobility, such as the baroness of Sieradz and the viscount of Rouen. Baron Ziegler and the archduke were notably absent. The orchestra finished their interlude and Maximilian stood to give introductory remarks.

"My friends, allies, and aides," he said. "Tonight we come together to celebrate an exciting and powerful union. The joining in matrimony of my daughter, Lady Sophie of Bavaria"—he gestured to Sophie on his right—"and my son-to-be, Prince Philip of Spain!" he said, raising his arm to Philip on his left. The room broke into cheers and applause.

Sophie was surprised—and a little indignant—at the joy of all the guests, including the servants lining the room who broke character and cracked smiles. She wished it was genuine.

"I am eager to strengthen our relationship with Spain," Maximilian continued. "You may recall that my grandfather was close friends with Prince Philip's predecessors, and so Bavaria already has a rich history with the kingdom . . ."

Next to Sophie, Claudia fidgeted. Sophie glanced at her

stepmother, but Claudia didn't seem to be paying attention to Maximilian. Instead, she was watching the faces of the guests.

"I thank Duke Maximilian for his kind welcome," Philip said, taking the floor from Maximilian. "I look forward to serving the people of Bavaria as I do the people of Spain."

Sophie frowned but saw nothing out of the ordinary in the crowd of people. It was the usual assortment of nobility from Bavaria, the Holy Roman Empire, and beyond.

Sophie turned her attention to Philip. He was discussing the history of Spain and Bavaria's relations, and she wanted to understand this, to hear the background she was so interested in through his own words. Sophie was certain, though, that neither King Ferdinand's matzlfangen strategies nor the battle of Milan would be mentioned.

She was sorry that Philip had no friends or family members at the banquet—no one close to him, anyway. Of course, there was no way any of them could be here, since the wedding was so rushed.

Then again, Duchess Maria was not here either.

"And thus, on the brink of this new union, I would like to propose a toast," Philip said as his speech came to a close. He stood and lifted his goblet. "Without further ado . . ."

Amid the clamor of all the guests standing to join him, Claudia leaned over to murmur something into Sophie's ear and pointed into the crowd. But Sophie couldn't hear what she said.

What? she mouthed.

Claudia only shook her head and raised her own goblet of wine.

". . . I pledge that we shall serve you as Prince Philip of Spain and my betrothed, Lady Sophie of Bavaria!"

Sophie looked for her wineglass but did not find it at the right setting, so took the nearest one. She lifted it high, grinning wide and drinking deeply as the room toasted and cheered. The drink was sweet and acidic and heady all at once.

Then a scream cut through the noise of the crowd.

Everyone turned as if in slow motion to see Duke Maximilian fall to the ground, unconscious, his silver chalice clattering from his outstretched hand.

"Papa?" Sophie choked.

A sharp ringing in Sophie's ears drowned out all sound. Hardly comprehending the sight of her father on the ground, she moved as though she were walking through thick mud, limbs heavy and vision warping. Sophie fell to Maximilian's side as his arms began to twitch.

"Give him space!" It was Philip, barking at the tight ring of guests that had appeared around the duke. "Dash it, give him *space*!"

Sophie tried to lift her father's head, her hands numb and tingling with the pricks of a thousand needles. But his body was stiff, and his arms and legs bent at strange angles. He was still alive but convulsing, a thick mess of saliva bubbling from his mouth.

"It must have been the wine. Or his glass," the viscount of Rouen said.

Voices murmured above Sophie, wailing, crying, speculating.

"Who could have done this? Lieber Gott!"

"It was in the goblets—Duchess Claudia's own goblets—"

"Dear lord, have we *all* been poisoned?"

No. No one else had been affected. Everyone else was alive, scared and hysterical, but alive. No one else had fallen.

"Max!" the duchess wailed, throwing herself upon her husband. Claudia was crazed, hysterical, but Sophie could only watch, mute, as her father did not stir.

The duke had been poisoned.

Then Philip pulled her away and the guards came through to rush Duke Maximilian to the infirmary.

CHAPTER TWENTY-THREE

THERE WAS A JEWEL BEETLE crawling along the stone floor of the palace. Its metallic aquamarine shell shone in the dying daylight as it tried to navigate the strange surfaces that were so unlike its home outside. Sophie had traced its circular, endless path as it looked desperately for some way back to the garden, watching it for what seemed like hours as she waited outside the infirmary.

Claudia was somewhere in her chambers—by choice or by force, Sophie wasn't sure. Her stepmother had collapsed after the disaster and was taken away by her nurses in hysterics.

"Sophie." Philip's soft voice floated over the marble floor and called Sophie into the door of the infirmary. He had not allowed her in as the alchemists and medical advisers performed their tests, instead keeping watch and promising to call her if something important happened.

"What's happening?" Sophie rushed to his side.

He shook his head. "They've finished. You can come in and see him."

Sophie entered the dark room with Philip's hand tight in hers, terrified of what she would find inside. But though she expected frightening contraptions and bubbling potions, there was only her father, reclined in bed and sleeping.

"Papa?" she murmured. She went to his side, but he didn't stir at the sound of her voice.

The palace physician cleared his throat as he made some final notes on a sheet of paper. "He won't respond," he said. "I'm afraid he's in a very deep sleep due to the poison he consumed . . . Yes, his drink was indeed contaminated," he added in response to Sophie's alarmed expression.

She felt all the blood drain from her face. "But—does that mean we have *all* been poisoned? The wine—"

"Fortunately, no. We've tested the other goblets and found the toxin to be coated along the rim of only his goblet, not in the liquid itself," the physician replied.

This did not make Sophie feel any better. Philip held her hand a little tighter.

"They were Claudia's goblets," she said flatly. "Claudia was in charge of setting everything up."

The adviser frowned down at his notes, his face troubled.

"Duchess Claudia was very insistent we use the goblets from her dowry."

Of course, Claudia wanted her family to be part of the occasion. Sophie chastised herself for even suspecting anything afoul in her motive. Claudia loved the duke. But Sophie remembered her stepmother scanning the crowd, and there was something she wanted to tell Sophie. Was it some kind of warning? Or was the duchess working with someone to bring down the duke? Sophie couldn't rule anything out.

"We shouldn't jump to any conclusions yet," Philip said quietly. "But any unanswered question is worth looking into."

"When will my father wake up?" Sophie asked. She felt that if he would just open his eyes and talk this through with them, things would make sense. There had to be some sort of explanation; it had to be an accident. Maybe some spoiled meat had touched the goblet while it was still in the kitchens. Maybe he'd only fainted from the stress of the engagement. Yet even as the thoughts came to her, Sophie knew these explanations were a reach.

"There's no telling," the adviser said with a sigh. "This seems to be a state on which there is very little research. Some are beginning to call it *comatose*. It means that the body has shut down to focus every other effort on healing itself."

"So—so *when* will he be healed?" Sophie pressed again.

The adviser cleared his throat and looked away from her. His expression forced fear through her every limb, and she squeezed Philip's fingers until he flexed his hand in pain.

"No one knows, my lady. And I must warn you, it is possible that he will never wake up at all. If he doesn't revive and take in water and food within three days—maybe four—he could die of starvation."

"No," Sophie said. "That can't be right. Papa!" She raised her voice, expecting him to stir at her call. But of course, he did not.

"The alchemists are attempting, as we speak, to create an elixir that will revive him—"

"An elixir! Yes! An antidote to this poison! Papa!"

"Sophie, let's let him rest," Philip said.

But she broke out of his grip, went to her father, and shook him. Yet he would not move at her touch.

"Come now, please!" she cried, raising her arm and smacking the duke hard on the face.

"Sophie!" Philip said, lunging forward and pinning both of Sophie's arms.

It was no use. Duke Maximilian's head merely lolled to the side as the physician rushed to straighten it.

Sophie allowed Philip to drag her out of the room, black spots flaring at the edges of her vision.

As she emerged back into the hallway, Sophie looked up to see Claudia waiting her turn to enter the infirmary. Claudia stared at Sophie, her eyes hollow and rimmed bright red. Claudia's face was blotchy and gaunt, its beauty newly tainted by something foul. "He's gone, isn't he?" she whispered, like a ghost.

"Your goblet," Sophie accused. "It was your goblet that poisoned him!"

Claudia's eyes snapped into focus. "What? What are you saying?" She reached for Sophie. "How can you possibly think—"

"Leave her be," Philip whispered, guiding Sophie around them.

But Sophie held Claudia's gaze a long time, trying to read her thoughts, then cut her eyes to the floor.

There she saw something tiny and blue-green—the body of the jewel beetle—crushed by Claudia's shoe.

❧

Sophie and Philip held vigil through a long and sleepless night, taking turns nodding off while they sat in the library together and sipped coffee and tea in silence.

"Sophie," Philip said sometime around three in the morning, his voice cracked and rough. "There isn't anything special about your father's seat at the head table, is there?"

Sophie set her tea down and rubbed her eyes. "How do you mean?"

"Visually. My father has something ornate, almost like a throne, at his spot, but your father's chair is the same as the other ones, isn't it?"

"All the chairs at the head table are gilded and carved, but they're identical, yes. What of it?"

Philip looked long and hard into his teacup, thinking aloud. "At your father's wedding to Claudia, there had been only three chairs, so a fourth was added for me tonight. And you and I were the guests of honor, not the duke and duchess. You were next to Claudia—"

"I'm not following."

"You and your father switched places, Sophie, remember? Duchess Claudia insisted on it. I don't mean to worry you, but—but do you think it's possible that poisoned goblet was meant for you?"

Though her nerves were already shot, a current of alarm cut through Sophie, forcing her to sit up straight on the sofa. "I don't—I don't think I have it in me to consider that right now."

"I know they were Claudia's goblets, and that doesn't look good for her. But if we don't even know who the poison was intended for, we can't yet think of motive."

"She would never harm me," Sophie murmured at last. After the initial panic, Sophie was calm and could think clearly. "She is my stepmother. She loves me." It was true, Sophie could feel it in her bones.

Philip, stiff, leaned forward and set his teacup back in its saucer with a *clink*. "Are you certain? She is not your mother, after all."

Duchess Claudia was not her mother, true. She was a stranger from a foreign land, a poor province. Who was she before she arrived? She declared her love for the duke, but did she really love him? And now that she was pregnant—did Claudia think she could rule the duchy with her son? It was absurd to think of, but Sophie suddenly realized there was a lot she didn't know about her stepmother.

"I can't think about it anymore. I'm too tired."

Philip nodded. "Please, get some sleep. You'll be more ready to face whatever happens tomorrow if you're rested. I promise to wake you if anything changes."

She was too numb to protest.

Duke Maximilian's condition had not changed by morning. Sophie sat alone in the library while Philip took his turn sleeping. She kept twisting and twisting his ring around her finger. It glittered cheerfully in the bright pool of sunlight coming through the window, a beauty that seemed wrong, given the circumstances. But before Sophie could begin moping again, the sound of clattering silver filled the air. Lotte was there with tea, breaking Sophie's reverie.

"How are you feeling, Lady Sophie?" the maid murmured.

"Alive, I suppose."

Sophie reached for the cup, breathing in the familiar smell of chamomile. While she slept, Philip had asked that a guard be assigned to Sophie for the time being, at least until they had assessed whatever threat surrounded the palace. Knowing that the guard had already inspected—and probably tasted—the drink made it slightly less appealing, but still welcome.

Stirring cream and sugar into the tea, Sophie remembered the unfamiliar concoction Claudia had given her several days ago. Hadn't there been something strange about it? Hadn't it altered Sophie's consciousness? Not in a bad way, of course. But if Claudia was capable of spiking drinks . . .

The goblets were Claudia's. She had insisted they use them for the banquet.

"Lotte," Sophie called before the maid left the room. She beckoned her closer, speaking low. "Have you heard anything more about Duchess Claudia lately?"

"Yes, my lady, but it's rather grim." Lotte's mouth set in a line. "Are you certain you want to hear it?"

Sophie sipped from her cup and nodded.

The glee that Lotte had once taken in relaying the gossip was gone from her voice now. She fidgeted with the cuffs on her dress as she spoke. "Of course, you can imagine the rumors that are going around. No one likes her anyway. Even though she is carrying the duke's heir. Or not anymore."

"What do you mean?"

Lotte leaned over conspiratorially. "Your father called for his councilors the other night. After you said you would not marry Lord Manfred."

"And?"

"I heard the valet say that the duke changed his will."

"What?"

"The duke named you his heir. He had received a dispensation from the emperor. I don't think he meant to have you marry anyone you didn't want to. And so, he changed it for you," Lotte said excitedly.

Sophie felt her heart begin to race. "My father changed his will—and the law—for me?"

"Yes."

"And you know this for a fact?"

"Well, it is just a rumor, but the valet swore that's what he heard."

"But even if it was true, why would Claudia want to poison me?"

"For her baby, of course!" Lotte shook her head. "Your father basically disinherited him. The doctors are sure it is a boy."

Would Claudia do that?

Resort to poison to keep her unborn son as the next duke?

"I don't believe it," Sophie said. "That seems very risky. She was in charge of the whole banquet, so suspicion would immediately fall on her, just as it has. She must have known that, were she the one behind it."

Lotte shrugged. "I don't know, my lady. But that is what they say—that she is out to get you, and now, perhaps, after he changed his will, your father as well."

Sophie chewed hard on her thumbnail. It was true: In the absence of herself and Duke Maximilian, Claudia would gain full control over the duchy as the sole ruler of Bavaria. Perhaps the young duchess was stronger and more sinister than Sophie believed. And the strange figure in the woods—what color was Moldavian livery anyway? And that strange affection for that goblet of cordial that afternoon while Sophie was getting ready . . . Was there poison in there as well? Claudia had changed the duke's and Sophie's places at the table, but the duke had reached for her chalice out of habit since it was where his was usually placed.

The goblet was meant for Sophie.

Which meant the poison was as well. Philip had already come to this conclusion earlier.

She could no longer deny it.

"Has Duchess Claudia been assigned a guard at her room this evening?" she asked Lotte.

"Yes. Prince Philip requested that last night."

Sophie tipped the teacup back and forth in its saucer. "Good. That's just . . . in the interest of our safety. Including hers."

"Of course, my lady."

CHAPTER TWENTY-FOUR

IT WAS HARD TO SLEEP that evening. Sophie tossed and turned as she wrestled with the idea that Claudia would try to poison her. Could her stepmother be responsible for such a vile act? Would she truly try to eliminate Sophie just to keep her son's inheritance intact? It was impossible to believe, and yet . . . there seemed to be no other explanation for the poison on the goblet. And the servants were convinced it was their new duchess who was responsible for the duke's illness.

But Sophie could not bring herself to believe that Claudia would be so callous. She was Claudia's only friend in the palace, and it was inconceivable to think the young, nervous woman who had shown her such kindness could harbor her such ill will. It was harder to convince Philip, however.

When she told Philip what she had learned about the duke's will, Philip strode around Duke Maximilian's study in a rage. "You must send her away!" he urged. "For your sake—and mine! I cannot leave you here if she remains."

Now it was Sophie's turn to be the voice of reason, seeing as Philip was nearly blind with anger, shoving his fingers into his hair.

"Hush, Philip, I'm all right," she said, leading him back to a chair for the third time that morning. She was still shaken by the thought, though the feeling had since evolved into a desire to *do* something. But what? She could not send a pregnant woman away, especially one who was carrying the duke's son. And she was still unconvinced Claudia was behind the whole thing.

His hands fell to his sides and tightened into fists. "You cannot trust her, and if anything happens to you—"

"Nothing will happen." Sophie sighed.

"You don't know that," Philip said darkly. "And if it does . . ." He buried his face in his hands.

Sophie went up to him and pulled his arms away. "No one will harm me. She is under armed guard. She cannot even leave her room without me knowing."

But at that very moment, the doors of the study opened to reveal Claudia herself, as though summoned from thin air.

Sophie almost jumped back, while Philip stepped between her and her stepmother.

Claudia looked even more ghostly than usual, pale-faced and wide-eyed and shaking.

"Claudia?" Sophie stood, her heart suddenly thrashing against her rib cage. "Is everything all right? Is it Papa?"

Claudia quickly shook her head. "No, but—I was just there. Nothing has changed. The guard allowed me to see him when I asked to leave my chambers." She nervously glanced at Sophie, who felt a well of guilt rise in her chest.

"This was delivered while I was with him." She held out a letter to Philip.

He accepted it with a grim, apprehensive look and scanned the page quickly. Then, face flushed and contorted, he balled up the note and threw it into the cold fireplace hearth.

"Philip?" Sophie whispered. "What's wrong?"

He did not meet her eyes but stared at the floor. A moment later, Philip broke the silence with a gruff voice.

"England has declared war on Spain."

And so it was that the next morning, Sophie watched through a filmy cloud of tears as Philip suited up in armor and heavy boots, preparing to leave for battle. "Don't," Sophie begged, her voice tired and hoarse. "Please don't go. Don't leave me again. Stay."

Philip wouldn't look at her. "We've been over this."

"Please. Philip."

"My father cannot fight alone. I have to fix what I started." He gritted his teeth as he shoved chain mail over his chest.

"It is *not* your fault!" Sophie shouted, her own voice grating angrily on her ears.

He buried his head in his hands. When he lifted his face again, his eyes were red and wet. "Don't you see? If I had just stayed away and listened to my father—"

"You'd be miserable in a loveless English marriage, and I would spend the rest of my life alone," Sophie finished, shaking her head vehemently. "Philip, you can't doubt for a minute that you saved me. But none of this is your fault. You said so yourself that England was just looking for an excuse to attack." Her throat closed up as she said it.

Philip did not answer but pressed his forehead against her own, eyes squeezed shut. She breathed him in. "It breaks my heart to leave you," he said. "Especially knowing you are in danger here."

She shook her head. "I know it looks bad for Claudia, but it is not her. I know it in my heart; she would never wish me harm. She is not behind this; she cannot be."

Philip stared at her. "But if not her, then who?" Suddenly his face turned ashen and he shook his head. It could not be; he would not think in that direction. If he did, he would have to stay and protect her, and he could not. He knew where his place was. He was still Prince Philip of Spain. "You must promise me you will watch out for yourself and keep safe in my absence."

"And you must promise me the same," she said.

He nodded. Then he pulled away and picked up his sword, sheathing it into its scabbard with force, and left the room.

Sophie marched after him. She could not bear to see him go. An awful certainty hung in her chest that she would lose both her father and her fiancé in short order. She couldn't help but think of a chessboard with only pawns, a wicked queen, and a vulnerable king left on her side, ready to be demolished.

Sophie grabbed at Philip's arm, tears streaming down her face. She planted her feet to pull him back from the stairs.

"Please," Philip said, wrenching his arm from her grasp. "You're making this so much harder than it needs to be."

"I'm always watching you leave. I've done it so many times I can't stand it. If you must go, I must go with you!"

He turned around and grabbed her by the shoulders, his face filled with a terrifying emotion she couldn't read.

"You cannot. I must fight for my country," he said through a clenched jaw. But when he saw her face, he softened. "I will come back. I promise. I've come back before, and I will again."

She let him go then, feeling as though she'd been punched in the gut.

Sophie spent the rest of the day lying on her bedroom floor. She didn't eat, she didn't drink. She simply held still and felt the cold stone against her cheek. Sophie didn't want to think; she was just so tired. She longed for sleep but knew that if she climbed back into bed, she would only worry about Philip, and thinking of her father's face—or even Claudia's shattered one—would keep her up. Claudia seemed to understand that she was under some kind of house arrest and had accepted it without question, which made Sophie feel even worse.

At last, Sophie knew where she had to go.

Sophie stood and pushed her hair, unkempt now, away from her face. She reached under her bed for her mother's dagger, safe in its box, and slipped it into the scabbard at her hip. Carrying a weapon seemed more justified now than ever. Though what good had a dagger done against a poisoned goblet? She would have to start carrying a whole alchemy lab of antidotes, apparently.

Sophie smoothed her dress and tentatively pushed the door open. The guard outside looked at her with eyebrows raised.

"I'd like to go to my mother's room," Sophie said.

Duchess Maria's quarters were an open secret in the palace. They were located in the southwest turret tower, which had given her a sprawling view of the Alps and the setting sun. The duchess had loved to paint and read, so Maximilian presented her with rooms that could inspire her. Sophie had spent many evenings taking tea with her mother in the golden light as the sun sank below the treetops.

When she died, the duke closed off her rooms and hung a large tapestry—which depicted the myth of Orpheus and Eurydice—over the entrance to her chambers. The weaving hung in such a way that those who didn't already know of the entrance wouldn't realize it was there. He had forbidden anyone to enter the quarters and kept out of them himself from the moment he closed the door, preserving it as a sort of memorial to his wife and attempting to freeze the rooms in time. It remained a part of the palace like the dead limb of a still-living tree.

But what Maximilian didn't know was that Sophie came here sometimes, only when she absolutely needed it.

Sophie and the guard reached the tapestry in the southwest wing and Sophie took a breath. When she lifted the edge of the cloth, the guard stepped forward.

"Please," Sophie said. "It's safe."

"I have clear orders," the guard said. "I'm not to leave you alone, and for you to go into those rooms without proper protection—"

"Orders? From whom?" she challenged.

"Prince Philip, of course," said the guard.

Of course. Now that her father was unconscious and the duchess under suspicion, Philip still outranked her.

"It's *safe*." She gave him her most intimidating look. "You also have orders not to enter these quarters or acknowledge their existence."

The guard was quiet for a moment, clearly trying to work out this paradox. Then he nodded and stepped to the side, giving the impression that he was guarding a different door a few feet down the hall.

Sophie slipped behind the thick tapestry and fitted a key she'd stolen long ago into the old iron lock. She eased the heavy door open as quietly as she could, and soon she was on the other side.

Sophie took a deep breath. Though fainter and fainter each time, this space still smelled like her mother. Or maybe it was her imagination. Duchess Maria's comforting scent must have disappeared years ago, slowly replaced by stale air and fine layers of dust. But to Sophie, it was as though part of her was still here, fresh with lilac soap and ink and oil paint.

This was why Sophie never visited the quarters unless she could help it—she worried she'd somehow contaminate it with her own presence. It shouldn't be disturbed. She'd come soon after her mother died and on several other dark nights while her father traveled far away. Beyond that, she saved it for emergencies.

All her mother's things remained, too. Sophie had considered secreting small trinkets or mementos back to her own quarters, but she could never bring herself to do it. Removing anything from the room or bringing anyone else inside would break its spell. Apart from the dust and the sun bleach on the easel by the wide bay windows, it seemed as though Sophie's mother could enter it at any moment, cheeks still red from a brisk walk in the woods.

Here, in her mother's room, she felt safe, as if Duchess Maria were still there to protect her and soothe her troubles. She climbed into her mother's bed, pulled the quilts up high around her chin, and immediately fell asleep.

Until there was a hard rapping on the door.

It was Lotte.

"Wake up, my lady! It's the duchess! I think she's hexing the palace!" hissed her loyal maid.

Chapter Twenty-Five

Sophie walked down the hallway at a fast clip following Lotte and tailed by a new guard who had relieved the former. Her petticoats swished as she made her way from her mother's quarters to Claudia's.

"What is she doing?" she asked Lotte.

"I don't know, but it sounds . . . unnatural!" Lotte replied.

Sophie didn't like it one bit. Didn't Claudia know that this was no time for strange goings-on? With everything that had transpired and the entire duchy already against Claudia, Sophie couldn't understand why the new duchess would invite any more scrutiny upon herself, nor could she guess what the suspicious activity might be.

She stopped outside of Claudia's quarters and motioned for her own guard and Claudia's to remain back a few paces. Carefully, Sophie put her ear to the door. She would get to the bottom of all these rumors herself.

At first, she heard nothing. She closed her eyes and let her breath slow, feeling the thumping of blood in her ear.

Gradually, chanting rose behind the great oaken door. There

were voices, as though Claudia was speaking with someone, and the sound of rustling. Then Claudia cried out.

"See! I told you! Unnatural!" said Lotte.

"Claudia?" Sophie knocked on the door. "Claudia, are you all right? Let me in!"

The wailing continued. The guard rushed forward, and Sophie pushed the door open, leaning hard on the wood against some resistance. The room was dark, and it took a moment for Sophie's eyes to adjust.

Once they did, she swore under her breath and sent Lotte and the guards away from the door. It would do nothing for Claudia's reputation to let them see the scene inside.

The duchess was lying in the middle of the room in a circle of polished stones with only candles to give her light. A bundle of herbs and incense burned in a shallow bowl next to her, and there was a chalice of dark brown liquid spilled on the floor. Claudia was dressed in a thin tunic, which clung to the sheen of sweat on her body. She was shaking.

An image of her own father convulsing flashed before Sophie's eyes, and she took a step back, clinging to the bed frame in fear. She felt panic overcoming her but bit the inside of her mouth hard, focusing on the pain instead. As her eyes took in the room clearly, she realized Claudia was not convulsing but shaking with tears.

Sophie broke through the circle of stones and knelt next to her stepmother.

"Claudia, what's happened?" She picked up the chalice, smelling its briny contents. "Please, Claudia, please tell me you haven't poisoned yourself." Sophie could hear her voice falter as she said the words.

Claudia grasped Sophie's hands with a grip so hard it hurt, and shook her head, sobbing.

"Are you injured?" Sophie asked.

Claudia shook her head again. Retrieving a pillow from the bed, Sophie eased it under the head of the duchess and pressed a hand to her lower back, hushing until Claudia quieted a little.

"The baby," Claudia whispered. "I am trying to keep him."

"What?!"

Claudia pulled at the skirt of her tunic, showing a dull red stain. "I am losing him."

Sophie's heart broke at that. She leaned over Claudia and brushed matted hair away from her face. "Oh, Claudia, I'm sorry. I'm so sorry."

They stayed like this for a few moments, Claudia breathing slowly in the dark room, Sophie brushing her stepmother's hair back with her fingers. When Claudia was able to heave a sigh and raise herself, painfully, to a sitting position, Sophie gestured at the strange objects surrounding them.

"Claudia . . . what is all this?"

The duchess looked bitterly around the little circle. "It's from the witch in the woods."

"Excuse me?" Sophie murmured.

Claudia pressed her fingers along her browbone and then rested her jaw in her hand. She squeezed her eyes shut tight and shook her head, another wave of tears threatening. When it passed, she spoke once more. "I have been seeing a witch. I thought it would help."

"Oh, Claudia . . ." Sophie put her arm around Claudia's shoulders. She'd heard stories of witches and magicians, dragons and other lore as a child. In fact, her mother's library was full of these stories. But it had seemed that was all they were—stories, of people who may very well have once existed, but who were now long gone from this time.

"I'm sorry, how did you— Did you say a witch?" Sophie asked.

Claudia nodded, gesturing limply to the trinkets surrounding her. "She's given me all these tools, these potions. She gave me potions to 'open my womb,' and when I got pregnant, I thought she was a miracle worker. And then I started bleeding and I ran to her for more. She gave me some herbs to keep the baby, but I can't tell if they haven't been working or if I'm not using them correctly or maybe she's a fraud, but—"

She waved her hand at the body that seemed to betray her.

"I'm so sorry, Claudia."

Claudia sighed. "I was—I was so worried that maybe one of her potions had made its way into that goblet somehow and that I *was* somehow responsible for the poisoning, like everyone in the palace seems to believe."

Sophie went still. "I didn't . . . I didn't believe that."

"But you doubted me," said Claudia.

"I did, I apologize, I was overwhelmed," said Sophie. "And at the party, you were scanning the crowd—and you were trying to tell me something?"

Claudia's eyes glazed over, trying to remember. "Oh! Yes! I thought—I thought I saw someone I recognized . . . but I can't for the life of me place who it was. It is gone, I am sorry."

Sophie nodded. Then something else came to mind. Something she wished she had noticed or realized before. After telling Claudia about Dietrich's cruelty, her father had seen to finding her a match with Manfred, and then after telling Claudia that Manfred was still un-acceptable and threatening to run away, the duke had changed his will to name her his heir.

Claudia.

Claudia had seen to her, had protected her, had put her above her own child. Her stepmother loved her.

Sophie felt a wave of emotion at the weight of this new realization. She rested her hand atop Claudia's.

"Do you want to keep trying whatever it was that you were doing?" Sophie asked. "Maybe it will save the baby."

"I've done everything the witch told me to do," said Claudia. "Now we just need to wait and see."

So Sophie moved from window to window and pulled open the drapes, pushing back the panes and letting the mountain breeze carry the heavy stuffiness and smelly smoke out of the room. There was still some light in the sky that illuminated Claudia as she gathered the tools back into an unusual bag, dark purple velvet embroidered with tiny silver designs.

"How did you know about the witch in the woods?" asked Sophie. "I thought she was just a village myth that the servants talked about."

Claudia crossed to her dressing table and pulled a small object out of the drawer. "I found this guide for a useful fertility root tucked away in the library."

Sophie gasped. "This is my mother's book! She wrote this. This is her handwriting."

Claudia laughed nervously. "Oh—I didn't know. Are you upset with me?"

"Of course not. I'm just glad it was helpful."

Claudia shook her head, continuing. "There's a note in the margin, do you see? It led me right to the witch's cave."

Sophie took the book and brought it to the window, the tiny scrawling handwriting becoming clear in the pale and fading light. It read:

Where the Pöllat meets the Deut. Bach · Marshy ground near cave in cliffside

She touched it lightly, tracing her mother's handwriting with the tip of her finger. It could only be referencing the point where the

Pöllat and Deutenhauser Bach rivers converged, higher on the mountains and north of the palace.

"Claudia, I've never seen this before," she said. "I've been through this guidebook hundreds of times."

Claudia took a step back and looked hard at Sophie, running her eyes up and down. Her gaze was hungry.

"What?" Sophie said warily.

"You say it was your mother's book?"

"Yes."

"If that is so, then she must have consulted the witch as well."

Sophie pressed a hand to the window casement to steady herself. She wasn't naïve; she understood there were things she hadn't known about her mother. Though they'd been close, Duchess Maria had lived a whole other life before Maximilian and Sophie; her time with her daughter had been short. Sophie wished she could have had her mother for longer, and this marginal note was a clue to the parts of the duchess Sophie never knew. Was this witch someone the duchess had worked with? Could she tell Sophie more about her mother?

"Maybe," Sophie said. "Or maybe it's just a coincidence. We might never be able to say. However . . ." She kept her voice as gentle as possible. An idea was forming in her head, but she wasn't sure that it was a good one.

Sophie let Claudia take the book and tuck it back in a pocket next to her heart. The duchess watched Sophie closely. "What is it?"

Sophie set her jaw. "I want to go see her."

"You do? Really?"

"If my mother worked with this witch, then she's probably— hopefully—a respectable woman, yes? It seems possible that her charms and potions worked before. Don't you think that she could have something to help Papa? Anything at all?"

"Actually—" Claudia said slowly.

"What? What is it?"

The duchess took a breath. "When I told the witch of the duke's poisoning, she jumped up and began gathering all sorts of herbs and powders from her stores."

"What?" Sophie had to stop herself from seizing Claudia's bag. "What did she make? Is it something that could wake my father?"

Claudia rummaged through the bag herself. "No, I'm afraid that's not quite it. But she said it would keep him alive at least, while he slept, until another solution could be found."

"Why didn't you tell me sooner?" Sophie cried.

"I'm sorry, I—I brought it to the head medical adviser and he practically called me a madwoman." She shook her head ruefully. "But maybe I'd have better luck if you were with me."

Claudia found what she was looking for and pulled it out for Sophie to see. It was a spherical glass jar, corked at the top and large enough to fill her palm. Inside was a thick, dark green paste.

Sophie wrinkled her nose. "What is it?"

"Some sort of poultice. She said a teaspoon should be placed at the base of his throat each day, and under his nose as well, so he can breathe it in. I was going to come to you next but then, well—I started bleeding again."

Sophie took the bottle from Claudia and examined it carefully. She popped its cork and sniffed, an earthy, swamplike smell filling her nose.

"Do you trust this witch woman?" Sophie asked.

Claudia took a breath. "I don't know enough of her yet. But, Sophie, we mustn't forget what we've discovered: that your mother *did* trust her."

"And we have no other choice," Sophie agreed.

"We must go to the infirmary at once," Claudia said, taking the bottle from Sophie and gripping it tightly in her hands.

CHAPTER TWENTY-SIX

THEY RUSHED THROUGH THE HALLS. Though Maximilian had been stable over the past two days, Sophie was terrified they would arrive a moment too late to save him. But when they burst into the room, everything looked the same as ever, with the palace physician and a couple alchemists deep in conversation while they held watch next to the sleeping Maximilian.

"Duchess Claudia," the head adviser said, standing.

Sophie noticed Claudia drawing herself up taller, as though she was bracing for a fight. "I would like you to reconsider my solution," the duchess began. "This is a natural poultice, made by a practitioner of herbal medicine, that is said to keep the duke's condition stable until he is able to be woken. I have her word that it will not harm him."

"I've given you my answer, Duchess Claudia. And I told you to stay away from that sorceress!" The physician growled with such anger that Sophie took a step back. Claudia must have consulted with him about the witch in her attempts to conceive a child. Clearly the topic was not met with an open mind.

"She wishes to help us," Claudia said, her voice calm.

"She is nothing more than a fool in a cave—and one with evil intentions, at that!"

"Have you any better ideas?" Sophie broke in. "Would you simply let my father die?"

"I will not expose my lord to possible toxins from an old tramp, shut up in the mountains concocting God-knows-what all day—"

"But how do you know that it won't—" Sophie started.

Claudia put a hand up and stepped forward, her face beautiful and terrifying in its coldness. The room fell quiet. "Who is your ruler when the duke is indisposed?"

Nobody answered. The physician's face turned bright red, and a vein throbbed purple on his neck.

"Who is your ruler?" Claudia repeated very quietly.

"You are, my lady," he said at last.

"Very good," she said. "I will tell you how to apply the poultice, and I will watch to ensure that you know how to do it. It must be done every day to keep the duke alive."

The physician said nothing as his vein pulsed. He simply went to the side of the bed and clasped his hands behind his back as Claudia repeated the instructions the witch had given.

"Fine," he spat as he reached for the jar. Carefully, he swiped a bit of the poultice on Maximilian's upper lip and throat with a wooden spatula. As he did, everyone leaned forward, anxiously awaiting a result.

Very slowly, almost imperceptibly, Maximilian's shallow breaths became deeper and more relaxed. Sophie thought she saw some of the color return to his cheeks.

"That looks better," Sophie said softly. The physician did not respond.

After a few more minutes of waiting and watching, Claudia ordered everyone but Sophie out of the room.

"For what reason?" the physician asked. "So you can cast more spells upon him?"

"You don't need to know my reasons," Claudia said, and ushered them through the door. Then she collapsed in a chair next to Maximilian's bed and let out a long sigh.

"He'd never have spoken to my father that way," Sophie said quietly.

"Of course he wouldn't," Claudia muttered. "But I must thank you. You gave me the courage to say what needed to be said."

Sophie nodded, and they sat quietly, listening to Maximilian's breathing. Claudia stowed the poultice by the bed.

At length, Sophie spoke again. "I'd like to go visit the witch myself to see if she's come up with another solution, one that might be able to wake him up."

Claudia looked up, aghast. "You cannot! It is dangerous."

"But you go yourself."

"I am older than you by far," said Claudia. "And no one will miss me if I'm gone. But you are the duke's daughter. No harm can come to you. Not on my watch."

"But—"

Claudia hesitated. "When I saw the witch, she told me . . . she warned me that this would happen. Your stepdaughter will want to come see me, she said. But you must not let her. She said she foresees something very dark if you come."

A shiver twitched down Sophie's backbone. "What do you mean by *dark?*"

"She doesn't know for sure," Claudia said, shaking her head. "She only sees misfortune. She described it like a sort of blot or smudge on a mirror—a feeling that was unclear, but strong. She told me you must not come."

Sophie sat on the edge of her father's infirmary bed with her chin in her hands, taking care not to jostle him. She crossed her legs and felt the shape of her dagger in its leather sheath slide against her hip. Sophie sat up straighter. "If you didn't poison me, Claudia, then who did?"

Claudia nodded. "Exactly. We still don't know who was behind the poisoned goblet. It is too dangerous for you."

Sophie thought over the mystery.

"Claudia—do you think—" She shook her head. "Never mind."

"What were you going to say?"

"Philip never said that his father consented to the marriage," she said in a rush, because it pained her to think that she was not accepted by his family. "He only said King Ferdinand had no choice."

"The strangers in the scarlet livery . . . the servant who brought the cordial . . ." Her stepmother grew agitated, twisting her fingers. "The goblet . . . that face I thought I recognized at the party . . . I thought it was Spanish somehow. Do you really think it could be Spain who has done this?"

Sophie could not avoid it any longer. "Who else would want me dead? King Ferdinand has never met me. For all he knows, I'm just some Bavarian wench who ensnared his son. His men must have followed Philip, of course they did. They would never let the prince walk around undefended. The king knows exactly where we are. We're here, in the palace. One of them already infiltrated our security, and we don't know how many others might do the same."

Claudia looked at her with growing dread.

"What I mean to say is that I'm in as much danger here as I would be in the forest," Sophie continued. "It's even easier for me to hide out there. I've spent more time out there than King Ferdinand's men have. And if I'm disguised as a servant, how would they know to follow me in the first place?"

"You make strong points. Though I'm biased and inclined to agree," Claudia said. "But you are not going alone."

"We shall see about that," said Sophie.

Two hours before the sun rose, Sophie woke in the darkness and dressed in a maid's outfit that Claudia had procured for her, placing Philip's ring on a chain to wear next to her mother's necklace. She stopped in the infirmary before she left, glaring at the guard there as if daring him to ask her a question.

Duke Maximilian was still unmoved, sleeping, looking as though he could wake at any moment. Sophie watched him for a few minutes, just to see if he would. She pressed her fingers to his wrist, feeling the warm pulse of a man who already seemed to be fading from her life.

"You don't worry about me, Papa," she whispered. "I'll be right back. You just concentrate on healing." Ignoring all thoughts of a final goodbye, she bent and kissed him on the cheek.

As Sophie left the infirmary, she pressed a hand to her hip to make sure her dagger was there. In truth, she'd lied to Claudia: She felt much safer in the palace. And the duchess couldn't have guessed how little time Sophie had spent outside of it, especially in the past few years. Her memories and knowledge of the mountain terrain were old, left over from the hikes she took with her mother as a child.

Now the mere thought of the forest brought her back to that rainy night, the silhouette of a dark figure sending her stomach churning.

But the prospect of finding a cure for her father and learning more about her mother ate away at Sophie. She had no other choice.

Sophie had agreed to meet Claudia in a back stairwell, which led down toward a rarely used door off the end of the palace. Her stepmother insisted on seeing her off.

"Did anyone see you?" Sophie whispered.

As Claudia shook her head, Sophie realized she was wearing similar traveling clothes.

"What are you doing? You can't come with me," Sophie said. "You have to stay here."

"I told you, I can't let you go alone. With any luck, we'll be back before anyone realizes we're gone," Claudia whispered.

Sophie saw it was useless to argue.

They slipped out the door and onto the banks of the Pöllat, which curled alongside the palace. The soil was wet and muddy with autumn dew, holding imprints of their shoes. Claudia motioned for them to walk in the river, staying close to the low-hanging branches of trees. Sophie bit her cheek as the freezing water soaked through her boots and stockings. Wading up to their shins, they left no trace as they worked against the flow of the water, heading north into the mountains.

Sophie turned to look at the palace once more before they rounded a bend. But its looming silhouette was still dark, sleeping in the predawn.

CHAPTER TWENTY-SEVEN

AS CLAUDIA LED SOPHIE THROUGH the shallows of the river, the two women moved slowly in their attempt to stay undetected, either by palace guards or, if they were around as Sophie feared, by King Ferdinand's men. When they got far enough from the palace, they climbed out of the river and traveled along a deer path instead of the main trail.

The sky was still dark but growing ever lighter, and soon the forest was alive with early-morning birdsong. Sophie caught herself grinding her jaw and realized she was listening hard for any noise beneath the chorus and the loud rushing water that would signal an intruder approaching.

As for themselves, the women traveled quietly. It was for safety, but Sophie could tell Claudia was also lost deep in thought. Sophie worried the duchess might overexert herself, especially after her bleeding incident. But the duchess led the way in her usual silence, often lifting her arm to point out an easier path or push back branches so Sophie could pass through. Otherwise, she walked with her head down, brow furrowed.

Sophie felt a similar apprehension as they continued up the Pöllat. Though she had high hopes for this visit, she wasn't sure what the witch might reveal about her mother. What if she told Sophie things she didn't want to know?

But in the end, the most important thing was a potion to wake her father. Everything else would come second to that.

Sophie couldn't pretend she wasn't also a little frightened. What if the witch did have evil intent as the palace physician believed? Few, if any, of the stories she'd heard about women who dealt with magic were good; most told of spiteful old hags who stole livestock, poisoned wells, and ate children. There was plenty of cause to be nervous.

As the sky grew lighter and the birds began to fly, Claudia paused at the riverbank.

"Should we take a moment to rest?" she said. "I usually have a drink of water somewhere around here."

Sophie nodded, so they found a flat rock to sit on and stretched their legs. Claudia brought out loaves of bread and apples from her satchel, and they scooped handfuls of water from the stream. "It isn't much farther," she said.

"Are you sure you are okay?" Sophie asked. "What about the baby?"

Claudia nodded. "I'm fine. But I can't shake this feeling that someone is watching us. I keep getting a bristling at the back of my neck, though there's nobody I can see." She peered over her shoulder, into the thicket of trees behind them. "The forest is dense enough here that someone could conceal themselves."

Sophie wrapped her arms more tightly around her knees and glanced around. The first few shafts of sunlight were beginning to break through the leaves, but the foliage still grew thick and dark in the underbrush. Though the morning promised a warm day, the chill was strong in the air. Sophie began to feel exactly as Claudia was describing; she pushed the thoughts away.

"But I think we are worrying ourselves about things that aren't actually there," Claudia said. "You'll feel better if we keep moving. Are you ready?"

They gathered themselves up from the bank and continued their journey to where the ground beneath their feet grew springy and damp. They were close to the witch's cave and the highland marsh just before it. It became difficult to walk along the river, so they moved farther over toward the main path.

"That tea you gave me the other night—that was from the witch, wasn't it?" Sophie murmured.

Claudia looked back, her eyes wide and guilty, but Sophie smirked at the expression. She wondered how she had ever suspected the duchess of any evil when she gave herself away so easily.

"Yes," Claudia admitted. "It was a calming potion I put in that tea. It seemed like you needed it."

"To be honest, I was grateful. Seems as though you're able to work a little useful magic yourself."

Claudia sighed. "I wish I could work something useful enough to get us out of this mess."

As the roar of the water quieted to a whisper, Sophie became more in tune to the sounds of the forest. There was the crunching of their feet over dry grasses and sticks, the chirring of squirrels in the trees, and the *swish* of the wind through the branches.

Then she heard another noise that made her stop short—a soft crack somewhere behind them, as if a branch had been stepped on.

"What was that?" she whispered. They both stopped.

"I didn't hear anything," Claudia said.

"I thought—" Sophie said, searching the thick trees. The familiar uneasy feeling crept up her spine. "Maybe it was just an animal."

Claudia nodded, but her face was on high alert.

As the mid-October sun rose higher, the dew evaporated and the forest grew muggy and warm. Sophie took down the hood of her cloak, shaking out her hair and rolling up the sleeves. Claudia did the same.

Suddenly there was another crack, louder than the first and much closer.

"Stop!" Sophie hissed. "We're being followed."

Claudia's face went white, and she moved closer to one of the broad tree trunks for protection. "Oh God," she whispered. "What do we do?"

"I don't—"

Thwack. Sophie felt the displacement of air near her cheek as an object rocketed past her and lodged in the tree, inches from Claudia's arm.

It was an arrow. Claudia looked at Sophie in horror.

Run! Sophie mouthed.

They took off through the forest, dodging trees and leaping over roots. Their pursuer didn't even attempt silence now, crashing through the underbrush and gaining speed. Chancing a look over her shoulder, Sophie saw the dark figure of a man sprinting toward them. As he ran, more arrows showered down around the two women, missing their marks by mere inches.

Sophie pounded feet to the ground, cursing her heavy dresses and willing Claudia to go faster.

Then a hidden root caught Claudia's stride, sending her tumbling to the forest floor. She hit it hard; Sophie saw blood as she split her chin. Claudia's eyes were wide in fear as she cradled her belly and struggled to push herself up. Sophie ran to help her.

"*Go*, keep going!" Claudia shouted as Sophie slowed. "It's you he wants, not me!"

But Sophie backed up and stood like a statue behind a small tree, just off the path. Her brain replayed the target practice she'd had in the clearing again and again as the figure advanced. She pressed her hand to her hip, face filled with concentration. Behind Claudia, the sound of their attacker grew closer.

Claudia clambered to her feet, arms out, and lurched toward Sophie as if to tackle her to the ground.

But at the last moment, Sophie let the dagger fly past her—an incomprehensible flash of silver. A strangled cry rang out through the forest. Claudia turned, but Sophie was already rushing forward, grinning with wild triumph.

"What—" Claudia spluttered.

The man fell to the ground, face-first, dagger plunged in his shoulder. He was dressed as a huntsman, with a quiver of arrows on his back, but the colors of his costume were scarlet and gold, the unmistakable livery of Spain.

Sophie knelt and turned him over, removing her dagger in the process.

It was Sir Rodrigo.

"That's him!" screeched Claudia. "I saw him at the banquet! That's the man I recognized!"

Sophie nodded. She had been right.

King Ferdinand did not take to being told what to do. He had sent his soldiers with Philip and they were still here, even if the prince had already left. So now there was a huntsman who hunted for Sophie. Sir Rodrigo groaned and rolled off his injured arm.

"Sophie, stay back!" Claudia cried.

"He can't hit us at this close of a range," Sophie argued. "I had to get my dagger!"

With a roar, Sir Rodrigo struggled to his feet and pulled a sword from the sheath at his hip.

"Oops," Sophie said. She whirled around and picked up a fallen branch with her other hand. Backing away from the man, she held it out like a spear as Sir Rodrigo brought his blade down on its middle.

Sophie wielded the branch, but he slashed off its end, sending woodchips flying.

Sir Rodrigo swung again, narrowly missing Sophie's neck as she ducked his blow.

"I warned you!" he roared. "Why did you not listen?!" He raised the sword over his head for a fatal blow as Sophie clutched what was now a twig of wood. She tossed it aside and ducked, striking at his shin with her precious weapon. "You cannot marry the prince!"

The tip of the dagger hit the hard bone of his leg, but slid off and into the meat of his calf. Sophie's muscles moved on instinct and pushed the blade forth all within a split second. Deep into the flesh, like Chef had taught her, then withdraw it for the next strike.

Sir Rodrigo roared out in pain as Sophie scrambled out of the way of his sword.

"SOPHIE!" Claudia cried.

Sir Rodrigo lunged again, and Sophie ran her dagger straight into his chest. She jumped back as he fell to the ground once more. The women froze, waiting. The forest around them felt cold and silent.

But after an agonizing moment, Sir Rodrigo still did not move. When Sophie nudged him with her toe and received no response, she braced herself and grasped the hilt of her dagger. Squeezing her eyes shut, she counted to three and yanked, doing her best to ignore the feeling of the blade pulling away from his heart. Sophie gulped deep breaths and cleaned her dagger on the grass.

"Is he dead?" Claudia whispered.

They eyed him closely, but there was no sign of life.

Claudia pulled Sophie backward, staring in shock. "That dagger, how did you know to—"

Sir Rodrigo rolled onto his side and gasped as though he were drowning. Claudia and Sophie jumped and backed up quickly, Sophie holding the dagger blade out.

Sir Rodrigo opened his eyes, but blood poured out of his mouth. "Lady Sophie," he whispered.

"Yes?" she asked.

"I am sorry. The king—the king sent me to kill you."

Sophie slowly lowered the dagger even as she felt her pulse start to thrum in her chest. "Are there more men in the forest? Any nearby?" she asked.

"Yes."

"Sophie, we should run," said Claudia. "If the others find us—"

"Tell Philip I am sorry," said Sir Rodrigo. "I am sorry."

Sophie watched as the life drained out of the king's man. "He wanted to kill me," Sophie said, holding Claudia's hand.

"The king of Spain wants to kill you. The courtier was just doing as he was bid," said Claudia. "But we cannot linger. The witch's cave is in that cliff up ahead."

Sophie followed her gaze. There, across an open meadow, was a bluff that sat shelflike between the forested tree line and the rockier peaks of the mountain beyond. Improbably, there was a marshy area along the edge of the Pöllat, damp and dark under the shadow of the cliff face. Sophie squinted and shaded her eyes with her hand. She could just barely see the mouth of a cave half-hidden behind a grove of pines. The sight made her nervous and impatient all at once, allowing her to put what she had just done out of her mind.

Sophie and Claudia reached the edge of the forest, which opened onto wide, vulnerable space.

"I don't like that field," Claudia said. "We will be seen too clearly."

"But there's no other way to get there," said Sophie. They had to find a cure for her father. Sophie put her head down and marched out into the field. No sooner had she taken three paces than movement to the left caught her eye: On the bank of the Pöllat stood a man, all in black, with a bow in his hand and an arrow trained directly toward them.

Sophie and Claudia froze.

Then another figure appeared on their right—a second archer, cresting the hill above them.

"Oh blast," Claudia cursed. "Blast it, blast—"

Sophie faced the first man, the two women's backs to each other. But Sophie was far out of range for her dagger to do any good. Sweat poured down the back of her neck. The meadow was silent except for the warm wind whistling through the grasses.

Before anyone could move, a third man emerged from the forest behind them and a sickness nearly overtook Sophie. He must have been following them the whole time. The third archer was just as large and gruff as the others, a thick silver beard and a smug expression on his face.

He released his finger from the string and let his arrow fly.

Several things happened at once, though not in any order Sophie could comprehend. In an instant, she saw the arrow coming toward her and felt Claudia's body collide with hers, tackling her to safety.

"You must run! I will run back to the palace," said Claudia, speaking quickly in the chaos. "I will lead them away, and when they see I am not you, they will leave me alone."

"How can you know that?"

"I am the duchess of Bavaria; they will not touch me. Their orders are to hunt you. The king of Spain wants you dead, not me. But you cannot come home. You are not safe in the palace. He will not stop until you are dead, war with England or not."

Sophie could not argue with that logic.

"Run, Sophie. Into the mountains where Ferdinand's men cannot follow. I will take care of the rest. I will keep you safe. And when the danger has passed, I will send for your return."

Sophie tried to answer but could not find her voice. The three attackers were charging toward them, and another arrow plunged into the ground inches from Claudia's arm. Sophie felt suddenly that she could not move, frozen to the spot where she lay. But Claudia's hands were on her shoulders; Claudia was forcing her to rise and run.

"Now go!" Claudia cried. "GO!"

Before Sophie could grasp what was happening, she was back in the forest, surrounded by pines, alone. She could still hear the shouts of the men in the field. But something was crashing through the trees; something was pursuing her.

Sophie had no choice. If she wanted to live, she would have to run and hide, leave everything she'd ever known. She took a few steps forward, made sure she still had her dagger, then ran until she was swallowed up by the deep, dark woods.

CHAPTER TWENTY-EIGHT

SOPHIE HAD NEVER RUN SO much in her life.

She crashed through the forest, legs pumping and lungs gasping for breath. Though she eventually lost the huntsmen, every rustling breeze and moving shadow seemed to her like another assassin descending from the trees. She moved without knowing where she was going, but somehow kept her feet, miraculously, from catching on the tangled foliage of the forest floor.

But Sophie was tiring. Though living in the palace involved walking, hiking, and climbing stairs, she wasn't used to the constant, oxygen-depleting exertion that this morning's run required. Fueled by adrenaline, she put a good distance between herself and the meadow near the witch's cave, but soon her muscles ached, and her throat felt raw.

She slowed to a jog, then to a brisk walk with spurts of speed every now and then. Finally, after what seemed like hours, she stopped and took stock of her surroundings. By some stroke of great luck, there were a few apple trees, still with a bit of fruit on their branches, in a sunny clearing. Realizing how hungry she was, Sophie tore apples from the branches and quickly ate two. She slipped a few more into the pockets of her maid's uniform, then looked around, sweaty clothes clinging to her body.

Judging by the still-thick forest and rockier peaks in the distance, Sophie wasn't quite above the tree line, but she was getting close. She was miles from the palace now, with no escort, no guard, no Claudia. The witch was out there somewhere but just as far away as everybody Sophie loved.

Guilt squeezed her insides tight—she'd let Claudia return to the palace by herself.

Sophie took a deep breath and tossed the apple core back down the path, watching it roll down the gentle slope.

This was the most alone Sophie had ever felt.

How long would she have to stay out here? Going back to the palace was out of the question. And the branches of the trees, soon to be bare of their leaves, were not lost on Sophie. Cold weather was coming fast.

Sophie buried her face in her hands, counting her breaths. She squeezed her eyes shut and tried to clear her mind until her pulse slowed and her heartbeat returned to a normal pace. If she gave up so easily, soon all would be lost.

Philip said he would return, that he would not die in battle.

She had to live for him, for her father, for her stepmother.

Sophie looked at the forest around her, trying to see it from her mother's eyes. Though it had been a few years since she'd gone out into the mountains with Duchess Maria, there must be some things that Sophie could remember. Her mother would say that the forest contained everything she needed. There were apple trees—those were obvious—but there must be more if Sophie looked hard enough.

There—behind the red of the fruits were other, taller trees dropping green pods. Sophie picked them up and rolled a few in her hands, cracking through the bumpy outer layer: walnuts. Satisfied by her find, she gathered up handfuls of the nuts and added them to her pockets.

She continued to follow the path along the Pöllat, taking stock of her situation. There had to be somewhere she could hide safely until the king's men were gone. And as she had promised, Claudia would send a sign, or messenger, when it was safe to come home.

Soon she saw another clearing up ahead with a stone structure in the middle. It was a hiking shelter, with three walls to block out the wind and the fourth open against the slope of the mountainside.

Sophie frowned. Though it was tempting to stay and make a camp here, the site wouldn't work long-term; she would need more warmth and other food than just apples and walnuts. She didn't like that it might be used by other travelers either. The clearing itself was vulnerable enough.

No, Sophie wanted to be alone. She would rest here for the moment, but she couldn't stay.

She found a small stream that branched off the river and drank deeply, filling her hands with water. She ate another apple as she sat in the sun and eyed the shelter, which was very old.

As Sophie brushed the juice off her hands and peered closer at the structure's walls, something caught her attention: There were etchings there, little carvings and markings left by other hikers. She ran over the stones with her finger, feeling their grooves. There were mile markers, pictures of the mountain peak, and some hikers' names. Her curiosity growing, Sophie followed the north wall all the way to the left, then crouched to inspect its corner. There, close to the ground, was a symbol that wasn't like any of the others: a small but thick arrow unequivocally pointing west. It was drawn in a place that wouldn't be noticed at eye level.

Sophie scratched at it with a nail, thinking. She looked around the corner of the next wall, but the arrow didn't seem to be referencing anything there. She examined it again, then looked out into the clearing. To the right of the shelter was a large boulder lodged in the grass, one that looked as though it had rolled down from the rockier peaks long ago.

Picking up her skirts, Sophie walked over to the boulder and circled it, running her hands along the stone to feel for anything unusual. But the rock was relatively smooth. She stood back, considering the boulder's shadowed side. It was then that she noticed a notch close to the grass; another arrow, the same as the first, pointing toward the southwest corner of the glen.

Sophie peered at the edge of the underbrush surrounding the clearing. What could it mean? There was no break in the foliage, which thickened everywhere except for the main path she'd come down. Sophie touched the arrow again, trailing her finger away from the rock and pointing it straight in the direction it indicated. She walked forward along that line until she reached the wall of brush and branches. Sophie frowned, then pushed against them with her hand.

To her surprise, they parted to reveal a clear and well-kept trail. It twisted before her, disappearing quickly into the deeper woods.

Sophie glanced back at the sunny clearing. Its cheerful openness both tempted her to stay and warned of easy discovery from any of Ferdinand's assassins. Anyone, friend or foe, could have made this secret path—and it seemed they didn't want it to be found. But it was an excellent way to throw the king's men off her scent, and whatever awaited Sophie at the end of the path had to be better than a poisoned goblet or an arrow to the back.

Sophie looked around to make sure no one was watching, then slipped through the wall of branches.

∿

Once inside, it was as though she'd never been in the clearing at all.

Sophie walked slowly along the secret trail that meandered and zagged, thin enough to look like a deer trail at certain points. Though it was clear of most obstacles, it was far less traveled than the main path she'd left, which seemed more like a road now. She had to be wary of the many lodged stones and hidden roots that threatened to flatten her on the forest floor.

Before long, Sophie had lost any sense of direction or idea of where on the mountain she was headed. She hoped the king's men would be as lost as she and would never find her here.

As she continued, another memory came to Sophie of her mother taking her on secret mushrooming missions. *Chef likes to think she knows the most about food,* Duchess Maria had said long ago. *But she doesn't know how to look for mushrooms like I do.*

They would search in spots just like this, where the forest was shadowed and the ground was damp, especially after the autumn rains came. Straying off the trail, Sophie found a fallen spruce that was beginning to decay and sink back into the ground. She examined the tree from above, then moved beneath it on the slope of the hill, brushing dead leaves from its underside.

When Sophie saw the ribbed gold of chanterelles, she almost shouted for joy. There were dozens, clustered on the trunk near the dark soil, and chestnut boletes, too, with thick pancakey caps ready for harvest. Sophie cut as many as she could with her dagger and put them in her pockets, which were growing quite bulky. She continued to stop and pick at edible plants and seeds as she went, the knowledge her mother had imparted flooding back as she moved along the path.

The sun was just beginning to sink behind the mountain and the wind was blowing colder when Sophie noticed a large shape among the trees ahead. She peered through the dusk, putting her hand to her hip as she drew closer.

It was a cottage.

CHAPTER TWENTY-NINE

THE STRUCTURE WAS OLD AND dark, sagging into the sunken ground beneath it. The space in which it sat was hardly a clearing, with the trees twisting their branches close to the building's old stones, and vines slithering upward as if they wanted to swallow the little house back into the earth. The cottage had two stories, tiny windows, and a rotting thatched roof that had taken on the greenish hue of the forest. It gave Sophie the sense of a place that had once been happy but was now derelict.

Sophie crept behind the trunk of a nearby tree, watching, waiting. She could neither see nor hear any sign of life on the inside. She moved closer, keeping her footsteps as silent as possible on the forest floor. If abandoned—which it looked to be—the cottage would be the perfect place for refuge. But finding such a hiding place as this felt too good to be true.

Standing in front of the house, she again listened for noise and heard nothing. Sophie pressed lightly on the mossy door and felt it give, unlocked. Pushing gingerly, she eased it slowly open on groaning hinges.

"Hello?" she murmured to the darkness. "Is anyone here?"

No answer.

As her eyes adjusted to the low light, she saw an interior that looked abandoned indeed. An old wooden table and chairs were strewn about and covered in dust. Dishes littered the fireplace mantel and hearth, where ashes were piled. The rotting rafters were threaded with thick spider webs.

Keeping her hand at her dagger's hilt, Sophie carefully went up the stairs to the second floor, testing the strength of each step with her foot. They creaked loudly but held her weight.

The murky green light of the vine-choked windows revealed a similar scene upstairs: several beds in disarray, with sheets covered in grime and pulled halfway to the floor. Ancient-looking candles stuck fast to the windowsills in gluey pools of wax. Certainly, it seemed that a long time had passed since the room was used.

Then something in the corner caught her eye.

Next to the farthest bed was a little oak chair that gleamed in the low light, apparently polished and free of dust. On the seat was a sleeping tunic, neatly folded, and beneath that, a book. There was a small pair of leather slippers.

Sophie crept over and ran her finger along the backing of the chair; it was clean.

Her hair prickled on its ends before she knew why. But she soon registered the sound of whisperings downstairs.

Sophie turned silently, frantically, looking for an escape—but she was trapped. Her instincts told her it was Ferdinand's men. And unless she wanted to slice herself in two by launching out the windows, she would have to fight through them.

She edged down the first few steps with her back against the wall, dagger drawn, sweat pouring down her brow. She heard careful foot-steps nearing the landing.

Then a long shadow shot up the stairs.

Sophie rounded the landing, arm reeled back to throw, and shrieked at the last moment. She grabbed her own throwing arm with the other, afraid it would discharge of its own will. The dagger clat-tered to the floorboards and was swept up by a tiny, dirty hand.

Standing before Sophie was a small figure holding a miner's pickax.

A child.

The boy had the pick raised above his head in one hand, skinny arms trembling slightly, and wielded her dagger in the other. Behind him, several other children peered in through the doorway. They were all thin and covered in grime.

"It's—it's all right," Sophie stammered, holding her hands out and backing up. "I mean no harm. I'm sorry for scaring you. Truthfully, you scared *me*."

"Who are you?" the boy asked. His voice was stern around its tremor. "What are you doing here?"

"I'm—" Sophie stopped short, casting around for an identity. "I'm—my name is . . . Snow. Snow White," she said, using her old nickname. "I've run away from the palace."

"That's an unusual name," the boy said.

"My mother gave it to me." It was true. Duchess Maria had also called her Snow White long ago.

The boy narrowed his eyes. "Why did you run away?"

"I was frightened. There are some terrible things happening there right now. I was afraid."

"Hmm."

The boy lowered the weapons and nodded at the others, who crept into the dim room, never taking their eyes off Sophie. There were seven in total, all young boys. The one with the ax was clearly the oldest, but he couldn't have been more than twelve years old. The tiniest boy cowered in a corner, no more than four or five. Sophie sat down on the stairs, careful not to make any quick movements.

"And who are you, if you don't think me rude to ask?" she said to the oldest boy.

He leaned on the pickax, surveying her suspiciously. Finally, he decided to speak. "Anselm," he said. "We live here."

"All of you do?" Sophie asked.

He spat on the floor and nodded.

"Are these all your brothers?" Sophie asked.

"No." He scowled. "If you're no friend to the palace, then you're a friend to us. These boys have all been orphaned, mostly on account of the copper mines. They know they can come here and be taken care of."

It all clicked to Sophie then—the layers of dirt coating the children, the dirty beds, the low placement of the carved arrows in the clearing, hidden from adults but obvious to anyone at a child's height.

"I see," Sophie said. She and Anselm looked at each other for a long moment, neither sure what to do next.

"Well," Anselm said doubtfully. He looked around at the other boys, who had relaxed a little but still hung back. Then he nodded. "If you have nowhere else to go, I guess you can stay. Just for the night."

It was a start, at least. "Thank you. I'd be very grateful," Sophie said, though she didn't move from the stairs and the children maintained their distance. "So, you're Anselm. Who else do we have here?"

The boy cleared his throat. "Well, I'm the oldest. Then there's Klaus and Willem; they're brothers by birth." He nodded at two children who had similar curly black hair. "That's Bren," he said, pointing to a stocky boy with a round face. "And Markus . . . and Johann . . ."

One of the younger boys had remarkably gray hair, until he

shook the soot from it furiously to reveal light blond locks. The other sneezed.

"And the smallest here is Thomas." As he said the name, the tiniest boy of all ran from the corner and clung to Anselm's leg.

"It's lovely to meet you all," Sophie said, bowing her head low to them. "All of you work in the mines together, then? Even Thomas?"

"Course," Anselm scoffed. "No other choice 'cept starving. Speaking of . . ."

Anselm gestured to Markus, who deposited a large roll of bread onto the dusty table, more likely than not from Sigrid's own bakery in town. All the children rushed forward at once.

"Hey, hey, hey!" Anselm bellowed. "Like we've practiced!"

They glowered at him. Then Johann shoved the roll toward Thomas, who took a hungry but measured tear with his teeth. He passed it back to Johann, then Johann to Markus, going in order of age until a small corner reached Anselm. He held it and looked at Sophie, his eyes defiant and unsure.

"Please, no," Sophie said, knowing he was debating whether to offer her any. "In fact, I have more."

She emptied her pockets of the apples, nuts, berries, and mushrooms she'd gathered as she'd made her way along the trail, placing everything on the table. All in all, it was a considerable pile, and fourteen wide eyes stared at the foraged food hungrily.

"We should save some of it," Anselm said, while rubbing his jaw and hopping from one foot to the other.

"No. Listen," Sophie said. They all turned to look, their expressions holding the world-weariness and suspicion of tiny grown men. She could already tell that Anselm had the weight of a parent on his shoulders and wouldn't appreciate condescension or charity. Her proposition required careful wording. "I need a place to stay. I know you can take care of each other; it's clear you've been doing that already. I know you probably want to continue living as you are now."

Anselm frowned at her but gave a short nod.

"Keep on as you are, but let me help," Sophie said. "I know you're hungry. You have little time to gather food or keep the place clean. Let me stay, and I'll help you with that. I can take care of things while you're away."

"We don't need any coddling," Anselm said slowly. "We're not babies."

"Of course not. It's clear you're not. But let me work with you. Let me earn my keep. We can work together, and we'll all get good things out of it."

Anselm glanced back at the others, who stayed silent, and ran his hand through his hair, letting it fall over his forehead. Then he set his jaw.

"It's a deal," he said, shaking her hand with surprising grip. "Fall to, boys."

The children lunged for Sophie's findings, chattering among themselves. Though it would hardly be considered a meal in the palace, Sophie wondered if it was more food than they'd seen in a long time. Biting her lip, she vowed to gather as much as she could tomorrow to give them a feast.

The drafts blowing through the little cottage reminded Sophie that she was running out of time before the snow came and the ground hardened and died. She hoped she would be able to uphold her end of the bargain and find food before then.

Sophie touched her hip by instinct, surprised to find the scabbard there flat and empty.

"Anselm," she said. "May I have the dagger back? It's important to me."

He eyed her, slipped it into his boot, and pushed the hilt until it was almost out of sight. "You're here on a trial basis. Maybe later."

Sophie almost rolled her eyes, sure that she could cross the room in two strides and wrest it from him in less than a minute. But if she wanted their hospitality, the trust had to be mutual.

That night, Sophie turned one way and then the other, but her shoulder bones pressed painfully into the floorboards no matter which position she tried. She'd been granted a blanket from the boys, now asleep upstairs, and balled up her cloak for a pillow as she stretched out near the cottage's hearth. It seemed impossible that only last night she'd been in her own bed at the palace; it felt as though years had passed since then. But her body easily remembered the soft eiderdown and plush mattress it was accustomed to. Thinking of the luxury she'd lived in while these seven children fended for themselves, guilt bit at Sophie's conscience.

Despite the thick swaths of ivy covering the cottage and the heavy trees above, moonlight poured in through the windowpanes. Sophie squeezed her eyes shut and then opened them again, abandoning the hope of getting comfortable. Maybe in the morning she could find sweet grasses or old leaves in the woods and fashion a sort of mattress. There would be so much to do. Sophie's mother, with all her wisdom and knowledge of nature, would have known how to handle this.

If only Sophie had made it to the witch's cave before the huntsmen had come upon them. Maybe she could have gotten more answers.

Sophie hoped, at least, that Claudia had made it out of the ambush safely and gone on to consult with the witch before returning to the palace. There was no way to know what had happened; Claudia wouldn't risk sending a message even if she could, and Sophie didn't dare go back to the palace until she knew it was safe.

She brought her knees closer to her chest and thought of her father in his poisoned slumber. There was a chance, even if small, that

Claudia had already been able to wake him. But what could the reaction of the palace have been when Claudia returned without Sophie? Nothing good, Sophie was sure.

But most of all, Sophie thought of Philip, alone in some military tent, likely just as uncomfortable and worried as she was. Though Claudia would write and fill him in as best she could, Sophie was certain he would fear the worst. If he survived the war to that point, that is. Sophie's heart hurt so bad it felt like a physical pain in her chest.

Then she gasped. There was a ghostly figure staring at her in the moonlight, stock-still at the other end of the room.

The figure moved closer, and she realized it was the smallest boy, Thomas, tiptoeing toward her in his neat cotton sleeping tunic. His eyes were wide with fear as he approached, and he held something behind his back.

"Hello," she whispered, sitting up. "You're Thomas, aren't you?"

He said nothing, watching her carefully.

"How old are you, Thomas?"

"Can you read?" he asked, ignoring her question and sticking one knuckle in his mouth while he struggled to hold whatever it was he was hiding.

"Yes," said Sophie. "Can you?"

He shook his head. "Only Anselm can, but just a little."

"What's that you've got?"

He deliberated for a moment, then presented her with the thick book she'd seen when she'd first gone upstairs. It was a collection of folk stories, printed in careful script and bound simply with leather. She ran her hand over the cover.

"Is this your book? Where did you get it?"

He nodded. "From Mama."

Her smile fell, and she opened the inside cover. An inscription in spidery, careful script read, *To my dear Thomas.*

Swallowing hard, Sophie patted the floor next to her. "Would you like to learn to read?"

When he nodded again, she turned to the first page and began. "'There was once a poor widow who lived in a lonely cottage—'"

"Like us?" Thomas interrupted.

"Your cottage isn't lonely," Sophie said, smiling. "You have all these boys to take care of you."

"And you too? You'll stay?"

Sophie had only minimal interaction with children in the palace, and his plain expression of hope disarmed her. All she could do was nod and continue to read.

"'In front of the cottage was a garden wherein stood two rose trees, one of which bore white and the other red roses . . .'"

Sophie ran her finger along each word, speaking slowly and encouraging him to repeat after her. The first story was about two young girls and a strange little dwarf. The second was about a man who insisted his cow could talk. Soon, Thomas was giggling as well as tripping over the syllables.

"Thomas?" a voice called sharply from the gloom. Anselm emerged at the bottom of the stairs, boots still secured fast to his feet. "You all right?"

Thomas nodded rapidly. Anselm gave a long look at the two of them splayed on the floor, reading in the moonlight.

"Just making sure," he muttered, and disappeared back upstairs.

CHAPTER THIRTY

THOUGH SHE WOKE EARLY, MUSCLES stiff and sore, Sophie found the boys had already left for the mines. Thomas's little book of stories lay discarded next to her on the floor.

She blinked in the dusty sunlight and listened to the quietness of the cottage and the morning birdsong outside. With the house empty and nowhere to go, Sophie realized she had the entire day to herself. While she'd been an only child in Duke Maximilian's palace, never before had Sophie been so completely alone and free of commitments. Usually her days were filled with reading, classes, and long talks with Claudia that she already missed.

Here, there was nothing but the time she had to herself. No sounds except the creaking of the wood as it settled and the rustling of the forest.

As opposed to calming her, the quietude put her teeth on edge at first. To combat the feeling and to take her mind off the fact that she was essentially a fugitive on the run, Sophie threw herself into the repair of the cottage. She began from the top down, stripping the beds of their deplorable linens, taking them outside, and beating the dust from them as best she could. There were still a number of things left behind by whoever previously owned the house; Sophie knew the boys couldn't have purchased or built it on their own. Among these items, she found a frail old broom to sweep the cobwebs away from the rafters and tore the ivy back from the windows to let the light shine through.

One day turned into the next, and as the boys came and went from their work, Sophie fell into a routine. She spent each morning foraging for whatever food she could find. She'd found a bucket and rags in the cupboard beneath the stairs and followed the faint sound of water to a nearby stream. Whether it branched from the Pöllat or a different river, she couldn't be sure, but she was glad for the source that allowed her to bring water to the cottage. Now she could launder the bedsheets and her maid's uniform, which she'd worn longer than any other outfit in her life. Yet she was surprised by how little this bothered her, and how the longer she stayed at the cottage, the more she lost her sense of the direction from which she'd come. Though the path that led Sophie here was nearby, she shied away from it. It felt dangerous.

By the end of the week, Sophie had scrubbed down the interior wood of the little house with such gusto that it shone in the soft forest light. It was too late in the season to plant a garden, but she cleared a space of land in the sunniest area of the small yard just in case she had time to teach the boys how to, and gathered as many heads of wild garlic, nuts, mushrooms, and berries as possible. She reached again and again into her memory, pulling out things her mother had told or shown her about how to use and preserve plants. Whenever Sophie recalled something particularly important, she—with Thomas's permission—used the last endpaper of the folktale book to write down notes, creating a miniature nature guide of her own.

Sophie took most of her gatherings and left them to dry in the sun so they wouldn't go bad over the winter. She took the rest and extracted whatever seeds or bulbs she could, storing them in a dark cupboard of the cottage. Klaus and Willem repaired a fishing pole she found behind the cottage, then showed her how to bait a hook. With flour and ale that the boys brought her from town, she made bread they could dip in wild honey.

As Sophie learned more about the boys, it seemed to her that Anselm had some ownership over the cottage, though maybe that was only because he was the oldest and the leader. Sophie had to bite her tongue to keep from prying. While he watched the cottage's transformation with surprise and muttered gruff thank-yous when the table had food, Sophie knew he still didn't trust her. He hadn't yet returned her dagger, but he lent her a dull knife and the head of a broken ax so she could complete her tasks.

Sophie didn't push him; after all, questions might lead him to ask some of his own, and Sophie didn't think she could trust seven young children to keep her presence a secret. If news of her whereabouts got out among the villagers, it could easily reach the palace and lead King Ferdinand's men straight to her.

Sophie often struggled with her conscience, lying wide awake at night in the bed she'd fashioned for herself near the fireplace. She'd begun reading lessons with the children, choosing bedtime stories at night and encouraging them to take turns narrating. All of them seemed to enjoy the routine—except Anselm, who preferred to roll over in his bed and face the wall. Little Thomas had grown especially attached to her, gaining a reputation for feigning sickness so he could stay back with her during the day. Those were the happiest times, when Sophie would task him with sorting berries or bring him along in the woods while she worked.

But she felt bad about deceiving them. Much worse, she worried that she was putting them in considerable danger, should Ferdinand's huntsmen ever find her. Would their being children prevent the king's men from hurting those who had harbored her?

She hated knowing that she was taking that risk. But for the moment, there was no better option—so she kept her secret close to her chest.

One night, as she sat on the back stoop, clumsily trying to carve a new bowl from a hunk of wood, soft footsteps sounded behind her. Anselm appeared and sat next to Sophie, a thin blanket pulled around his shoulders to protect from the cold air.

"Hello," she said.

"Hi, Snow."

She waited for him to speak. She could tell that leading the boys was very important to him, so she always gave him space and let him come to her instead of the other way around.

"I heard something strange in the mines today," he said.

"Oh? What's that?"

"The duke's daughter, Lady Sophie, is missing."

Sophie accidentally dug the knife blade too far into the wood, but she kept her face flat and didn't look at him. "Is she really?"

"Yes. They say her pa is still asleep, and her step-ma is going mad but won't send anyone out to find her 'cause the king of Spain wants her dead. She was supposed to marry his son, but the king didn't cotton to that."

The knife slipped again, nicking Sophie's thumb. She pushed the image of her father out of her mind, and then she looked at Anselm. He was studying her carefully.

"She must really want to stay hidden, I suppose," Sophie said, but received no response. She shrugged. "It must be important to her and her family, if they're willing to go through that."

Anselm pressed his lips into a thin line. "She must need someone to protect her, then."

Sophie nodded solemnly.

The two of them sat looking at each other for a moment, quiet. The night wind rustled through the trees, but its sound no longer startled Sophie.

"Seems like you need a better tool," Anselm said at last, breaking the silence. He reached into his boot and pulled out her dagger, placing it into her hand. "Though I wouldn't dig at that wood with this."

"Thanks," Sophie said, trying not to show how relieved she was to have it back. The metal felt warm and familiar in the tight grip of her palm.

"Use the chisel end of the pickax to carve out the bowl," he advised. Then Anselm stood.

"Are you going to bed?" Sophie asked.

He tapped his hands against his pockets. "No, uh, not yet—"

He ducked quickly into the door to retrieve something. When he came out again, he held Thomas's book of stories. His face was beet red.

"Would you—I was wondering—" he started.

Sophie smiled, and the night seemed a little warmer. "Let's start on page one."

CHAPTER THIRTY-ONE

As the pleasant autumn afternoons hardened into chillier nights, Sophie began to feel like the forest was pressing in on her from all sides. Each day she worried there was something she had forgotten or another chore that still needed to be done before the season changed. Already there had been some flurries on the colder evenings and frost on the thatched roof in the mornings. She had never needed survival skills like this before, and as the days grew shorter, she felt ill-prepared.

"How have you made it through the winter in the past?" Sophie asked Anselm one night, when the darkness outside seemed blacker than ever.

He shrugged. "We just make do. Pile up a lot of firewood, eat whatever we have, sleep a lot. Like bears."

"We had to kill a deer once," Thomas said, his eyes wide.

"That was sure something," said Klaus with a haunted look on his face.

"Meat!" Sophie cried, slapping her forehead. "I'm good with my dagger, but I'd never get close enough to a deer." For all the berries and nuts and vegetables she gathered and the fish she caught, venison would provide them many times more fat and protein.

Anselm nodded. "We might be able to fix that."

But she wasn't even certain how to cut and preserve meat in a way that would last the months. She thought hard, trying to remember what Chef would do in the palace kitchens. It involved a lot of salt— of which the cottage had none. And as sharp as Sophie's silver dagger was, she was also sure that the work of butchering a deer would be a bigger job than the small blade was suited for.

She would have to go into town.

Sophie didn't want to think about it, but there were other, under-lying feelings that drove this decision. She was dying for news of the world. Going back and forth between the cottage and cave each day, the boys rarely had anything to share besides what they heard in the mines. The thought that Philip, her father, or Claudia could be dead without her knowing made her sick with worry.

Though the little house was comforting and safe, Sophie also longed for the sight of something familiar, especially when the snows would prevent any of them from leaving the mountain for weeks or months.

She spent a day or two debating with herself, weighing the risks of going down the valley while knowing that she was running out of time. Though a handful of the villagers had come up to the palace during her crusade with Claudia, most didn't even know what Sophie looked like and had never met her before. The exception was Sigrid, of course, but Sophie would avoid the bakery.

Sophie's maid's uniform was now so worn and dingy that she thought it would be unrecognizable as palace garb. She'd also fash-ioned a cloak from an old wool blanket the boys had, both to protect against the November wind and further conceal herself. Dressed like this, Sophie looked much more like a beggar than a noblewoman.

The expedition was too tempting to pass up. Sophie rose early one morning as the boys were getting ready to leave.

"Let me come with you," she said. "I have some things I need."

Anselm raised an eyebrow, and she knew what he was thinking. "Are you sure that's a good idea?"

"You don't want to carry back five pounds of salt by yourself, do you? What harm could it do?" she said lightly.

He lowered his voice. "There are palace guards that inspect the mines sometimes."

"I'll be careful. I promise."

Anselm shrugged. "Get a move on, boys, we'll be late!"

The wind blew cold as they made their way down the mountain, but the boys laughed and pushed one another, rosy-cheeked in the chill. Sophie knew they must make an odd-looking group, a bunch of children and a tall, cloaked figure following behind them. She was grateful for the tree cover, the overcast day, and the light fog that made them inconspicuous.

"Snow's coming with us! Snow's coming with us!" Thomas shouted, dancing around her and tripping over both feet. Bren smiled and lifted the boy on his shoulders.

Sophie did not know their route, nor how far they were from the caves that held the copper mines. This part of the forest was unfamiliar to her, though she knew they must be somewhere on the same side of the mountain as the palace, where the rock sloped down into Bavaria. The boys, however, were right at home, running off the trail for minutes at a time and popping up farther down.

All too soon, Sophie could see the clearing of the trees as they reached the valley. She held her breath as they broke through, eyes clouding over when she caught sight of the familiar village in the distance.

The boys hurried to the left along the bluffs, toward the entrance of the mines. Sophie hesitated at the point where the path forked to the right into town, and Anselm hung back with her.

"You sure you'll be all right? I can pick up the salt, you know? It's no problem," he said.

"Thanks, Anselm. I think I'll feel better if I do it myself."

She bid him goodbye, took a deep breath, and started slowly, picking up pace as she got closer to the village. Unfortunately, though she strained her eyes, the palace was shrouded in mist today. She could make out the large shape of her home looming in the foothills but little else.

Sophie sighed, wrapping her cloak more tightly around her as she reached the town square. She wondered what she would find if she went back up the hills right now. It could even be possible that her father was awake, healed and looking out from the high tower.

Sophie fought the wild urge to wave, to call for him. But she would risk her life doing that, and she knew her father could not see her anyway.

It took all the strength she had to turn from the palace and from the road that would lead her straight to its door.

Instead, Sophie headed for the cutler's shop. She hesitated as she entered, securing her hood around her face, but the thick-armed man barely gave her a second glance. He continued to hammer away at the metal he was working on, alternately running it through the small forge in his hearth and cooling it in a bucket of water.

It seemed to Sophie that all the shops were just as sparse as they had ever been. But luckily, this one still had a few knives hung up on the walls, many of them small, but better suited for butchering than her dagger.

"Good morning," she said gruffly, trying to disguise her voice. "Is that for sale?"

She pointed to a sharp blade with a carved wooden handle.

"It is. Four thalers," the cutler said.

"That much?" Sophie's supply of coins was limited; she'd planned to use two for the knife and three for the salt, which would be more expensive.

"That much, and I should be charging even more," the man grunted. "If you have a problem, take it up with the duchess up on the mountain. I'll have to make tools out of the coins themselves once my silver runs out."

Sophie's mouth went dry as she handed over the thalers, telling herself she'd figure something out for the next shop. She tried to keep her voice level as she spoke. "Has the duke woken up yet?"

"Of course not. That old turtle abandoned us in life, and he'll abandon us in his death, too. I can't imagine it'll be long now, with all that black magic the blasted duchess is subjecting him to."

Sophie wanted to ask more, but she couldn't. If she showed emotion, she would give herself away.

"Better spend your thalers while you can," the cutler grumbled, sliding the blade into a leather sheaf. "Word is after Spain defeats England, they're coming for us."

Sophie grabbed the covered knife off the counter and slipped out of the shop. She stuffed it into a satchel from the cottage, hugging the bag to her chest as she took deep breaths to recover from the man's words. This had been a bad idea. She would get the salt as quickly as she could and wait for the boys outside the mines.

The spice merchant's shop was slightly better stocked than the silversmith's, likely because spices were more expensive and not as crucial to the war efforts. Sophie was overwhelmed by the incredible smells of the dry herbs as she entered, making her suddenly homesick for Chef and the palace kitchens. Glass jars of seasonings lined the shelves in a colorful array. Sophie stood in their fragrance for a moment, breathing it all in.

Then two things happened at once. The merchant came out from the back of the shop, and someone else came in through the front door.

Glancing toward the entrance, Sophie nearly dropped the satchel she was holding.

It was Lotte.

Sophie quickly turned her back, hunching over a low shelf and pretending to examine the bright yellow jars of turmeric.

"Good morning," Lotte said to the merchant. "How have you been? I'll tell you how *I* am—some rabbits destroyed all our coriander, and now Chef has me running all her errands."

"I've not seen you here in some time, Mistress Lotte," the merchant replied. "But luckily for you, we've got coriander in stock."

"Yes, you know . . . my duties have changed." There was such sadness in her voice that Sophie wanted to turn and give her a hug.

"I was sorry to hear about your lady's disappearance," the merchant said. "Does it look very bad?"

"They think her dead," Lotte said quietly. Then she piped back up to normal volume. "Lady Sophie is gone, Duke Maximilian is no use—what more can we stand to lose? Unless this is what the duchess wants, that Lady Sophie never be found."

"She was the one to lead Lady Sophie into the woods, was she not? It seems certain that she left her there to die. Someone ought to do something about her, or we'll all pay for it," said the merchant.

Sophie bit the inside of her cheek to keep from saying anything.

"News is Spain is losing," Lotte continued. "It's said they're getting battered out there."

Sophie froze.

"Prince Philip is still alive, though; he wrote to the palace," said Lotte. "Asking about Lady Sophie. Wonder what the duchess told him!"

"Well, I'll tell you what I— Just a moment—fie, beggar!" the merchant barked. "Either buy something or get the blazes out of my shop!"

Sophie half turned in surprise, realizing he was speaking to her. The blood rushed to her face. Her first instinct was to bolt out the door, but she needed that salt. Without it, whatever game they did manage to hunt would be rotten after a few days. She couldn't go back to the cottage empty-handed.

Sophie pulled the hood even tighter around her head and kept herself turned away from Lotte. Her stomach roiled at the merchant's insolence.

"Salt?" she rasped, doing everything she could to keep from sounding like herself. "Five pounds?"

The merchant scoffed. "Five pounds! You expect me to believe you can pay for that?"

Sophie nodded. She had only one thing to barter that she hated to let go, but she had no choice.

The merchant rolled his eyes, reached for one of the jars on the wall, and shook a measure of small, round seeds into a pouch.

"Here's your coriander," he said to Lotte. "I fear I'm going to have to squabble with this hag for a long time."

"It's no trouble," Lotte murmured, frowning. "Good day to you both."

As soon as the maid left the shop, Sophie straightened up, reached beneath the collar of her dress, and yanked off her mother's silver necklace. It had stayed with her since the night of her father's wedding and her own debut, but the jewelry would do more good in a trade for salt than hidden beneath her clothing. Besides, Sophie had what she needed of her mother—the dagger, memories, and knowledge that would keep her and the boys alive. Sophie slapped the necklace down on the counter.

"Five pounds of salt. Now."

The merchant stared open-mouthed at the delicate and expensive object, then sprang into action, weighing out measures of salt.

"And include a half pound of those boiled sweets, please."

Just as Sophie reached for the heavy packages, there was a clamor outside the shop. She looked through the window to see all seven boys milling about the town square with a number of other children. Thomas was running from store to store yelling for Snow, and Anselm was trailing him, trying to quiet him down.

"What's happening?" Sophie called, leaning out the door.

Thomas caught sight of her and bounded into the shop. "We don't have to work in the mines anymore! We don't have to work in the mines!"

"What? You don't?" Sophie asked.

Anselm joined them, speaking in a much lower voice. "We've just received word from Duchess Claudia. She's shutting down the mines!"

Sophie grinned from ear to ear. It was clever of her stepmother. Maximilian would never have stood for the decision, but with him indisposed, the advisers could say nothing against Claudia's orders.

"Well, that's no good," the merchant grumbled behind Sophie, as he'd overheard. "How are all the miners supposed to survive the winter without their wages?"

Anselm held up a jingling bag of coins. "We've been given an allotment."

Sophie could have clapped for joy; the advisers must be livid. She scooped the packages of salt and candies off the counter, assisted by Thomas and Anselm. In her haste, her hood fell off, revealing her young and refined face.

The merchant jumped back, apparently having expected a withered old crone.

"Wh-what are you?" he stammered. "Some—some kind of witch?"

Sophie re-donned her hood and lifted her chin at him before sweeping out of the shop. "Yes. And I hex thee."

The ground was hard and cold as Sophie crouched in the brown underbrush. She pressed back a nearby branch that obscured her view, trying to see deeper into the dark forest. Sophie's visit to the village had given her everything she'd hoped for, and none too soon; today, the clouds were gathering swiftly and looked heavy with snow.

Sophie had many reasons to be grateful. Though her father was not yet awake, she knew Claudia and Philip were safe—for the moment. She knew that the boys would be nourished and warm with her throughout the winter, thanks to Claudia. Maybe the cold would be able to freeze out the war efforts, too.

For now, there was one last thing she had to do.

Sophie shifted her feet and tightened the grip on her dagger. She'd had several decent shots, since she'd begun practicing, but today she could not afford to miss. Likely enough, Sophie would only get one chance.

From somewhere farther off in the forest, there came a low, clear whistle. Then another, then one more: the signal.

The sound was followed by shouts, whooping, and boots crashing through the underbrush; fourteen human feet chasing after a deer's spindly four.

Sophie saw them coming from all sides, waving their pickaxes, and making plenty of noise to scare the poor thing directly into Sophie's path. They closed into a tighter and tighter circle as the animal bolted straight ahead. Sophie grimaced, suddenly remembering Lord Peter and the squirrels.

They had to eat. And so, when the deer was less than ten feet away, nearly on top of her, Sophie sprang from the underbrush and released her dagger with deadly aim.

It was her best throw yet, borne of determination and duty and the most primal instinct to survive.

Sophie watched as if in slow motion as the blade spiraled through the air, finding its mark in the deer's chest in just a fraction of a second.

"I'm sorry, I'm sorry, I'm sorry!" Sophie yelped as the animal fell to the ground, kicking a few times before becoming still.

Thwack.

In all the things Sophie had imagined for her future and the possible paths she could take in her life, not one of them involved butchering a deer outside a tiny mountain cottage at dusk while five little boys watched from inside. Being the oldest and strongest—and having done it once before—Anselm helped, but even he had a difficult time stomaching the task.

Poor Thomas, who'd wanted to keep the deer as a pet and name it, was upstairs huddling beneath the bedsheets until it was all over.

They used every part of the animal that they could, tossing the byproducts far enough into the forest that wandering carnivores wouldn't come too close to the house. Anselm put aside the tender and tasty loin to cook right away. He then poured the salt in a pine box, where they buried the meat and left it to cure.

He and Sophie made their way to the stream just before dark, breaking a thin layer of ice from the surface so they could scrub the grime from their hands in the freezing water.

"Thank you for all your help today, Anselm," Sophie said. "That wasn't easy work."

"I should be thanking you. I know you did it for us." He peered at her in the darkness. "Everything go all right in the village today?"

Sophie nodded. "I'm glad I went."

"Good."

They walked slowly back home. Sophie pushed open the cottage door, where a warm fire crackled in the hearth. Anselm and Sophie set the venison to cook on a spit over the fire.

"Welcome to your first night of freedom, boys!" she cheered. "What would you like to do first?"

The children looked at one another uncertainly. Their short lives up to this point had been devoted to work. Then Thomas appeared at the top of the stairs, eyes puffy from crying. "Read us a story!" he demanded.

It was a popular request. Everyone huddled near the hearth, draping themselves over chairs or sprawling on the floor. Sophie glanced out the window as she opened Thomas's book, seeing the flakes of the first heavy snowfall begin swirling through the night.

But at last, she felt ready for winter to come.

Chapter Thirty-Two

THE SNOW PILED ON THE mountain and over the trees, blanketing
the little cottage and making its days and nights flow together into one.
Passing as a dream would, the winter seemed sometimes to last for
years and others only for a few weeks. But the inside of the house was
cheerful, filled with firelight and laughter and all the stories told as the
snow raged on, first by Sophie and then by the boys, who learned to
spin the tales themselves. The world outside the house slept, halting
all its strange events until the days began to grow longer once more.

One morning, the boys took a trip into town and Sophie stayed
behind to make some repairs to the cottage. After re-thatching bare
spots on the roof, she went back inside to have a cup of tea and something to eat. Sophie rested and enjoyed the coolness of the dark room
as she sat by the hearth.

Then there was a movement outside.

She glanced out the window but saw nothing. It wasn't unusual
for deer or fox to slip by the house during the day. Standing stock-still
in the garden once, Sophie had seen a buck pass only feet from her, so

close she could see the fine fur on the points of his antlers. Yet there were no animals in the yard now.

Sophie returned to her tea just as a shadow fell over the room's floor. She looked up once more and dropped her cup, reeling back as it shattered—a very tall woman was standing in the doorway.

"Wh-who?" she stammered.

Beneath a heavy hooded cloak, the woman wore black robes that had an iridescent sheen of deep green in the pool of sunlight. Her hands were folded and the fingers long. She removed the cloak, releasing white hair that hung loose and trailed down her back. It was impossible to tell her age by her face. She was very old—that was clear—but her features seemed to shift every time Sophie looked back at them, from grizzled to smooth and back again.

The woman seemed almost to float, pristine and out of place among the cottage's humble surroundings.

Sophie knew there was no one else it could be: This was the witch. She felt her hair standing up all over and heard her blood thrumming loudly in her ears. The magical woman could be here for any number of reasons—good or bad.

"Good morning, mistress," Sophie said, her voice quavering. "Did my stepmother send you?"

"Oh yes, Lady Sophie, I am here to do the bidding of Duchess Claudia," the witch said. Her voice sounded like sheaves of dried barley, shifting and rippling in the breeze.

"You know my name," said Sophie, less a question than an observation. "May I have yours?"

"It isn't important," the witch sniffed. "But on to what is: I have a message for you."

Sophie struggled to collect herself. Something about the woman was indeed familiar; her movements and the shape of her face tugged at some very old thread in Sophie's mind. She felt she should be terrified, and at first, she was certain she was, but there was nothing in the woman's demeanor that suggested a threat. Sophie picked up the broken pieces of her teacup and placed them back on the hearth.

"Is it safe to return to the palace now?" Sophie put a hand to her throat. "Is that why you've come?"

"I'm afraid it's just the opposite."

"Oh!"

"Calm yourself. I need to tell you some things that aren't so pleasant."

Calm yourself. Sophie could have laughed aloud. Though her whole body seemed to be on fire, she offered the good chair to the witch and forced herself to sit still on the hearth, twisting her fingers together to keep them from shaking.

"First, the thing you wonder most about: I'm afraid I've been unsuccessful in waking your father, child. Your stepmother was able to see me, and I gave her another potion for him." The witch grimaced, as though it was painful for her to admit it. "However, he is in a very deep sleep that puts up a fight against my skills. But I will continue to try."

"Thank you," Sophie murmured, not sure what to say.

The witch waved Sophie's gratitude away with her hand. "Now, I have been working with your stepmother, Duchess Claudia, and keeping very close watch on your—"

"Oh, her condition? The baby? Is she well?"

The old woman nodded and continued. "Though you have been well hidden for quite some time and the snows slowed King Ferdinand's progress, I'm afraid that his men have discovered your location."

Sophie whipped her head to the window as though she would see spies crawling through the bushes and dropping from the trees. She'd been in the cottage so long, with such a sense of safety, that she'd nearly forgotten about them, and now the terror came back in full force.

"Not yet," the witch said, shaking her head. "There is still time. But—"

"Are the boys safe?" Sophie asked, a pit opening in her stomach. They were out there right now, perhaps among the danger themselves.

"It's *you* the king wants, not them," the witch said.

"How did Ferdinand's men find me?"

"Going into town as a beggar was not the most inconspicuous thing you could have done," the witch said, raising an eyebrow. "To my knowledge, the spies used information from a certain spice merchant to learn your whereabouts."

"Oh, damn him! And me—I shouldn't have been so foolish."

The witch clucked her tongue. "Not your fault. It seems even while waging a war in England with his son by his side, this Ferdinand is the obsessive sort—half-mad, if you ask me. But here we are, after all. And so, my dear, you must be removed from the picture."

Sophie leaned back against the hearth, uneasy at the woman's decisive tone and quick change of direction. What had made Sophie think she could trust her? Just because Duchess Maria had known the witch didn't mean they'd been on any sort of friendly terms.

"What does that mean—'removed from the picture'?"

"The Spanish king cannot hurt you if you are already dead," the witch said plainly.

"So, you've come here to kill me?" Sophie cried, heart-stopping fear shooting through her limbs. Now the woman's face seemed warped and frighteningly sinister.

"Only in a fashion."

The witch lifted her arm in a sudden movement, but Sophie responded with her own. In a flash she was on her feet, hurling her dagger through the air. But it clattered harmlessly to the floor.

The witch rummaged in the sleeve of her robes as though nothing had happened. "That isn't what I meant, child," the witch said, sounding irritated. "I told you to calm yourself."

Sophie took a deep breath, bewildered and uneasy. As she watched, the witch procured an object, holding it tightly in her hands. "This is a very complex piece of work," the sorceress said, keeping her eyes down. "I've spent a great deal of time developing it, as I had a feeling it may be useful in the future."

"What do you have?"

The witch opened her hands to reveal a palm-sized fruit: an apple. But it was like no apple Sophie had ever seen. Its unnatural deep red shone in the dim light of the cottage like glass. It was strangely perfect in its shape, not lumpy like those Sophie had gathered in the fall, but symmetrical all the way around.

The witch smoothed a thin finger over the skin of the apple. "When you eat this fruit, it will not kill you. You will be fine. But it will send you into such a deep sleep that, for all purposes, you will appear dead."

"Like . . . like my father?"

"Yes, my dear," the witch said quietly. "You will not wake without intervention. Ferdinand's men will find you and report your death back to the king, who will—it is our hope—back down from his assault."

"Are we certain they'll find me? How can we possibly know nothing will go wrong?"

"We can't. We can only hope that it will work. But there is no other way—if we do not do this, the king's men will find you and kill you for certain."

Sophie lowered herself onto the hearth once more. The plan seemed to involve a great deal of risk. And there was one very glaring point missing from the scheme.

"How will I wake up?" Sophie asked.

"Philip will come with the antidote when it's safe."

Philip. Just hearing his name made Sophie feel a little better. But not quite enough.

"I'm not sure," Sophie said, her mouth dry. "May I think about it? How long do I have?"

The witch studied the floor, avoiding Sophie's gaze. Finally, she spoke. "My dear, I'm afraid I must tell you that the king's soldiers are on the mountain at this very moment."

"No!" Sophie breathed, picking up her dagger. She wished for Philip, for her father, for Claudia—for anyone who could tell her what the right decision was. She could try to fight the assassins, but how many of them were out there? She could never win. Worse, she could never put the lives of the boys in danger like that.

"Remember that your stepmother sent me; she said it was the only way to keep you safe. She bid me to help," the witch said.

Sophie thought of Claudia's outrage on behalf of the miners and the children, her adoration for the duke, and, most of all, the love she had for Sophie—the long nights they spent together, talking in front of the fire.

"Do you trust her?" the sorceress asked.

"Of course I do," Sophie said. She sheathed her weapon.

The witch held the apple in her outstretched palm. "Then eat."

"Wait!" Sophie ran to the table and scrawled a short note on a piece of paper, folding it and placing it near the door.

Then she glanced at the witch and took the apple, its shining skin smooth like porcelain in her palm.

"Just a bite," the witch whispered. She looked much younger than she had before, her face serene and eyes bright.

Sophie sank her teeth into the fruit, surprised at how soft it was. It had the taste of honey and cinnamon, the sweet tang of its flesh undercut by something earthy and bitter. It was unlike anything Sophie had ever eaten.

She felt nothing at first. Then the room began to dim as though the sun was going down early, and Sophie felt a heaviness overtake her body. The witch suddenly floated above her—no, it was Sophie who had fallen to the floor.

A memory shot through Sophie, something that she had forgotten to ask. She fought against her eyelids, which were closing of their own accord.

"Did you know my mother?" Her speech came out thick and muffled in her ears, as if she were underwater.

"Yes, I knew Maria," murmured the blurry figure above her. "And I will tell you all about it when you wake."

Then all was darkness.

CHAPTER THIRTY-THREE

ANSELM HAD RUN DOWN FROM the foothills to the villages, whistling an old lullaby he thought he'd forgotten long ago. The air was still cold, but the spring already looked so green. Even the mines were suddenly a marvel to him, their labyrinths tunneling deep into the earth.

While the copper caves were still closed, Anselm and the boys heard talk of great improvements in their visits to the towns. The burliest men had been sent from the palace to help the children and villagers; there was more money devoted to gunpowder, and they now even had a carriage of horses to help them move the coal. Their friend Snow had made the cottage so comfortable, it was a home now and not just a place to sleep.

As they spent the day in town, Anselm knew the boys could sense the change in him, too. They gave backward glances as he ran after them, grinning and hoisting Thomas on his shoulders with extra strength. For the first time in a long time, they climbed the mountain at the end of the afternoon singing an old folk song, one that Anselm used to lead when he was trying to cheer everyone up. With festive harmony and the happy discord of little boys being loud, their voices echoed off the foothills and valleys as they hiked through the forest.

It wasn't until they were close to the cottage, their thoughts filled with the anticipation of supper and after-dinner stories, that Anselm cut the singing off sharply.

Something was wrong.

All through the winter, the little house had been lit from within and cozy in the dusk. On the evenings when they ventured out for a walk in the woods, they could often hear Snow bustling around inside and humming to herself even before they reached the yard.

But now the house was dark. There was no wood smoke rising from the chimney, no cheerful light or familiar, homey sounds, though Anselm knew that Snow White had planned a busy day of chores. Even the dusky sky looked somehow duller, more muted than the fresh air that usually hung over the cottage.

"Where's Snow?" Thomas asked.

"Quiet a moment," Anselm said. The other boys looked to him nervously, and he motioned for them to stay back.

A terrible sense of dread came over him as he crept toward the dark house. He held his breath as he pressed the door with one palm. It was unlocked and slightly ajar. For a moment, everything was black as his eyes adjusted. But slowly, slowly, the shape of a figure on the floor became clear.

Anselm opened the door farther to let in more light, then squeezed his eyes shut. It was *her*.

The room tilted as Anselm reeled, holding on to the door handle for support, fighting the wave of nausea that kicked up inside of him. He stumbled forward, and as he did, his foot caught at something that crinkled on the floor.

A piece of folded paper, with his name on it in Snow's hand-writing: *Anselm.*

He tore it open, head spinning. He could only read it because Snow had taught him so patiently for many months.

Dearest Anselm,

So sorry to do this. What timing! But you are right about who I am. And I am not dead, only asleep . . .

Anselm's head shot up. He looked carefully at Snow's—or should he say, Lady Sophie's—motionless body on the floor. He crouched down next to it, floating his hand just above her rib cage. Then he winced and pressed it against her.

Her body was so cold; there was no way she could be alive. And yet, she had written this note herself. Gritting his teeth, he took two fingers and pushed them against her neck, just under her jaw. He could feel no pulse there, nothing to indicate life. He pressed harder.

Then, softly, ever so slightly, something very slow and inconsistent pushed back against his finger. It was almost imperceptible, but it was a beat all the same.

Anselm let out a long breath of air. Relief flooded his body, and he turned back to the letter.

. . . and have agreed to be so according to the plan of my stepmother, Duchess Claudia, and the witch of the woods. Spain's men must believe I am dead. King Ferdinand must believe he has won. The witch will give you further instruction.

You can do this.

All my love to you and the boys.

Anselm shook his head once, twice, then read the letter again. He rubbed his eyes, trying to understand. He had not met any witches in real life, but there were plenty in Thomas's book of folktales— and they were often terrible tricksters. But clearly, Snow White had trusted this one, since her words in the note rang true and Anselm would recognize her handwriting anywhere. He would need to trust the witch as well.

He glanced around the dark room, almost expecting the woman to emerge from the shadows. When that didn't happen, he turned to the letter again, examining it closely and flipping it over.

On the other side, someone else had added a message in thin and spidery script. The ink shimmered slightly as though it was still wet. Anselm caught his breath and read the words with care. When he was done, he went back outside, where the boys were waiting in the darkness, frightened and restless.

"We've got an important job to do," Anselm said.

CHAPTER THIRTY-FOUR

IT WAS NOT PHILIP'S FIRST experience of war. Since his father's reign, Spain had been involved in so many endless battles, and endless wars it seemed. The kingdom fought the Aragon elite, the Dutch colonies, and now England once more. The defeat of the Spanish Armada in 1588 by the English was still a wound that Philip's father could not abide. At this moment, Spain's army was bigger, faster, stronger. Their supply of weapons and equipment was endless, funded by the country's wealth and desire for revenge. Since the tide was turning and Spain was sure to win—or at least battle England to an uneasy truce—Philip decided it was high time to return to Bavaria to see his beloved.

The past few months had been unimaginable. Philip had received no news from the palace about Sophie. But the thing that kept him going in his time away from Bavaria was the belief that his beloved was safe; that no harm had come to her in his absence.

While he had not admitted it to Sophie, Philip had suspicions concerning the source of the poison Duke Maximilian had consumed.

He had attempted to talk to his father about it, but every time he brought up Bavaria or his impending marriage, the king dismissed him and refused to engage in conversation. As far as Ferdinand was concerned, Philip and Sophie's plans were of little consequence, and something to be handled only after England was finally defeated. It assuaged Philip's conscience, however, when he realized his broken engagement to Princess Elizabeth was not the true reason for the hostilities between the two countries. England and Spain were fighting over—what else—money, power, and trade routes. It was unlikely that even a marital alliance would bring the two nations to peace.

And so, suspicion gnawed at Philip. If Claudia had not attempted to poison Sophie—and Sophie strongly believed she had not—then who else would want to harm his beloved? The answer roiled in his gut.

As Philip's hope and patience grew thin, it occurred to him that one man could confirm or deny his worst fears—one man very close by.

The prince groaned inwardly as he approached the grand general's tent where his father held office just outside the battlefield. Philip felt, as he always did, like a small boy in the presence of King Ferdinand. The feeling grated on him more and more as he grew older. And now, could he really march in there, practically accusing his own father of attempted murder?

But he set his chin and squared his shoulders as he brushed past the guards at the entrance, determined to find the answers he was looking for. He would do anything for Sophie.

Ferdinand sat in a thronelike chair at the head of an oaken table littered with maps, charts, and steel-cast models of the war front. Scrolls spilled onto the floor, where the dirt of England's soil was covered with dozens of thickly woven rugs.

"Yes?" Ferdinand asked, looking sharply up at the intrusion.

"Father," Philip said. His heart was racing as he tried to find the words. "I must talk with you about Lady Sophie—my betrothed."

His father smiled thinly. "What can possibly be said about her?"

Fury leapt in Philip's heart, but he pressed on. "I know you may not approve of our union, but you have taught me to be my own man. And I fear for her life—someone has put a target on her back, and I don't understand why."

Ferdinand shrugged. "It seems she should be careful, then."

"Have you sent any scouts to Bavaria lately?" Philip asked, switching tack and watching his father closely. "I know you keep close watch on me. We both know."

The king bristled; Philip had never spoken this plainly to him. But he lifted his chin and narrowed his eyes. "I can't recall."

Philip laughed, a loud, cold bark. "Can't recall! That's the most ridiculous thing I've ever heard. You keep record of every movement you make. Isn't that how you stay so sharp—all the intelligence you gather?"

"Careful, son," Ferdinand said softly. "Mind your tone. You'll hang yourself trying to untangle threads that don't concern you."

"Why, just look at all these maps and charts," Philip continued, ignoring him. He began riffling through the papers, rattling off their purposes. "Funds for battle. How much grain your soldiers ate. *Can't recall?* Just look right here!"

"Stop it," the king snarled. "Put those down!"

"Maps of England," Philip cried. "An order for troops to the east, an order for a platoon to—"

His heart stopped cold. Ferdinand had sent a platoon to Bavaria.

The king snatched the orders out of Philip's hands and ripped them to pieces, his face unreadable.

"It was you," Philip whispered. "You have sent our men to assassinate my bride."

"You still think to marry that mountain girl?" Ferdinand roared. "When you are meant for royalty! You could have ruled England and Spain!" He threw a scroll to the floor and shook his head. "Enough. You have returned to me like a sensible son. Forget about the girl. She will be taken care of."

"What have you done, Father?" Philip whispered, fists shaking. The strange man in the scarlet livery. The poison on the goblet meant for Sophie. He knew his father well. He knew. He just did not want to face it.

"Only what is necessary," the king said smugly.

Philip could have attacked Ferdinand with his bare hands, but he knew he had to think—for Sophie. His mind whirled as he tried to keep his composure, fighting the sick feeling that flooded his limbs. Sophie was still alive. She had to be. He would have heard if she was dead. And there was no news of such ill tidings.

Yet.

Philip drew himself up to full height. "You will not win this. She is stronger than you could ever know."

"Then she may have a chance."

Philip did not answer but turned and marched toward the door of the tent before he could do anything he would regret.

"Where are you going?" Ferdinand bellowed. "Don't forget: Your duty lies here!"

But the prince shoved out of the tent with a roar. His heart lay far from these battlefields.

Philip had never traveled so fast in his life. He had to go back to Bavaria. He had to find Sophie, to call off his father's men; only he could reverse their orders. After two strenuous days of travel—aided by the first mild weather of spring—Philip returned to the duke's lands, clinging to his horse's neck as it limped along the road through the villages. As his exhausted steed climbed the foothills, Claudia came out of the palace doors, tears streaming down her face.

Philip gasped at her change in appearance. Her face, though still beautiful, had the beginnings of permanent worry lines from stress and sleepless nights. Claudia's already-hard features were sharper and colder than ever before; the palace had not been kind to her in his absence. The dress she wore was black for mourning, full in the skirts and concealing her pale skin with dark satin.

"Philip! Thank God you're back," she choked, running up to him with surprising speed. She helped him off his horse with improbably strong limbs. "Please come quickly—it's Maximilian. I can't be alone."

"Sophie," he asked, "where is she? Duchess Claudia, my father was behind it all. We must act fast—"

Claudia shook her head. "She is safe—but not here. I will tell you later. Please, come with me, I beg of you. We don't have time to spare," she said as she led him to the duke's chamber.

Philip sat next to the duchess as they watched the duke's breath get shallower and shallower. His head and chest were smeared with a dark green poultice, which Claudia told him was meant to keep the duke alive, as well as a thin gold oil dabbed around his nose that was supposed to wake him up. Still, the duke looked gray as a corpse. He had been sleeping for months. Philip couldn't comprehend how he had held on this long.

"It's not working anymore," Claudia said between sobs. "We use more and more of the poultice, but I can tell he is slipping away. And the potion he is breathing should have woken him by now. The witch said it might, but it hasn't."

"The witch?" he asked. "What witch?"

Claudia did not explain and only continued to cry.

"Whatever this stuff is, whoever gave it to you, surely it can only do so much when the duke's time has come," Philip said quietly.

He studied his hands as Claudia sat next to him, weeping quietly. The skin on his wrists and knuckles had become rough, aged by the bitter winds on the battlefield and scarred in combat. The index finger of his left hand was even jagged now; it had broken when the hilt of an English sword had slammed into it. Philip squeezed his fingers into fists and shoved them beneath his cloak, out of sight. His hands looked like his father's.

Duke Maximilian must have ingested a toxin of great strength all those months ago. That he had not died—even if this state could not be called living—must have meant he had a great deal of determination. But it didn't matter now. Sometimes Sophie's father made little movements as though he was about to wake up, but mostly he gasped and labored for air.

"Please, my dearest," Claudia murmured, going to the duke. "Just open your eyes. Just open your eyes."

No sooner had she said it than his struggling stopped. He drew one soft breath, held it for a moment, and let out a final rattling of air.

And then, at last, he was still.

"No!" Claudia screamed, collapsing over his body. "No!"

Philip went to her and placed his hand hesitantly, soothingly on her back, trying to find the words to say.

"Oh my dear God, he is gone, and Sophie did not get to see him," Claudia cried. "Our baby will never see him."

Philip wanted to scream *Where is she?* but knew it must wait in respect of the duke's passing. "Claudia?"

But Claudia did not answer him. Instead, she lay beside the body

of her husband. "Oh, Max, Max, it cannot be. You cannot leave me."
She kissed his face and neck and hands, her tears turning into wails.

The physician came in to confirm Maximilian's death and enter it
into record. Even he, no-nonsense man that he was, looked at Claudia
with pity as he sent her away with her maids. Then Philip was left
alone in the room while the palace began the burial preparations.

He looked at Maximilian's still form, feeling as though he should
say some words. The man lay right there, yet the room was completely
empty of another human presence. This shell bore little resemblance
to the man Philip knew when he was alive, he who had been in this
room mere minutes ago.

"I don't know where you are now," Philip murmured, feeling
rather awkward and devastated at the same time. "But I promise you,
I'll take care of them. You have my word on that. I will defend your
country from mine."

He glared at the ground, shaking his head quickly as if anger
could prevent tears. "You may not have been perfect, my lord, but
you were a better father than I've known myself. I—I wish you well."

꩜

Philip didn't know what to do with himself. He'd come back to warn
Claudia about the imminent threat to Sophie, but his heart ached to
burden her with bad news now. She had said Sophie was safe—for the
moment, at least. He resolved to speak with Claudia the first moment
she had calmed from her husband's passing.

Philip went outside and paced the garden angrily, sometimes
ripping off the fresh buds of new plants just to throw them on the
ground; other times, bursting into angry tears. He was ashamed.

The marble bench beneath the Norway spruce was the only thing
that brought him comfort. Try as he might, he feared he was losing

the memory of Sophie's face. At times, he could picture his beloved, her lovely eyes and serene smile staring back at him. But when he looked too closely, her features rearranged themselves and blurred.

Yet he recalled with sharpness their first nights together, when things had seemed easy and promising. Philip could remember the smell of the roses floating among them here in the garden as he fell for Sophie, the folk song they first danced to, the feel of her hand in his, her waist beneath his touch.

Philip twisted a sinewy strand of ivy around and around his finger. It didn't break; it only kept fraying and fraying until there was a mess of thin, dark green strings in his hands.

He would not let his father win.

As he sat, he became aware of the sound of hoofbeats coming up to the palace from the valley. They were going at a fast pace, galloping at such a clip that he wondered who it was. He doubted any servants would have reason to ride so quickly.

Philip rose and headed toward the front of the garden to get a clear view. Presently the rider came through the trees, and he could see it was one of Maximilian's trusted men, the captain of the guards. On seeing the prince, the rider's face fell, but he urged the horse on faster.

"Prince Philip! Prince Philip!" he called, his voice high and frightened.

"I'm here!" Philip said, jumping in the path of the horse, then stepping back quickly to grasp the bridle and calm the horse. "What's happened? What's wrong?"

The man shook his head. "Your Highness—no—" He seemed unwilling to relay the news.

"Well, out with it! Please!"

The captain dismounted, but couldn't look at Philip. "My lord, Bavaria's men have been tasked with combing the mountainside, searching for spies. We defeated a platoon we found of—well, of Spanish soldiers, sir," he said reluctantly.

"Yes, I hear you," Philip said impatiently. "And then?"

"And just now, my men—they said—they said—it's Lady Sophie. But"—he opened and closed his mouth a few times, as though he could not find the words—"but she's dead."

"No." Philip shook his head vehemently. "No, you're lying."

"I'm sorry, sir. We found her in a glass coffin on the mountainside . . . she's gone."

Philip's knees gave out, and he sank into the dirt of the road.

CHAPTER THIRTY-FIVE

THERE WAS NO SOUND, ONLY Philip's breath. He rose and turned away from the guard, shaking his head so quickly that his eyes blurred.

"Wait, my lord!" the man cried.

Philip walked, nearly ran, without knowing where he was going, simply trying to get away. He didn't understand. He couldn't understand. Claudia had said Sophie wasn't here, so why was she on the mountainside?

And dead? It was impossible.

He couldn't believe it.

He wouldn't.

It wasn't true.

Philip would know, surely—if Sophie was dead? If she was gone from this earth? He would *feel* it. She was alive. She had to be.

The prince found himself somewhere on the third floor, near Duke Maximilian's study. He could not go any farther. He sat down, in the middle of the corridor, and buried his face in his hands, pressing his eyeballs with the heels of his palms until it hurt.

He sat like that for a long time, trying to shut out the world. He whispered to himself, "Sophie, my love, I know you are alive. That man is wrong. You live; I know you do!"

After what felt like hours, a warm draft overcame Philip. It smelled like cinnamon.

He lifted his head, rubbing at his swollen eyes, and squinted to find an oddly dressed woman standing in the hallway before him. She was tall, taller than seemed natural; her iridescent black skirts brushed the ground as though there was nothing beneath them. She was a young woman or perhaps—as Philip looked closer—someone very old. Someone who had lived since ancient times.

"Hel-hello?" he said, embarrassed to be found crying on the ground like a child. He shoved his hand across his cheeks. "Who are you?"

"I'm a friend, Your Highness," the woman said brusquely. "I have been a friend to Bavaria and the duke's family for a long time."

"Who are you?" he demanded.

"I have been called a sorcerer, an accursed hag, depending on the circumstances—"

"You're the witch," Philip said.

"That too," she said. The woman grinned wickedly and suddenly looked young again, her features shifting and hair and robes rippling though there was no breeze. Philip reeled back in shock. Growing up, his father had told him terrifying stories about magical women, relaying their vile deeds and appetite for children's flesh. They were a species who used to exist on earth but no longer did—or so he was told.

Claudia had mentioned the poultice was from a witch, and it had kept the duke alive until it hadn't. And the woman's strange appearance here indicated she was something more than human. But she seemed little like the monsters that he thought witches to be. Philip

237

shook his head; his despair was so great he was willing to accept anything at the moment.

"My lady, whatever you may be, I need help," he said, and could not stop the tears from falling fast as he spoke. "My betrothed is dead. So is her father. Claudia is broken, and I don't know what to do—"

"Stop." The witch closed her eyes and held up a hand. "Do not despair, my boy. This is what I've come to tell you: Your lady is not dead."

"What?"

"Indeed, she is not. Sophie sleeps like her father did, but she *can* be awakened. Your instinct was right. She is alive."

Philip merely stared at her, his emotions rearranging themselves left and right. "I— How did you read my mind?"

"I have an approximate understanding of many things," the woman said. Then she smiled slyly. "Plus, I heard you say it."

Philip pinched the bridge of his nose and leaned against the wall of the corridor, elbows resting on his knees.

"I put her under a spell, yes—a strong one. You were meant to find her yourself, but the duke's soldiers found her first." She lowered herself to the floor with Philip—kneeling or floating—Philip couldn't tell. "It was the only way to keep your father from trying to kill her."

Philip stared at her and rubbed his hand along his jaw. He could feel adrenaline returning with the witch's every word.

"So, it was him," Philip said, hushed. He knew it, but he didn't want to accept it. It was too awful to bear, that his love for her had brought this terrible fate upon Sophie. Philip shook his head bitterly, swearing under his breath. "This is all my fault. This never should have—"

"Enough of that now," the witch said. "Self-pity isn't helpful. You must act quickly." Her serious expression remained unchanged, but her eyes were bright.

"Who are you, really?" he murmured. "Why should I trust that what you say is true?"

The witch lifted her hands in a shrug, her face entirely calm. "You don't have to. But I only wanted you to know what happened before you acted rashly." She frowned at him sternly. "Lovers have ways of bringing harm to themselves when they fear their beloved is dead. I am here to tell you, yours is alive. Or she will be when she takes this."

She tossed something above his head—a little golden something that flashed in the sunlight. Straining to catch it, Philip clasped the object in his hands from midair. It was a thin vial made of glass. Inside was a honey-colored liquid, thin and splashing against its confines as he turned it this way and that.

Philip studied the antidote before tucking it safely in his inner vest pocket.

"Courage, my dear boy," the witch whispered. "Now go!"

"I don't feel very courageous right now," Philip said. He studied the veins and patterns of the marble floor beneath his feet. They were to him like clouds, as diffuse and amorphous as his thoughts. "And how do I use—"

He looked up, shocked to find he was suddenly alone in the hallway.

Philip whipped his head left to right, but there was no trace of the strange woman. It was as though she had never been there at all.

Chapter Thirty-Six

Philip set out within the hour on a new steed from the palace stables, following directions from the captain. Before leaving, he checked on Claudia and told her he was going to get Sophie. He would not give her any more news of death today. He refused anyone's company. He would go alone to save his love. He could not bear to be with anyone if the antidote did not work. As he charged up the road that followed the Pöllat, even *he* could not explain what he was feeling. His grief for the duke, rage toward his father, love for Sophie, and fear that something had already happened to her all congealed into a hard, sharp point that drove him forward like the broadhead of an arrow.

There was something else below this mess of emotions, too. Would Sophie still want him, after all this time? She had suffered so much, and in many ways, he had been the cause. He did not know whether there would be room left in her heart for love.

He saw the peak of the mountain growing nearer and noted the change of the land around him into a marshier shelf as he galloped. The beautiful river of summer was now a rushing torrent, fed by the melting snow. His horse reared up at the unfamiliar terrain of the highlands, nearly bucking Philip from the saddle.

Philip scanned the path and the surrounding trees, memories of war setting the frayed edges of his nerves on fire, but no enemy appeared. He leaned down, murmuring some calming commands into the horse's ear.

The trail became rockier as he continued, but he urged his horse forward. He had sometimes been unnerved by the dark, tangled woods of Sophie's duchy. But now the forest felt kind toward him, opening itself and guiding his horse's step.

Spring was visible everywhere in tender, tiny green tips. Shimmering shafts of sunlight spilled through the branches, and in the whispering hush of the wind through the trees, Philip wondered at his own doubt in magic.

At last, Philip came to a clearing with a hiking shack and dismounted his horse as he was told. Stretching, he looked around but could not see the way to go.

All at once, a cloud of something like dandelion seeds rose up in the air and blew toward the far end of the clearing. Philip grasped at the fuzzy bits in awe, seeing no dandelions in the field and knowing it was too early for them to take seed, but they swirled away from his fingers. All he could do was shake his head in wonder and follow the cloud where it led, to a concealed trail hidden behind a wall of brush and low branches.

"Just incredible," he murmured.

As he walked, something in him sensed that he was not far from Sophie. Philip noticed a familiar fluttering of nervousness in his chest, the same he had felt when he returned to Bavaria from England those many months ago.

He pushed fear and doubt away from him with every step. He avoided thinking of the news of her father he would have to tell

Sophie when she woke. But there would be time for that later. First, he would make sure she was safe.

Suddenly, Philip heard voices nearby. He paused, realizing he had no idea what he was actually looking for.

Moving slowly, carefully around the next bend in the trail, Philip came face-to-face with the very last thing he expected.

Before him was a tiny boy, no more than five years old, holding a huge pickax that made him look even smaller. On his face, he wore the most vicious of scowls.

"Halt!" the boy squeaked.

Philip raised his eyebrows. "Good afternoon," he said.

"Why have you come here?" the little boy snarled.

"I'm looking for someone. A young woman named Lady Sophie. Have you seen her?"

"No, sir." The boy shook his head. "All we've got is our Snow White here, so off with you, now."

"There can't be that many young women in this part of the forest, can there?" Philip smiled. "What does your Snow White look like?"

"None'f your business." The little boy narrowed his eyes. "You've come to take her away, haven't you? That's why I'm on the lookout—to keep any scoundrels from taking our Snow White away." His face became very solemn. "It is my sworn duty."

Philip crouched down a little so he could level with the boy. "I'd just like to have a visit with her, that's all," he said. "Though, if I am being honest, we love each other and I'm hoping she'll come back with me to where we belong."

The boy looked surprised, then screwed up his face as his bottom lip wobbled.

"Anselm!" he shouted, and burst into tears.

"Oh," said Philip. "Oh no, come now—"

More footsteps and voices approached. Behind the boy appeared six others, larger than him and holding equally dangerous-looking mining equipment. Though each looked skinny and haunted, they were clearly ready for a fight. Philip took a few steps backward, holding his hands up in peace and noting their fierce expressions.

The tallest stepped in front of the little boy. "Who are you?" His voice was rough and gravelly. He phrased it as a statement, not a question.

Philip cleared his throat. "Please, my friend," he said. "I'm Prince Philip. I've come for Lady Sophie, to rescue her from her deep sleep."

"Prince Philip of Spain, aren't you?" The boy spat. "Wasn't it your father what sent men to have her killed? Isn't it your father who threatens us now with war?"

Philip sighed, then drew himself up to full height. "Yes. That was my father. But I am not him. I am on the side of Duchess Claudia and Lady Sophie—and you."

The boys looked at one another, then back at Philip, sizing him up.

"Give me one good reason to trust you." The oldest boy lifted his chin.

He raised his pick higher, ready to strike, as Philip reached into his pocket. Then Philip pulled out the witch's vial and held it up to the waning sunlight.

"I have the antidote that can wake her up," he said.

A murmur ran through the little crowd. The oldest boy stared at Philip a while longer. "So—so it's true? She isn't really dead?" the boy finally said, and Philip was surprised to see his eyes welling up with tears.

"She isn't. And I wish to wake her," Philip said softly. "Will you help me?"

The boy lowered his ax, letting its blade hit the ground with a *thud*. "All right, then. Follow me," he said at last. "Boys." He nodded to the others, and they seemed to understand an unspoken command. Two flanked Philip and two went behind him; the rest watched him and held their pickaxes at the ready. The smallest boy ran to the front and took the eldest's hand.

They led Philip into a small clearing where the forest floor was matted down and littered with blankets. In the middle was a wooden bier draped with cloth and a long box covered with a glass dome, as if it were a coffin.

"Sophie!" Philip let out a strangled cry, seeing her lying as if lifeless inside. He ignored the boys with their axes and ran to her side.

She could not hear him, of course. Hesitating, he pressed his hands to the glass. Before Philip's eyes, the barrier melted away at his touch and dissipated into the air.

The boys gasped and rushed forward as Philip stumbled against the table.

"I suppose you *are* who you say you are," the oldest boy muttered. "That's the witch's doing, I'd wager. It held fast for the other men. Go on, then."

Philip nodded at him, thankful. He turned to examine Sophie.

She looked just as though she could be sleeping, her skin still soft and flushed from the blood that pulsed in her veins, but her chest did not move with breath and a stillness had set into her body. Her hair was much longer than when Philip last saw her, laid out dark and thick beneath her and reaching down to her waist. She was dressed in the white-and-light-blue servant's uniform of Duke Maximilian's palace, but its colors had long gone dull, and the fabric had been patched and repaired in many different places.

In her hands, she held a silver dagger across her heart.

Just looking at her, Philip's heart swelled with an unfamiliar pain. How brave she was to have fled; how resourceful she must have been to survive the winter. And her kindness was evident in the faces of all these children, who had obviously sworn their allegiance to her.

He carefully touched Sophie's arm, then pulled back. It was colder than expected; some instinct almost made him want to recoil. What if the witch had been wrong? What if she was like her father and couldn't be saved?

Circling around the bier, the boys watched him gravely.

He had to try. But Philip had no idea how to use the antidote. He held the little vial up to the light, peering at its contents. There wasn't much there; he wouldn't be able to experiment.

Very gently, as delicately as possible, he placed his thumb on Sophie's chin and pushed downward, trying to open her mouth. But her jaw was stiffly shut, as though she were made of marble.

Sweat broke out along his forehead. He wasn't even sure if she was supposed to drink it, though that seemed like the only plausible option. If what the witch had told him was true, Sophie had also ingested the initial poison through the flesh of the apple. It would only make sense that the spell would be undone by the same mechanism.

Hands shaking, Philip pulled the cork from the vial and placed it against Sophie's lips, pouring a small measure between them. Most of it disappeared, but some slipped out and dribbled along her chin.

"No," he whispered. "Please, Sophie."

They waited, the air in the glen unnaturally silent, but there was no change. Philip could feel fear boiling up inside him like water over a fire. He poured a little more, but the same thing happened.

"Come now," he said through gritted teeth.

He pressed drops to his fingertip, anointing her eyes, forehead, and base of her neck, but nothing helped. She remained as still and cold as ever.

At last, close to tears and nearing the end of the vial, Philip poured what was left of it in his own mouth and pressed his lips gently to Sophie's, trying to breathe life back into her. He had never kissed her before, but he kissed her now as if her life depended on it—because it did.

"Come now, Sophie," he murmured, squeezing his eyes shut and pressing his forehead to hers. "Please, my love."

He smoothed his thumb over her cheek, wishing for warmth to grow beneath his touch.

For a moment, all was still. Philip could sense the boys holding their breaths; the only sound in the glen was the wind rustling in the trees above them.

Then Philip felt something move against him.

When he looked down, he saw Sophie's dagger placed threateningly between his ribs.

"Sophie!" he cried.

Her eyelids fluttered and suddenly flew open.

Sophie blinked a few times and peered at Philip's face. He stood stock-still, frozen in her gaze.

"Oh, it's you," she said, and smiled. The dagger came away from Philip's side.

Philip could only throw his head back in laughter.

Then he leaned close and pressed his lips against hers once more. But this time, she kissed him back. He cupped her chin gently, and she brought her arms around his neck, pulling him closer.

The boys all rushed forward. The littlest one clung to Sophie and would not leave her side. The children cheered and teased as Philip and Sophie kissed again and again.

❦

After Philip made sure Sophie was healthy and fed and that all the boys had been taken care of, Sophie led Philip up along the stream until they reached a high point overlooking the valley. From there, they could see the walls and towers of Duke Maximilian's palace rising in the distance.

He held her hand the whole way there. He felt he could not let go. He had lived this moment in his dreams for months, and now he could not believe it had come.

They sat together on a fallen log. He held her very close and spoke as gently and clearly as he could.

"Sophie," he said, tracing his thumb over hers. "I must tell you. Your father—"

She pulled back from him, fear in her eyes. "Is he—"

Philip stared into her eyes, then dropped his gaze and nodded. He had battled through the winter, seeing many of his countrymen die and losing faith in his own father. But this was one of the hardest things he'd ever done. "The duke succumbed to the poison. He held on so long—he did it for you. I know he did."

A long, heavy sigh escaped Sophie. She leaned back into Philip and hung her head.

"I knew, somehow," she whispered, even as tears spilled over her cheeks. "I don't know how. I had the strangest dreams while I was sleeping, and I never knew what was reality, prophecy, or just nightmare. But I can't say it's come as a shock. At the same time, I'm so grateful that you're safe, and so worried about Claudia. I don't know how to feel, not at all—"

And she buried her face in his shoulder while he rocked her in his arms for a long time.

When she pulled back, he smoothed her hair and looked her in the eyes. "I know it will be hard to go home," he said. "But the duchy needs you—the duchy, Claudia, and me. More than ever."

She looked at him, then nodded slowly and pulled at a thin piece of jewelry around her neck that he hadn't noticed before. "I will do my duty. But we can do it together."

On the end of the silver chain was his mother's ring, the one he had given to Sophie so many months ago. She took it off and held it in her hands.

"You—you still have it?" Philip said, emotion overwhelming him. "You've had it all this time?"

"Of course," she said with a small smile. "I have learned so much about myself since you and I first met. I have fought for my people's well-being, fended off attackers, survived through the winter with nothing but the mountain and the love of those seven boys to sustain me." There was a glint of something in her eyes, a look of strength that Philip had never seen.

"I marry you not because I need to, but because I want to," she continued. "I lose no power through this union but gain a lifetime of happiness with you . . . if you will have me."

She placed the ring in Philip's open hand.

"I would have no other," he said, struggling to keep his voice steady. "You have been my confidante, my best friend, and my equal in ways I have never known before. I would do all of this again if it meant I could stay by your side." He gently slipped the ring onto her finger once more.

"You saved me," she whispered.

"And you saved me," he said. "Without you, I would never have had the courage to stand up to my father and become my own man."

Sophie threw her arms around his neck and he held her so tightly, as if it were she who rescued him.

And she had—in more ways than one.

CHAPTER THIRTY-SEVEN

LEAVING THE NEXT MORNING WAS the most difficult thing Sophie had done in a long time. Though she had imagined her departure for many months—and even longed for it, on the darkest and coldest nights of the winter—now it was hard to believe it was really time to go. The days and hours that had passed like nothing between her bite of the witch's apple and her revival by Philip made it feel even more like she was jumping ahead in time.

The cottage had given her safety and security when she was in danger; the boys had become her little family. And she had no idea what she would find on the other side of the forest. Though she did not say so to him, Philip had changed a great deal since they'd last been together. His hands were rough and scarred; there was an empty look in his eyes she would catch when he didn't notice her watching. His face and body were all sharp angles and hard muscle; he looked so much older than the boy who'd left her.

Beneath that toughened exterior, he was thin. The winter

battlefields had not been kind to him. He spoke quieter and moved more decisively, cautiously. His youthful brashness was gone.

It was not all bad; Sophie knew change was inevitable and that both of them would experience it again and again throughout their lives. But it was unsettling to have missed out on so much. Philip was only a small piece of the upside-down world that awaited Sophie back home.

When he told her about her father, she had accepted the news, but now she felt herself falling apart as it sunk in. Her father did not survive. That poison had been meant for her. She should be dead. Instead, her father was.

She was afraid to see Claudia in her grief, afraid to return to a home without her father.

She'd hoped to prolong her time in the little cottage by packing and making sure everything was prepared for the boys to take over the household themselves. But she'd arrived last autumn with nearly nothing, and they'd already done a spectacular job keeping things running while she'd been asleep. All too soon, Sophie stood at the door with seven sad faces looking up at her, trying to keep her own lips from trembling.

"Now, come," Sophie said, swallowing hard to clear the lump from her throat. "We will not be apart for long. You will come to the palace the very moment it is safe for you."

Thomas ran forward, eyes streaming with tears, and grabbed on to Sophie's leg. The lump in her throat overwhelmed her, and soon her face looked just like his.

"Oh, now," she said sternly, lifting him up in her arms. "I'm less than a half day's walk away—so Philip tells me. It's going to be all right."

She kissed Thomas's head and set him down, hugging each of the boys in turn and ruffling their hair. When at last Sophie got to

Anselm, his face was hard and his lips were pursed, though his eyes were glistening like hers. He held his hand out for a firm shake, but she pulled him in for a hug. She pressed her hand to his back, hearing his sniffling.

As she pulled away, he turned to lift a thick object from the table. It was a collection of mishmashed sheets of paper, carefully folded and sewn together, covered by a piece of leather.

"What's this?" Sophie asked.

"It's our stories," Anselm said. "All the ones we told over the winter. We figured you might leave once you woke up, so we wrote them down. We thought you would want to remember."

"But—but it's your work! All your hard work..." It was too much. She leafed through the book, their careful handwriting and sprawling words and detailed drawings soon blurring together from hot tears.

Anselm shook his head. "We'll write more."

Now a mess of emotions, Sophie went around and hugged all the boys once more.

"All right," she said, wiping her eyes on her sleeve with a laugh and taking a deep breath.

Philip put his arm around her. "Ready?"

She nodded.

They walked into the forest to cheers and much fanfare from the boys, who waved and jumped up and down until they were out of sight. Sophie's chest ached at the final glimpses of the cottage that had held both home and family for her for so many months. But she turned forward to face the dim path before her, taking Philip's hand.

They made the journey by foot, letting Philip's horse rest after that tremendous gallop through the mountainside. Though Sophie had always imagined they would have a million and one things to say to each other when they reunited, it felt better, now, to walk in silence.

What could be said after the months they had endured? War and death and so much loss. What could be said about the uncertain future that lay before them?

Before Sophie was ready, the palace walls loomed high in front of her once more. She gazed up at the building, familiar but somehow completely changed. Sophie couldn't imagine that her home no longer held her father; the thought was absurd. And yet, it seemed as though some light within the architecture had died.

She tried to remember the last thing she had said to her father, but nothing came to mind. Everything had been full of chaos the night of the engagement banquet. When was the very last time she told him how she loved him?

Before the memory could overwhelm her, Philip stopped them at the trunk of a large oak alongside the bank of the Pöllat to rest for a bit.

Then Sophie saw Lotte, coming through the woods with a canvas bag, pressing a fist to her mouth as though trying not to cry.

"Lotte!" Sophie exclaimed. The maid broke into a run and crashed into Sophie, who held her in an embrace as Lotte's back shook with tears.

"Oh, Lady Sophie," she whispered. "I'm so sorry. I followed the prince out, I thought he was on his way to you. I'm so glad you're back. Oh goodness, we've missed you. Here, let's get you out of that filthy thing—why are you wearing that . . ."

Leading her behind a thicket, Lotte helped Sophie change into a clean dress, which felt incredibly uncomfortable after the softened fabric she'd been living in. Sophie grimaced, knowing that her regular palace clothes would be much worse and wondering how she'd ever lived like that.

Lotte worked through Sophie's hair, grown tangled and wild, as best she could with a boar-bristle brush. She wound it tightly into a thick, low bun.

"There," said Lotte. "Now you look like yourself again."

They made their way into the palace through side doors, back stairwells, and little-used corridors. Every sconce and stone once familiar to Sophie felt entirely different from this perspective, as if she were seeing her home backward. At last, when Lotte was certain no one was following, they emerged in the hallway near the southwest turret tower. Before them was the tapestry of Orpheus and Eurydice.

Sophie stared at Lotte as the maid produced a key from her pocket. "How did you know where to find . . . ?"

Lotte looked back, a little guilty.

Sophie shook her head and then nodded, a little surprised to find that she *didn't* mind. Lotte carefully pushed back the tapestry and unlocked the door to Duchess Maria's room.

"After you," she said softly.

Sophie entered, feeling conscious of Lotte watching her cross this threshold she'd only crossed alone for the past six years. Here again was the familiar scent, the way the light came in through the windows, the feeling of calm that washed over her.

And in the middle of the room stood Claudia, in a black dress that seemed to engulf her small frame.

"Sophie?" she began, her voice small.

But Sophie was already running, already holding her arms out to Claudia as they collided in the middle of the room.

"Oh, Sophie," Claudia said. "I'm so glad you're safe—alive—I had no idea what would happen—"

"Me neither," Sophie said, her face buried in Claudia's shoulder. "I'm sorry you had to go through this alone."

"And you. You've been so brave."

"It's all right," Sophie said. The two were squeezing each other so close that she barely had breath to say it. "I'm here now. I'm here."

At last, they broke apart and Claudia swallowed hard. "Your father—"

"I want to see him."

"Of course. I will take you to him immediately."

Then Sophie noticed something else. Claudia's dress was not just voluminous. Claudia herself was quite large. She stared at Claudia, at the large bump in her belly. "You didn't lose the baby."

Claudia's smile was bittersweet. "The witch said bleeding is common sometimes when one is with child."

"I'm so glad," said Sophie. It was a ray of light in a dark day.

After Sophie paid her respects to her father's body, Philip insisted they marry at once, and Sophie agreed. There was no more reason to delay the union between Bavaria and Spain beyond the reading of the banns over three weeks. On the third Sunday, they would marry. If Ferdinand still strove to threaten Sophie, it would be as though he was inciting war on his own son. This meant no wedding feast. No banquet. No invitations. There would be no fanfare, no glittering ceremony like Maximilian and Claudia had. Just a priest and the two of them, with Sophie's nearest and dearest as witnesses. Claudia, Chef, Lotte, and the seven boys. Together they all awaited the priest's arrival.

Sophie was glad Lotte had thought to make her look presentable. Her loyal maid had taken in one of Duchess Maria's most beautiful dresses and used Claudia's veil from her ceremony.

"I am so sorry your father is not here," Claudia whispered, blinking rapidly.

Philip cleared his throat, peering into his cup. "His last thoughts were of you and Claudia. I know that they were," he said. "When we talked before the engagement banquet, he all but ordered me to take care of you, Sophie, and to be a good partner and husband. I know he was speaking of our immediate future, of the engagement, but . . . it was almost as though he knew what would become of him. He loved you so much. Both of you."

Sophie nodded, gripping Philip's hand tighter. She would not think of this now—she would think of it later, after the wedding, or next week, or maybe never at all. She would store it somewhere far back in her mind.

"I don't believe I'll ever wish to leave your side again," Philip said. "But I should run and see if the priest has arrived. He should have been here by now. Will you be all right? Just for a few moments?"

"Of course." Sophie smiled. "I have my friends with me." She nodded to Claudia. Chef was wiping tears, and Lotte was shushing the boys, who were fidgety.

He kissed her hand and took his leave. When Sophie turned to look at Claudia once more, she was surprised to find there were tears flowing down her cheeks.

"Oh, Claudia," she murmured, going to her. "Oh no. Please don't cry."

"I can't help it." Claudia covered her face with both her hands. "I thought I would never see you again. And I felt like it was all my fault."

"Never! You saved me. Don't you realize that? You saved my life. I would have been dead long before now if you hadn't sent the witch."

"I just—I just don't know how to go on without Maximilian. I don't know how to do any of this."

"I'm trying not to think of it myself. But it's all right." Sophie crossed the space between them and put her arms around Claudia.

"We're going to figure it out together, you and me and Philip. We have one another."

"I'm the one who's supposed to be taking care of you," Claudia said, crying even harder.

"I spent months in the woods with seven children." Sophie chuckled. "If you need to be put down for a nap, I know how to do that, too."

Despite herself, Claudia laughed. Then she clutched her stomach and a gush of water pooled at her feet. "Oh my goodness," she said. "The baby!"

CHAPTER THIRTY-EIGHT

A WEDDING AND A BABY were momentous occasions indeed. But right now, all of that was far from Sophie's mind; she had much more important matters at hand. She prided herself on being a sensible girl, one who was not squeamish or silly about such things—and as she had told Claudia so loftily almost a year ago now, she was not a stranger to the realities of what was expected on a wedding night. But now Sophie was nervous. And excited as well. Her stepmother and Lotte had been kind enough to prepare a trousseau in the short time between the ceremony and the small candlelit supper that she and Philip had enjoyed.

Sophie was alone in her bed, waiting.

There was a knock.

"Come in," she said, sitting up and pulling the covers to her chin to hide the filmy nightgown she wore.

Philip poked his head in and grinned sheepishly, then shut the door gently behind him. He was wearing a robe over his sleeping garments. He too looked nervous, and his cheeks were red in the candlelight. He pushed his hair out of his face and walked determinedly toward the bed.

"Is this all right?" he asked.

She nodded, too overcome to speak.

He moved closer. He removed his robe, then slid under the covers with her. His shoulders bumped next to hers, and his hands entwined with her own. In the hearth, a log popped and hissed as it kindled the fire. Both of them stared at the light flickering against the dark velvet underside of the four-poster canopy. Sophie's heart was already at a gallop; both heat and goose bumps shivered up and down her chest. She could feel a warmth emanating from Philip's body too, burning her up in more ways than one.

Then Philip turned to her. "Sophie?"

"Yes?"

"Can I pull the covers down?" he asked.

She nodded.

Gently, he pulled the covers away from her body. She froze. She had never worn so little clothing in front of anyone other than her maids before. The cool air of the room washed over her bare arms.

He caught his breath. In the firelight, his eyes were sparkling. "You're so beautiful," he murmured.

She reached for him then, drawing him closer, and he rolled so that his body covered her own. He rested on his elbow and looked down at her reverently. "Sophie," he whispered, his voice now a growl. "I . . ." His hands reached for the straps of her nightgown and soon she was bared to him.

Sophie reached forward and pulled his nightshirt over his head, and then it was just the two of them, their bodies pressed tightly against each other's, and there was no more need for words.

Instead, she held him closer, so much closer, and he knelt down, and when he entered her, she felt no pain, only a sharp sensation that grew into pleasure.

She kissed him ferociously, matching his movements with her own.

"Oh God," he whispered. "Sophie." Her name was a prayer, a benediction.

"Philip, Philip . . ." She said his name over and over as they shuddered together, everything becoming blind and hot and immediate and impossibly ecstatic.

It was not enough. All through the night they reached for each other, and for that sweet sensation. In the morning, they became one again, the experience entirely new in the tender, early light.

"We're getting good at this," Sophie teased, tracing a finger against his spine as he dressed.

He laughed and turned to kiss her, grinning wickedly. "Surely you're not saying you think we've had enough practice? There's always room for improvement, Lady Sophie. We simply must keep working at it. And the kingdom wouldn't mind a child or two—or ten—or twenty—"

"Oh yes—I suppose we must do it for the kingdom," she said, dissolving into giggles.

"How many children should we have?" Philip wondered.

"Seven," said Sophie. "Seven is the right number."

There was something Sophie knew she still had to do. One afternoon, rooting through her father's study, she found what she was looking for. It was Duke Maximilian's last will and testament: the one that named his daughter the heir to the duchy, instead of his unborn son.

But Sophie already had everything she needed, and Maximilian had proven his trust in her. She would not wrest Bavaria away from her own flesh and blood, half siblings though they may be.

Sophie threw the paper into the fireplace, watching it burn. Her stepmother loved her. Her father loved her. Philip loved her. Her new brother would love her.

The duke was dead.

Long live the duke.

They named the newborn after his father, Maximilian.

CHAPTER THIRTY-NINE

JUNE WAS THE MOST BLISSFUL month in their lives. The baby was healthy and happy, and Claudia declared it was time to celebrate. Since Philip and Sophie did not have a wedding banquet, they would have a feast to honor Maximilian's baptism as well as Philip and Sophie's marriage. As preparations were underway, a messenger came from the Spanish royal palace.

Philip was in the duke's study with Sophie when he unrolled the message. His face was inscrutable.

"What is it?" she asked.

"The Treaty of Madrid has been signed. War with England is over," he told her.

"And so—what of your father? Will he come to see us?" asked Sophie. She could not hide the strain in her voice. While she never wanted King Ferdinand to step foot in Bavaria, Sophie couldn't help wishing that king and prince could reconcile somehow. If only for Philip's sake.

But her husband shook his head. "No. He will never visit us here."

Sophie exhaled.

When Philip looked up from the letter, his eyes were shining with tears. "The king was killed by a stray arrow after signing the treaty. A few soldiers did not know the war was ended. My father is dead."

Sophie hugged the prince—now, king—and held him close. "I'm so sorry."

Philip's shoulders sagged. "I am not. My father would have terrorized us, regardless. This is the best thing that could have happened. I am sorry to say it, but it is true."

"Still, he was your father."

Philip nodded. "He was that."

They were subdued for the celebration but glad to share their happiness with the rest of the court and the duchy. The baptism had gone well, and little Maximilian had only cried a little when the priest dabbed water on his face.

Now it was time to enter the banquet. The three of them stood at the top of the stairs. The nurse would follow with the baby.

"Let me just do one last check with the captain of the guard," Philip said, adjusting his coat. He left Sophie and Claudia together.

Sophie was wearing the gown from her debut—blue and red, with the golden silk. Claudia was dressed in red as well, her first time out of mourning, but it was a different dress than Sophie had seen her wear before. It had a low, square neckline and a bodice that cinched very tightly at the waist. Sophie thought perhaps Claudia wished to draw attention to the fact she was no longer pregnant; that her son had been born healthy and strong.

"Ready?" Sophie asked, glancing up at the dowager duchess, who was looking into space and wincing. Claudia took a deep breath and ran her fingers along her bodice with a frown.

"What's wrong?" Sophie said.

"Nothing." Claudia looked down, rubbing at the dress's fabric. "I just—I think one of the stays is coming loose. Let's go."

No sooner did they start descending the grand staircase than Claudia stopped again. "Now the other side's coming through, too. They're quite sharp—they must have come through the bodice." She smiled ruefully. "I should've known I wasn't ready to wear these things again."

A sort of numbness came to the back of Sophie's throat. "Claudia, are you sure you are all right? You look pale. I don't like this. Why don't you wear something else?"

Claudia shook her head even as she clutched the railing of the staircase for support. "No, it's too late. I'm fine."

"Claudia . . . where did you get this dress?" Sophie said slowly, trying to mask the mounting worry in her voice.

Claudia sucked in a breath. "One of the servants found it in my wardrobe. I hadn't worn it before. Don't worry—it just stings a little." She laughed, a strange gasping sound, and almost fell over.

"Claudia!" Sophie screamed. "Help me!"

The nearby guards hurried forward, bewildered, and Lotte rushed to Sophie's side.

"Did you help the duchess dress this morning?" Sophie asked.

Lotte nodded.

"Where did you get this gown? I haven't seen it before," Sophie said.

"I found it in your closet, my lady," said Lotte.

"Mine?" said Sophie.

"Yes—but I did not recognize it, so I assumed it was Duchess Claudia's and brought it to her."

Sophie reached for the tag at the collar of the neckline. There was a note on it: *A gift from Spain.*

"This—this must have been sent to me from the king of Spain after my engagement!" Sophie's blood ran cold. The poisoned goblet. The cordial. The huntsmen. And this dress.

"No," Sophie said. She began unbuttoning the back of Claudia's dress right there on the staircase. The handful of servants and guards that had gathered looked on, helpless. "No—"

"Sophie, please," Claudia said weakly. "What are you doing? We have to go . . ."

There were so many buttons. Sophie's fingers began to sweat, slipping on the silk again and again.

Finally, Sophie pulled the dagger from her sleeve and sliced through the back of the dress, cutting away from Claudia's skin.

Beneath the fabric, over Claudia's petticoats, the sharp stays had come loose and were digging into her abdomen.

"Claudia, you're bleeding," Sophie said, panic squeezing her chest even as she tried to remain calm. "Philip," she said, then again, louder. "Someone get Philip—please—"

Claudia's face went white. She closed her eyes, slowly lowering herself to sit on the stairs. With one hand gripping the dress, Sophie used the other to tear Claudia free so the gown hung loose.

"It's all right now," Sophie said, gathering Claudia in her arms. "They're just cuts, yes? Just a few cuts, we'll get you fixed up right away. Get you in a different dress."

Claudia shook her head, peering up at Sophie as though she was struggling to stay awake. "I'm a damn fool," she said, her voice raspy and thick. "Why did I wear this? I think I've been poisoned."

Poison.

Again.

"No," Sophie said. She heard the rushing of blood in her ears. "It can't be! No! Not you!"

"You and Philip—you are so happy together," Claudia said, lifting her hand with effort to Sophie's cheek. "You're going to do such great things, Sophie. Your father would be proud."

"Stop." Sophie shook her head again and again, rocking Claudia back and forth. "Stop saying that."

A look of confusion came over Claudia's face, and she traced Sophie's cheek with her fingers. "Take care of your brother, will you?" she whispered. "He only has you now."

Then her eyes rolled back in her head, and Sophie screamed.

CHAPTER FORTY

SOPHIE ADJUSTED THE CUFFS OF her long black dress as she sat on the bed in Duchess Maria's chambers. The past weeks had been filled with love and birth, and she had managed to contain her grief for her father—only for it to flood over again with Claudia's death. The night before, Philip had cradled Sophie as her body shook with sobs, both of them feeling like the world was breaking into pieces. But the dawn came, as it always did, clean and quiet and new.

This was what it meant to grow up, to rule; you held sadness in your hands and felt its weight, then set it aside so you could take care of others. Sophie had people depending on her, and she would not let them down.

The funeral would start soon. They would bury the duke and the duchess together. But for the moment, Sophie wanted to be alone with her thoughts. Philip was elsewhere in the palace making last-minute arrangements; along with the memorial for Maximilian and Claudia, they had agreed to hang a small painting of King Ferdinand at the back of the ballroom, covered with a black veil. They would mourn their parents together.

After the funeral was over and affairs were in order, Sophie would leave Bavaria for the first time in her life for their coronation in Spain. The thought filled her both with dread and with a tentative hope. She would finally do what her father had on all his travels—only she would do it better, putting the needs of the people first.

"We don't have to stay long," Philip had told her, watching her face nervously. "We could come right back. You could return to Bavaria every month if you want to."

But Sophie knew it was their duty to be in Spain; Philip, especially, needed to be with his people and establish his own reign. And she felt ready for time away from the palace that held so many memories of those who were now gone.

"We can split the year up," Sophie had said. "A few months here, a few months there. But I want to be where you are, where we can serve our people best. That's all that matters."

And Sophie would be the queen of Spain. She could only begin to imagine what this entailed, how different it would be from her life as a lady of the court in Bavaria. But even though she felt unprepared, Sophie knew she could meet the challenge.

She had her brother to think about, too. Maximilian, or Max, was growing fast, and already his cheerful shrieks and laughter echoed through the walls of the palace, making even the gruffest of Bavaria's guards crack a smile. Sophie and Philip had become new parents to him, such responsibility coming far quicker than they had expected. But the two of them responded with delight to his every move, and Lotte was always there to help.

Now Sophie held her mother's guidebook, which she'd decided to reunite with the others in Duchess Maria's personal library. After some long thought, she knew that she would no longer let her mother's chambers be a tomb. She would move in here with Philip, and they would start over, bringing back the life and happiness that had once existed in this space.

Opening the guidebook, Sophie ran her finger over the title page and noticed something that hadn't been there before. In looping, neat script, someone had written:

Compiled by the Duchess Lady Maria,
mother to Lady Sophie and guide to Duchess Claudia.

Sophie's eyes grew cloudy. Claudia had wanted to give credit to Duchess Maria as the author. Something about the wording spoke to Claudia's shyness, her hope to be included as a real part of the family. Sophie traced the handwriting with her fingers, an ache in her chest.

When she looked up once more, she gasped sharply.

The witch was standing in the room with her, a few feet away from the bed.

"You sure do like your entrances, don't you?" Sophie said, shaking her head.

"My apologies," the witch said. "It's a bad habit."

The sorceress's silver hair was in one long, thick braid, the end of which she wound around her fingers.

"How are you feeling?" she murmured.

"All right." Sophie closed the book gently and set it aside. "But I've been better."

The witch nodded. "I'll make you something later. Tea, if you'd like."

"Thank you. I would." Sophie folded her hands and sighed. "I'd like to ask you some things, while you're here."

The witch sat next to Sophie on Duchess Maria's bed, moving fluidly. Her soft, dark dress swished like river reeds, and in their black clothes, the two women looked alike. "Go ahead."

"If—if you can have premonitions and ideas about what's to come in the future..." Sophie squeezed her hand into a fist, digging the nails into her palm. "Why couldn't you save Claudia? I'm not blaming you, but—but I can't help to think, if only you had been there—"

The witch closed her eyes and nodded. "I wish it's something I could have stopped, too. I would have saved your father if I could, and . . . your mother as well."

Sophie's nails dug so hard into her hand it hurt.

"But death is a tricky thing," the witch continued. "And I have no power over it. I cannot stop it; I can only slow it down. I get visions about the *feelings* that different events may cause, but I rarely get specifics. And so there is often little I can do to prevent such tragedies."

The witch hung her head. She suddenly looked so small and helpless, poised there on the edge of the bed, that Sophie wanted to put her arms around her and give her a hug.

Instead, Sophie said, "Tell me more about my mother."

"My name is Brunhilde," the witch said and smiled. "Your mother was the only one in this duchy who cared to learn my name. She did the thing that I cannot—she saved my life. You would not remember this, as it happened before you were born, but in the old days, there was a war against witches. People feared them, eradicating them all across the land and casting them out. Your father came from a long line of men who did these deeds; King Ferdinand was one of them as well. But your mother . . ." Brunhilde shook her head. "She was my greatest advocate and friend. You are so like her. Maria was a scientist, so fascinated by my magic and determined to understand the world around her. She, too, struggled with infertility, but—just like

Claudia—through my medicines and her own concoctions, she was able to have you. And I was right there for her when you were born. She used to come visit me with you when you were little."

The witch's eyes grew misty, and she looked down at her hands.

"But—how can that be?" Sophie shook her head. "Why don't I remember you from my childhood?"

Brunhilde lifted her shoulders slightly. "Your father could never be convinced that I meant no harm—he banished me when you were still very young. I like to keep to myself, anyway."

Sophie slipped off the bed and held her hand out to the witch. "Brunhilde . . . that will change. From now on, you will be part of this palace. You will belong here. And you must protect my brother, for I cannot bring him to Spain with me. I will return often, but you must see to his well-being, and the kingdom's."

"Is it so?" the woman murmured. "You trust me to do that?"

"Completely," said Sophie, swallowing hard.

Brunhilde considered it. "I've always wanted to be a grand-mother," she said finally.

"You are the closest link I have left to both my mothers," Sophie told her.

The sorceress took Sophie's hand. "I am honored, my lady. Bavaria and the young duke will be safe with me."

Sophie and Brunhilde went down to the funeral together, using the door this time.

EPILOGUE

One year later

"FASTER, SOPHIE, FASTER—WE'LL MISS IT!" Thomas cried, jumping onto Sophie's back.

"Oof," Sophie said. "Sorry, Thomas, you're going to have to walk today."

"Thomas, go jump on someone your own size," Philip said, joining them on the path into town. He was holding little Maximilian in his arms.

Sophie smiled to see her husband with her brother. Maximilian had Claudia's complexion—all gold and spun silk—but his eyes were his father's and Sophie's.

They walked hand in hand in the warm morning, the seven boys and her small family.

The boys now lived in the palace full-time, and Sophie, Philip, and Max joined them five months of the year. Sophie had opened the doors of her childhood home to any children who needed a place to stay. Whenever the king and queen returned from their duties in

Spain, the youngsters would tear pell-mell through the halls and play games with Sophie and Philip late into the night.

Granny Brunhilde, which is what they called the witch, followed them with a smile.

Spring was on the brink of turning into summer, and the breeze was warm and sweet. Sophie breathed in deeply as they reached the edge of the town, savoring the smell of the flowering ivy that bloomed on the brightly painted, newly repaired homes. The street was bustling with people, especially some of the new families that had been drawn by the prospering copper mines and relocated to the towns.

As it turned out, many of the advisers had agreed with Sophie about the financial reform she proposed, save for a loud minority who had bullied the others into agreeing with their views. At least, this was the explanation they gave once it was clear that her brother would be duke and she the regent of Bavaria. Along with the advisers that remained in her favor, Sophie appointed Brunhilde, several other villagers, and qualified nobility to speak for local and national causes.

"Oh, Philip," Sophie breathed as they came into the square. "There she is."

In the middle of the square, the broken old fountain had been replaced with a large stone statue of Claudia, carved carefully from the mountain rock. Her likeness was beautiful and true to memory, with the statue bending slightly and pouring a pitcher of water over a miniature model of the villages. The fountain was still dry, waiting for its final dedication.

Sophie squeezed Philip's hand, then located Brunhilde and went to her side.

"Granny, it's perfect," she said, a little choked up. "I don't know how to thank you for the work you've done on this."

Brunhilde smiled. "It's a good tribute, my lady," she said.

Lotte added, "We weren't too sure about our duchess Claudia at first, but in the end, she gave us so much. It's the least we can do to remember her."

As the village clock tolled the stroke of noon, the villagers gathered around for the address. Philip gave Max to Lotte and helped Sophie onto a small wooden podium that had been placed next to the fountain. Sophie cleared her throat, fleetingly remembering the nerves she had felt when she first debuted. Looking into the eyes of her fellow countryfolk, she felt many times better.

"My good people of Bavaria," she began. "Thank you for gathering here today. After a year that has been much kinder to all of us than those previous—"

Here Sophie got several nods and some smatterings of applause.

"King Philip and I are very pleased to present this memorial to Duchess Claudia, who helped us to make great strides toward Bavaria's well-being. I was lucky to have her as my stepmother. She was a brilliant woman, but most of all, she was kind." Sophie's voice grew louder and more confident as she spoke. "We could all see how she cared for this land, which she came to call her home. May this fountain remind us of her goodness, and encourage us to look past our judgments, seeing the best in each other every day."

The crowd broke into loud applause.

At a signal from Brunhilde, several of the villagers stepped forward with buckets filled from the Pöllat and poured them into the fountain, with one man standing high on a ladder to send water rushing down through Claudia's stone pitcher.

"Wasn't she beautiful?" Sophie said, nuzzling Max's ear. He was such a bouncy, happy boy, destined to do great things.

Sophie was the queen of Spain. Philip would always be at her side.

They too would be blessed with children, someday soon. And if Sophie had a daughter, she vowed, her name would be Maria Claudia.

AUTHOR'S NOTE

THIS NOVEL IS LOOSELY BASED on the "true" stories that scholars think might have inspired the tale of "Snow White," one wherein a beautiful Bavarian baroness was poisoned by spies of the Spanish king who wished to thwart her marriage to his son, as well as another story in which young Lady Sophia had a stepmother who owned a talking mirror that "only told the truth." I've also taken a few liberties with the history of Anglo-Spanish relations. *Snow & Poison* is a work of fiction. All artistic liberties were taken deliberately and with knowledge of the historical record.

But hey—it's a fairy tale, right?

ACKNOWLEDGMENTS

THANKS ALWAYS TO MY PENGUIN family. My editor, Polo Orozco, who has been so patient, kind, and handsome—Polo, we must meet in person! Thank you to Jen Klonsky, our duchess, and Jen Loja, our queen. To Anne Heausler, Cindy Howle, Misha Kydd, Jessica Jenkins, Natalie Vielkind, and all our friends in sales, publicity, and marketing—I'm so thankful for all that you do.

Thanks always to Richard Abate at 3 Arts. Friend and councilor. We miss you, Martha Stevens!

Thanks to my family and friends, especially Mike and Mattie, who are not snow and poison but love and laughter.

Love to all my amazing readers.

XOXO Mel